TO HOLD A HIDDEN PEARL

Rossingley, Book One

Fearne Hill

A NineStar Press Publication

www.ninestarpress.com

To Hold a Hidden Pearl

Printed in the USA

ISBN: 978-1-64890-296-3

First Edition, May, 2021

Also available in eBook, ISBN: 978-1-64890-295-6

CONTENT WARNING:

This book contains sexually explicit content, which may only be suitable for mature readers, homophobic language used by a side character; grieving for deceased family members; depiction of a terminal patient with severe burns and disfigurement; mild eating disorder; alcohol use.

Prologue

Rossingley

Rossingley, also known as the **Rossingley Estate,** is located in <u>Allenshire</u>, a county in Southwest England. It is the ancestral seat of the Duchamps-Avery family, which is headed by the <u>Earl</u> of Rossingley. The estate covers over 6,000 acres (24 km²).

Originally built circa 1400, then destroyed by fire, Rossingley House was completed in 1641. The Grade I listed property stands in an estate park of 500 acres, featuring a fifty-acre lake, many specimen trees, and a trout stream, which is a tributary of the river Allen. Rossingley Church, a small family chapel thought to be built at the same time as the main house, stands at the north edge of the parkland. Rossingley's neoclassical façade was remodelled in the mid-seventeenth century, and although the name of the architect is not known, the influence of Robert Adam is evident in the grand Doric columns, emphasising the lack of adornment around the ten elegant upper-floor windows. The influence is also clear from the symmetrical interior floor plan which complements the geometric designs of the walled gardens to the west of the property. A wing on the north side of the house was destroyed by fire at the beginning of the 1800s and never rebuilt. Many windows at the rear of the third floor were bricked up during the period of the Window Tax in the 1700s and not replaced.

Duchamps-Avery Family

Rossingley has been the seat of the Duchamps-Avery family since its inception. Originally from Normandy, there is evidence the family had property on the land dating back to the 1100s. The first resident of the original house was Charles Duchamps-Avery (born c.1420). The first ancestor to reside in the current dwelling was Robert Duchamps-Avery (born c.1620); he was the grandfather of the first Earl of Rossingley.

A complete history of the Duchamps-Avery family can be found in *Rossingley: Ascent to Power*

The vast properties, lands, and holdings, including commercial land and property in London, have effectively solidified the Duchamps-Averys as one of the wealthiest families in England.

Recent History

In 2019, the family was struck by tragedy when Lord Edward Duchamps-Avery, fifteenth Earl of Rossingley was killed, along with his wife Lady Elizabeth, in a helicopter crash whilst attending a family event in

Morocco. His eldest son and heir, Oliver Duchamps-Avery and his pregnant wife, Isobel, also died in the crash. They did not have children. The inheritance consequently transferred to his younger brother, Dr Lucien Duchamps-Avery who now resides at, and manages, the Rossingley Estate.

Chapter One

LUCIEN

I don't do nightclubs anymore. It's not an age thing. Sure, I'm thirty-four, but there are plenty of men and women older than me in here seemingly having a blast. It's...it's just that I hoped I'd never need to, I suppose. I think I had this ridiculous notion I'd be happily settled with a great job, an even better loving partner, and a comfortable home. I have the job, and I certainly have the home, not that I particularly wanted it. But the loving partner? Not so much. To be fair, though, I'm quite difficult to love.

So here I am, propping up the wall in Spangles, a club I haven't visited in years, watching my pissed former work colleagues, Sam and Louis, make complete arses of themselves on the dance floor.

There's a whole gang of us here. I don't know any of the others, and I don't really want to become better acquainted with them either, but Sam has been begging me to come up to London for months and months. He's been a decent friend since the accident, as much as I've let him, and joining him for his boyfriend Louis's thirtieth birthday is the least I can do to show my appreciation. So

I'd downed a few colourful cocktails, which seem to have had no effect on my mood whatsoever, put on my glad rags, done my eyes, and now pretend to be the sexy guy I used to be before my former existence was comprehensively annihilated. And tomorrow, when it's thankfully all over, I'll whizz back down the M4 to Allenmouth, and having seen how absolutely spiffily I'm coping, they'll hopefully leave me alone for a while. I deserve an Oscar for tonight's performance, but I'm starting to flag. Another ten minutes of hugging the wall and my Campari and soda, and I'll be on my way.

An enormously tall, Italian Stallion kind of guy gives me a blatant once-over, and my eyes skirt past him. Thanks, but no thanks. Curly black hair, eyes like pools of melted chocolate, bulging shoulder muscles, and a broad chest threatening to break out of his tight white T-shirt. As if at any minute, the T-shirt might rip open and his skin turn an ugly shade of green. As he is, with T-shirt intact, he's what Americans refer to as a jock. Or an especially buff Danny Zuko. But I'm no simpering Pink Lady. He's absolutely not my bag at all.

My gaze settles on a little cutie chatting to his friends near the bar. Much more like it, exactly my type of guy. Perfect tight arse in the skinniest of black jeans, and he's demonstrating the grace of a ballet dancer as he reaches upwards onto his toes to speak into a friend's ear. Slight of build, and floppy, dirty-blond hair with pink frosted tips. Sensing my interest, he shyly smiles at me, and I look away. We all know the rules to this game, and a few seconds later, I glance back at him. He returns the look at precisely the moment that a protective, possessive arm comes to rest across his narrow shoulders, and the ruggedly handsome owner of that arm plants an adoring kiss on his cheek. With a regretful shrug, the cute guy turns to his companion and is pulled into a loving hug. A keeper for sure, only not my keeper unfortunately. Oh well, *c'est la vie.*

Gloria Gaynor is belting out 'I am what I am' at the top of her lungs. Most definitely my cue to leave. I finish my drink and head to where I last saw Sam and Louis. With a bit of luck, they'll be so engrossed in each other they'll let me slip out unnoticed to find a taxi to take me home. As I begin to push through groups of sweaty clubbers, the Italian Stallion guy blocks my path. And I mean blocks—he's broad and beefy. He's giving me another once-over, this time anxious, through thick black lashes, and his liquid-brown eyes are strangely as skittish as a colt's. I make to squeeze by. But his big hand reaches around, catching me unawares, settles firmly around my wrist, and I'm tugged towards a dark corner of the club. Granted, it's an unconventional hook-up technique, but I'm pissed enough and curious enough to go with it— perhaps in the dim light, he's mistaken me for my cousin Freddie; it wouldn't be the first time. We both have rather striking features.

So it seems that now he's got me here, he's not quite sure what it is he wants. He hovers in front of me, one hand resting lightly at my hip, and I can't tell if he's very nervous or very drunk. I'm happy to wait; I've nothing better to do. Anyway, I'm mildly intrigued as I have a feeling that, like me, he doesn't really belong. He licks his lips once—yes, definitely nervous—and it draws attention to his fine mouth, a full Cupid's bow, now glistening wetly. The sort of generous wide mouth made for laughing. Or cock sucking. I'm focusing on those lips now because the background thump of Ms Gaynor makes audible speech nigh on impossible.

"Can I suck your cock?" he asks.

Gosh, we must be acquainted after all, as this is one of my all-time favourite questions.

Okay, so I've not had any sexual activity in any of its manifestations for approaching *two years*, and I can't recall the last time I even bothered employing my own right hand. Months and months ago. So if there is a single man in the history of the universe in my current sexual desert who would answer his question in the negative, then I'd like to meet him and shake his hand.

I contemplate replying with a sarcastic "Yes, if you can find it, darling" because, frankly, it's most likely shrivelled up and died somewhere. But instead, I nod coolly and find myself mouthing, *Be my guest*, accompanied by a faintly ridiculous sweeping gesture of my arm as if inviting him in for afternoon tea. And that mouth is quite enticing, even if it is attached to a man built like Tarzan. Beautiful skin, too, a rich natural olive.

I don't know the extent of his lip-reading skills, but I think he gets the message. Still looks nervous as hell though. I'd go so far as to say bloody terrified. I've no idea why, as he's the one leading on this, and it's not like my cock is going to bite back. If he's afraid we'll be spotted and turfed out, then he need not be. This corner of Spangles might as well have a sign above it advertising Sloppy Blow Jobs Here, judging by the stickiness of the carpet and the blatant activities of the couples nearby. However, whatever internal battle he's fighting, his desire to suck me bizarrely wins out, and he sinks to his knees rather gracefully for such a big bloke.

All fingers and thumbs, he unfastens my belt, then wrestles with the buttons on my skinny Levi's. If we weren't in the situation we are, and if he hadn't made his rather forwards suggestion, I'd assume he'd never done this before because he's certainly making a hash of undoing my trousers. But eventually, they're open, and I give him a helping hand by lowering them slightly around my hips. I'm treated to a rather lovely whiff of good old-fashioned Fahrenheit aftershave; it's been years since I inhaled its woody, leathery aroma. With one last anxious glance up through his thick lashes, he slides his fingers inside the slit in my boxers and unceremoniously pulls out my cock. I think it's that endearing last look up that gets my juices flowing, a vulnerable mixture of fear and need, and thankfully, my cock is half hard and getting harder. Which is infinitely preferable to watching him endeavouring to shape his lips around something akin to a clammy slug, even if he is a total stranger.

And the blow job isn't half bad, even for someone who I'm utterly convinced hasn't ever done it before. There's a bit too much toothiness at the start, and some overenthusiastic sucking that has me wincing and nearly pushing him away, but then he settles and finds a rhythm and mmm...really not bad at all. What he's lacking in expertise, he's more than making up for in enthusiasm.

Should I have warned him against the perils of offering blow jobs to random strangers in dodgy Soho nightclubs? Probably. I am a doctor after all; surely it falls within the bounds of my Hippocratic oath. But I don't. Because looking down, I find myself suddenly mesmerised by the sight of that big dark head bobbing up and down on my cock, not to mention the rather lovely sensations as his raspy tongue lathes along the length. As my orgasm builds, I bury my hands in the mop of dark curls, arch my hips up, and forcefully fuck his mouth, my cock reaching right into the back of his throat, and he takes it all, bless him, he gamely takes it all.

And so for the first time in eighteen months, I'm transported out of myself to a place where Dr Lucien Avery, the reluctant sixteenth Earl of Rossingley, is reminded of what joy can feel like. To a place where he remembers what pleasure feels like, where he can smile, and his heart can briefly sing again. Because, finally, something good and pure and simple is happening, and he can believe just maybe there is a path leading out of this wretched sadness after all. And the boy who is making this all happen is some big lump of a creature, lacking in finesse, but with such soulful brown eyes and swollen red lips. A boy who even now is gazing up at me through his long lashes with such devotion to his task that my balls clench and my hips jerk, and without giving him the customary polite warning, I spurt again and again into his mouth until my legs wobble dangerously and I sink back against the damp wall.

I eventually open my eyes to find him standing in front of me once more. Well-mannered boy that he is, he's poking my cock back inside my boxers and putting my jeans back together, acts which seem somehow more intimate and sweeter than sucking my cock. After wiping a trail of my spunk off his cheek with a sweep of his hand, he gently smiles, and it's the smile of a fairy-tale prince. Such a charming smile that it could launch ships and incite men to fight wars; it sparks sensations in me I'd forgotten existed but want to experience again. I decide, in a moment, when I've collected myself—when I've come down from my unexpected high—I'll suggest we go back to my place so I can return the favour. I close my eyes briefly, wanting to hold on to this blissful forgotten feeling for as long as possible.

And of course, as in all good fairy stories, when I open them again, he's gone.

Chapter Two

JAY

"You're a fucking bastard, Jay. A fucking cruel, heartless bastard. If I didn't have an operating list, I'd come over to your house right now and stove your fucking, bastard head in."

Such an erudite surgeon. His patients would be so proud. I hold the phone a safe distance from my ear until he's finished his rant, deserving every single word of it, including having my head stoved in. Unfortunately, that volley of swearing was only a warmup. Already my headache throbs.

"I mean, what the fuck Jay-Jay? You've called off the wedding, like, six days before—six days! And you won't explain why? Are you mad? I'm surprised you haven't had your head smacked in already by Ellie's dad."

I'm surprised, too, but thankfully, he managed to restrain himself at the last moment for the sake of his successful legal career. And anyway, Ellie is quite capable of giving me a head injury herself, to be honest. She doesn't need men fighting battles on her behalf. I may have broken her heart, but she's still got a decent left hook—as I discovered yesterday, by breaking the news that after four years of togetherness, a mortgage, an engagement, and plans for wedded bliss, I'm pulling the plug. Suffice to say, Evan's current tirade isn't the first I've received on the subject, and I daresay it won't be the last.

"Fuck, Jay. I spent fucking weeks on my speech. It was fucking hilarious."

Evan is my best mate and was supposed to be my best man. We met on the first day of med school and got very drunk together at freshers' fair. Cementing our new friendship, I puked down his shirt, and he pissed in my wardrobe, mistaking it for the toilet. Neither of us have touched vodka since, although other alcoholic beverages are more than welcome to pass my lips, none more so welcome than now. As of yesterday, the role of best man is redundant, and he may choose to rescind the best mate position, too, since all my other friends have deserted me and taken root in Camp Ellie. Even my own parents and sisters are giving me the cold shoulder. But perhaps I've underestimated him because now that he's got it all off his chest, his tone is definitely softer.

"Just give us a clue, Jay. We all deserve that, at least. Have you been over the side and found another girl?"

"No," I sigh tiredly. "As I have reiterated several times, I haven't found another girl."

It's as if I haven't spoken.

"Because your Ellie is a fucking angel, mate. You can't let someone like her get away." He swears under his breath. "Listen, Jay, I've got to go; they've just wheeled the first patient into the anaesthetic room. We'll talk later, yeah?"

We probably will talk later, or rather, he'll yell some more, and I'll suck it up. That's all I can do because the truth is unpalatable to everyone apart from me, and even if I did have the balls to tell them what's going on, I'm not sure they'd believe me.

Chapter Three

LUCIEN

I never planned to end up working here. Not that it isn't a decent hospital, because it is. It's just that I was quite happy with my anonymous London existence. Being a square peg in a round hole is fine as long as there are other square pegs nearby with whom to compare notes. At St George's there were plenty, but here, in sleepy, provincial Allenmouth Hospital Department of Anaesthesia and Intensive Care, I'm the only one. Probably the only gay in the village where I reside, too, and certainly the only gay in the anaesthetic department.

I share my office with two glamorous forty-something female consultant anaesthetists, who seem totally oblivious to my unfriendly demeanour. My other colleagues received the message loud and clear yonks ago: Dr Avery has no desire to make friends. Friends ask questions one has no desire to answer, and then one grows fond of them, or even grows to love them, and I can't afford to lose anyone else I care about. I no longer have the emotional bandwidth to cope with that. The same goes for my intensive care patients; I try not to learn too much about them either. I prefer only to concentrate on the failing physiology of lungs and hearts and kidneys and my attempts to rectify it.

Believing I'd be the only consultant with an admin session this morning, I must have misread the rota, as Emily and Annabel are in the office, too, gossiping happily. Somehow, these two ladies managed to slip under the no-friends barrier when I wasn't paying attention, and while we don't socialise or anything, I like having them around every once in a while. Probably because they remind me of my mother and her old pals, how they used to share tea and cake in front of the Aga, putting the world to rights. Listening in on Emily and Annabel's conversations, an eavesdropper would have no idea they are senior doctors as they succeed in covering every conceivable topic apart from any remotely related to medicine.

Our office is not much larger than an average-sized toilet cubicle, and I endeavour to turn my back to them, hunching over my laptop as they cover the usual litany of book club, last night's telly, annoying husbands, the kids' latest achievements, and another female anaesthetist's appalling dress sense. This is the best bit, when they start to slag off our other colleagues and usually when I'm compelled to join in, especially if it concerns Dr Leitner, the head of department. Honestly? He's a total cock. Chauvinistic, misogynistic, bigoted, homophobic; you name it, he fits the bill. I'm convinced I was only offered the job as he was on leave that day, and Emily stood in for him at the interview. Fortunately, she is none of those things. In fact, both she and Annabel are absolute sweeties. Although they don't know it, they keep me sane. Sane-ish.

"And it's not just that skirt either!" hisses Annabel, sotto voce. The aforementioned colleague with the appalling dress sense uses the office next door, so she's keeping her voice down. "God knows who dyes her hair, but my eight-year-old could do a better job."

Listening to these women bitching about our colleagues is easily the highlight of my day.

"Honestly, Annabel," whispers Emily after a quick glance round. "I was in the theatre changing rooms on Tuesday, and I'm not joking, she has pubic hair down to her knees! It's like the Amazon rainforest down there! I'm not surprised she can't find herself a man."

"I'd love to take her somewhere for a makeover," responds Emily dreamily. "You know, decent haircut and colour, new clothes, a razor... She'd be all right if she sorted that lot out."

I can't stay quiet any longer. "Gosh, and a decent bra. She needs to go for a proper bra fitting. Her boobs flap around her hips."

"I knew you were listening, Lucien," nudges Annabel, delighted they've provoked me sufficiently to join in. "Maybe you could suggest that to her sometime."

"No, darling. Then I'd find myself embroiled in some sort of conversation with her; she'd corner me for hours, droning on about stationery or the new photocopier or another equally dreary topic."

"Good heavens, Lucien, you mean that you would actually have to talk to someone?" Emily replies sarcastically.

"It has been known," I respond.

Annabel butts in. "Stop bickering, you two. Look, I have an email here from the Education Lead. The junior doctors are swapping around this week, and we've all been assigned a new one to supervise."

Marvellous, a role I usually try to dodge. I'd rather not supervise a junior if I can help it, preferring splendid isolation in the operating theatre—just the patient asleep, the steady *hiss-pump* of the anaesthetic machine, and the Scrabble app on my phone. Or a copy of the *Telegraph* crossword. While the surgeon does all the work. But every now and again, the powers that be insist I show an interest in the education and training of the next generation. I'll probably be assigned a super-keen girly swot who bursts into tears the first time I give her a bollocking—sorry, some comprehensive constructive feedback. And she'll report me to Dr Leitner, and I'll have to pretend I'm bothered that I hurt her feelings or some such crap. Bloody strawberry generation. Annabel is still reading out loud from the email.

"Ooh, I've been assigned to supervise someone called Dr Wang Xiu," reads Annabel, hesitating over the surname. "Who is a complete anaesthetic novice and apparently has a needle phobia. Oh dear, that doesn't bode well for his future career choice. Who the hell gets on the interview panels at med school these days? Emily, you've got that girl we talked about in the meeting—you remember, she keeps on failing the final exam? I think she's on her sixth attempt."

Emily nods in a resigned fashion. At least I haven't been allocated that unfortunate soul; the level of patience required to mop up that ocean of tears is well beyond me.

"And you, Lucien my love, have the pleasure of a chap called Dr Jay Sorrentino, a first-year registrar.

Hmm…that's a name I don't recognise. According to this, he's been a doctor for six years, has completed three years of anaesthesia training already, has passed the final exam, and is interested in pursuing a career in intensive care medicine."

Okay, so it could be worse. At least he'll be able to vaguely recognise one end of a propofol syringe from the other. Inexplicably, Emily has started squealing and wriggling in her chair.

"Ooh, Lucien, it's Goldenballs! Remember? I told you about him. I interviewed him for the registrar job back in April. He wasn't supposed to be starting for another couple of weeks, due to his honeymoon or something, if I recall? Maybe they mixed up the dates as he's coming earlier instead. Oh, you are *seriously* going to love him! There was no way on earth I wasn't going to give him the job when we interviewed."

I disliked him already. "Pray, what gives you the impression I'll love him? I have an aversion to all juniors on principle."

"For goodness sake, Lucien, stop being so mean. For a start, he's bloody gorgeous. I mean, really gorgeous. His CV was quite impressive, too, and he was *so* nice." She nods happily. "It's about time this department had some eye candy—present company excepted, obviously."

"Obviously," I agree magnanimously. "The gorgeous, clever, *and* nice Dr Goldenballs. You make a boy giddy with anticipation."

"Now, now, don't be catty, Lucien. You're also gorgeous, and your CV was just as amazing. You only need to work on the niceness part, and then you, too, could be as lovely as Dr Sorrentino. Rather foxy shirt today, by the

~vay," Emily adds, looking me up and down. "Navy really suits your fairness. Is it Ted Baker?"

"Yves Saint Laurent."

No point having oodles of cash if you don't spend some of it on yourself occasionally. But she's right, navy does work with this ridiculous snowy hair and my pale complexion. Sighing in a world-weary fashion, I study my nails.

"So, when do I get to meet this amazing, gorgeous Dr Jay Sorrentino, then, so I can bring him down a peg or two? Or is he still enjoying a lavish honeymoon somewhere?"

Emily frowns at me. "Don't be so naughty, Lucien! No, he's not on his honeymoon; he's starting today with the rest of them, which you would have known if you'd listened properly and read your own emails! They are having an induction session this morning, and then Dr Leitner will be boring them with his welcome-to-the-department speech at lunchtime; therefore, I expect the lovely Dr Sorrentino will be joining you in the operating theatre this afternoon. And I'm confident you will give him a super, cuddly Dr Avery welcome."

Huh. So my afternoon plans to listen to the test match during the long spinal surgery case are completely scuppered. Instead, I'm going to have to make polite chit-chat with a cocky boy who thinks he's made of chocolate. And he will expect me to talk to him; I'll feel obliged to ask him about his previous anaesthesia training, his future professional development plans, and maybe even try to teach him something useful. Ugh, just kill me now.

*

Lunchtime. I don't really do food, not in the way everyone else likes to wolf down packets of cardboard sandwiches and bumper bags of crisps as if they'll turn into a pile of useless goo on the floor halfway through the afternoon without them. I'll maybe snack on an apple if my day is turning out to be particularly taxing, but truthfully, I haven't much of an appetite these days, and cooking for one lacks a certain appeal. I like marmite, and I like apples, sometimes I like them both together. And for supper, when I summon the energy to eat, I'm partial to Waitrose macaroni cheese. If the mood takes me, I'll occasionally swap the macaroni cheese for a bowl of organic granola. My diet has most of the basic food groups covered. The remainder of my calories and vitamin C come from Campari and orange, with a splash of soda. And on high days and holidays, I may treat myself to a slice of Battenberg cake.

But if I don't join the others in the departmental coffee room for ten minutes at lunchtime, then Emily and Annabel will accuse me of being unsociable, and frankly, I could do without the nagging. So when the time comes, I retrieve my apple from my Louis Vuitton briefcase and trail after them.

Comprehensively blocking the doorway to the coffee room is a wide set of shoulders tapering to a sturdy set of hips, covered in blue theatre pyjamas stretched pleasantly snugly over aforementioned shoulders and hips. Not strictly my thing, but appreciated, nonetheless. The dark-haired owner of the rugger-bugger shoulders and the fine, muscular derriere is studying a paper copy of the operating theatre rota and wrinkling his brow.

"Hello, Jay!" says Emily. "Welcome to Allenmouth; it's good to see you again! Are you finding your way around okay?"

The shoulders hastily move to one side to let us through, and the owner of the shoulders smiles politely, his mouth splitting into a naturally generous grin. Good teeth. "Hello, Dr Grosvenor, how are you?"

The voice is warm and deep, confident, with a Midland inflection. Not full Brummy, thank goodness, the vowels flattened on just about the right side of acceptable.

"Oh, call me Emily." She giggles, the flirtatious little minx, and then turns to me and Annabel. "Let me introduce you to everybody, Jay. This is my good friend and colleague, Annabel Creasey—she's our lead paediatric anaesthetist if you have a burning desire to follow that career pathway, and this..." She tugs me forwards by the sleeve. "And this lovely man is Dr Lucien Avery, one of my intensive care colleagues. More importantly, he has the pleasure of being your educational supervisor for the year!"

Since the dreadful day, eighteen months ago, when my beloved parents and brother were unexpectedly wiped out in a horrific helicopter crash, I've become quite adept at schooling my features into a bland mask of politeness. For instance, when well-meaning acquaintances tell me how sorry they are for my loss, and then, with concerned frowns, go on to enquire as to how I'm coping. Or, if I bump into a tenant from one of the estate cottages, who begins a lengthy reminiscence about what a delightful man my father was, and do I remember the time that...? The expressionless mask is essential in those circumstances because the alternative would be utterly unthinkable. *How do you think I'm coping, you stupid dumb wit? Yes, I know how wonderful my father was; I'm his fucking son. My brother and mother were pretty fucking wonderful too, just in case you think you need to remind me of that as well.* None of those are considered acceptable responses for Lord Duchamps-Avery, the sixteenth Earl of Rossingley.

The expressionless mask is also pretty handy when one is faced with the hunky olive-skinned chap who, approximately eleven days earlier, gave you an impromptu blow job in a seedy nightclub and swallowed mouthfuls of your spunk. I put my mask practice to good use and extend my hand.

"Hello. Jay Sorrentino, isn't it? I'm Lucien Avery; good to meet you."

Jay Sorrentino clearly has not practiced the mask. From Emily's brief résumé, it sounds like his life is perfect; he's probably never needed to acquire it. His rather lovely face turns from lightly tanned through a greyish white to a sweaty green. His large hand in mine is instantly clammy.

"Are you all right, Jay?" asks Emily with concern. "Has Dr Avery's reputation preceded him? Honestly, don't believe a word of it. He's a pussycat, aren't you Lucien?"

The Italian Stallion pulls himself together somewhat. "Er...yes. Thank you, Dr Grosvenor...er...Emily. I'm fine. I...er...it's...there's just a lot to take in."

"There certainly is," I reply gravely, maintaining a straight face. "An enormous amount to take in."

The innuendo is lost on the two ladies. Rapidly releasing my hand, my new protégé wipes his sweaty palm down his theatre scrubs. I make a show of checking the time. "So, Dr Sorrentino. Have a quick lunch now, and I'll see you in Theatre Seven at one fifteen. It's a spinal surgery list, but don't worry about assessing the patients beforehand; I'll do that."

He nods dumbly before making a sharp exit, possibly to vomit in the nearest toilet.

Well, this will be interesting. Maybe I'm not the only square peg after all.

Chapter Four

JAY

My head is all over the place. I get lost on the way to the operating theatres, even though I've been there already this morning and have a map of the hospital layout on the rota in front of me. It's him! Christ, the man from the nightclub, it's him! I can't believe it; of all the thousands, nay *millions*, of gay men in London, I had to pick one who doesn't even live in bloody London and is going to be my educational supervisor for the next year. Just fucking shoot me now.

Come on, Jay, I tell myself, get yourself together. It could be much worse. He could have recognised me, and he could be laughing right this minute about my amateur blow job to Emily and that other doctor, and then everyone would know what I'd done. But he didn't recognise me, I'm sure of it, he was cool as a cucumber. No, he definitely didn't recognise me, not a flicker of recognition. I'd have known. I'd have seen it in his eyes or something. Thank God it was so dark in that fucking nightclub.

If I were at some sort of Alcoholics Anonymous-type therapy meeting, I'd introduce myself like this: Hello, my name is Jay Sorrentino, and I'm a closet homosexual. Possibly homosexual. No, scratch that. Probably, definitely homosexual, although the extent of my homosexual experience is giving a beautiful stranger a blow job in a nightclub. Once. A week before I was due to get married to my lovely, long-term girlfriend, Ellie. Of course, it's not that I need therapy because I think I'm gay. Being gay is fine, like being born left-handed or having a lifelong hatred of mushrooms. No, I need therapy because I was too dumb to realise I was gay and nearly got myself fucking married to a woman.

After diving into one of the changing room toilet cubicles, I slump onto the closed toilet seat and take a few deep breaths. My pulse slows. First things first. Dr Lucien Avery is fucking stunning. The most stunning man in the history of stunning mankind. He looks even better than my hazy recollection from the club. And he's tall, taller than I remembered, slim and graceful like a dancer.

Evan nearly pissed himself laughing when I told him who I'd been assigned as my educational supervisor for the coming year. He's already been working at Allenmouth for six months on the surgical rotation and has plenty of tales about the legendary Androgynous Albino, most of them centring around the fact that he's scary as hell. He said it served me right for the wedding fiasco, and that after a day spent in the operating theatre with Dr Avery, I'd be begging Ellie to take me back, if only to mop my brow when I wake from recurring nightmares about him.

Dr Lucien Avery is not an albino, just very, very fair. His hair is white-blond, the same colour as Boris

Johnson's, but any similarity most definitely ends there. Dr Avery's hair is longish and sleeked back off his smooth, pale face, highlighting those amazing cheekbones. He's like a Jean Paul Gaultier aftershave model in a magazine advert, one of the not quite real, airbrushed, impossibly beautiful ones who are too pretty to be male but too masculine to be female. Um...androgynous, in fact. And his eyes—the palest shimmering blue. I hadn't fully appreciated them in the dark club when I was on my knees with my mouth stretched around his knob.

Quickly checking the time on my phone, I take a few more deep breaths. He'll be expecting me to join him in less than three minutes. I'll just walk right in there and brazen it out. I can do this; I'm 'Goldenballs' apparently.

I arrive in Theatre Seven's anaesthetic room ahead of Dr Avery and ahead of the patient. Thank God—it's always a good move to arrive before the boss. The anaesthetic nurse is a cheerful chap in his late fifties called Roger, and I introduce myself.

"You drew the short straw today, then," he remarks as we prepare the intravenous drugs together and perform a safety check of the anaesthetic machine. "He's never very straightforward. My advice to you? Only speak when you're spoken to and concentrate on the pint of beer you'll be having afterwards. You'll need at least one by the time he's finished with you."

Great. This day is getting better and better.

Just then, Dr Avery sweeps into the room, giving Roger a curt nod. I receive the same treatment. A diamond stud twinkles in his left ear, and from my recent engagement ring shopping, I can confidently estimate the stone as at least a carat, defying all the hospital health and safety rules. I hadn't noticed it when we were introduced in the coffee room as I was too busy focussing on not passing out. He's changed into theatre pyjamas, too, obviously. It's pretty difficult to look good in cheap blue cotton, but somehow, he manages it; they hang from his angular frame as though specially designed for him.

"Would you like to go and fetch the first patient, Roger?" he suggests. Actually, it's not a suggestion; from the tone, it's a definite command dressed up as a suggestion. He is soft-spoken, but his voice is clear, nonetheless, and unapologetically upper class. It's not camp exactly, but neither is it manly—more breathy, seductive. Full red lips, the briefest hint of the tip of his pink tongue. Fuck. Roger scuttles off.

"You can watch me anaesthetise the first patient, Jay, so that you know how I like to do things, seeing as we will be working together a lot. That way, I shan't be subjected to you demonstrating all the bad habits you've undoubtedly picked up from elsewhere."

He flashes me a small, slightly threatening smile, and I glimpse neat white teeth and pointy canines. If I wasn't feeling so het up, I'd be drooling. His looks and the aloof, moody thing he's got going are sexy as hell.

"I've drawn up the anaesthetic drugs, Dr Avery," I venture. Why am I so bloody nervous? I'm a twenty-nine-year-old bloke. And a reasonably successful, fairly popular doctor to boot. I remind myself that he's only a bloke too. "Roger told me your preferences, but if you could just check." Feeling bolder, I add, "Do you like to be called Dr Avery, or do you prefer Lucien?"

He rewards me with a sphincter-loosening look. Shit, I've overstepped the mark. Already.

"I prefer Dr Avery, thank you, Jay," he responds crisply. Stepping closer, he brings those delectable red lips to my ear. "Sucking my cock, darling, doesn't give you permission to use my Christian name. Especially as you didn't even perform that particularly well."

The cut-glass, whispering voice is menacingly low, and he throws the words out so casually that, for a split second, I'm convinced I must have misheard. He steps back again, seemingly unperturbed.

"You...you recognised me straightaway, didn't you?" I stutter, weak-kneed. My heart has leapt up to my throat.

"I'd recognise the top of your curly dark head anywhere, Dr Sorrentino. Your mouth, too, probably."

What an utter bastard.

He's waited until we're alone before twisting the knife. Bastard. But how the hell he managed not to reveal anything in front of his colleagues earlier, I don't know. I doubt he's a closet gay like me—he goes to gay clubs for a start, but he must have ice running through his veins not to have shown any shock at all when we met.

Fuck him. And his fucking taunt. I might be quivering like a jelly baby on the inside and about to see my whole life fall apart, but I'm not giving him the satisfaction of witnessing it. I'll disintegrate in private later. I've just got to get through this afternoon first. And then all the other afternoons we'll have to spend together. Those lips though. Fuck. I breathe deeply, steeling myself.

"I'm sorry if I disappointed you, *Lucien*. You didn't have many complaints at the time." I hope my voice sounds a lot steadier than I feel. "Hmm. *Lucien*." I roll the fanciful name round my tongue a few times. "I'm not sure about that, a little too similar to Lucifer. Living proof that nominative determinism is actually a thing."

Okay, so it's not the greatest of comebacks, but on short notice and chop suey legs, it could have been a hell of a lot worse. I mimic his own movement from a few seconds earlier and lean in close to those flawless features. "And considering I've never sucked a cock before in my entire life, I don't think I did too bad a job. It achieved the desired outcome pretty quickly at least. Trigger happy, I think is the term for it."

I'm satisfied to see a slight tinge of pink cross his lovely cheekbones. Not completely bloodless, then.

The doors open, and thankfully, Roger returns, pushing an elderly lady on a trolley before him. "There you go, my dear," he says to her. "This is the anaesthetic room, and here's Dr Avery waiting for you."

If I thought he had ice running through his veins a few seconds earlier, then he has pure warmth running through them now. His bedside manner is a masterclass in how to put an anxious patient at ease before surgery. Even his voice softens and relaxes, his upper crust accent less pronounced as Roger attaches her to the monitoring. Lucien inserts a cannula into her arm, all the while keeping up a reassuring patter. In the space of about three minutes, they've covered the latest happenings on Coronation Street and the price of lamb in Asda, and before she knows it, she's anaesthetised, and we're wheeling her through into the operating theatre.

This afternoon's operating list comprises two patients undergoing spinal surgery. Lucien—sorry—*Dr Avery* introduces me to the theatre team and to the surgeon, Mr Bayer, who is as smiley and open as Lucien is surly and uptight. Lucien expertly leads the team in turning the patient onto her belly, which isn't as straightforward as it sounds when she is anaesthetised and has intravenous lines, a breathing tube, and a catheter, but an essential task seeing as how the surgeon needs to stick a knife in her back. He keeps up an explanation of his rationale for all the steps he's taking as we go along. As we fall into the familiar teacher-pupil role, I calm down a little, and he responds to my, hopefully, sensible questions with comprehensive answers.

The best way to describe delivering anaesthesia is that it is like flying a plane, with the most challenging moments at take-off and landing or, in our case, drifting the patient off to sleep and waking them up again. For the vast majority of non-emergency surgeries, the boring bit in the middle—when the surgeon is operating—is straightforward. Apart from the anaesthetist required to be constantly present to monitor the patient and manage intravenous drugs and fluids, there is often an opportunity to sit back and relax. Unless the anaesthetist is me and I'm cosied up next to a very un-cosy Dr Avery, who has extended his long legs out on the adjacent chair and is writing up patient observations on the anaesthetic chart with a rather stylish fountain pen. There isn't a lot of space, and we are both wedged together between the anaesthetic machine, the X-ray machine, and the operating table. His knee accidentally brushes against mine.

"Tell me, Jay, are you a local boy?"

Okay, so we're doing the small talk thing and pretending our previous conversation never happened. I'm very cool with that plan. I explain that I moved down from the Midlands a few years ago, after I qualified, and bought a house in town.

"Live there alone, do you?"

His knee touches mine again, and this time, he leaves it resting there, outwardly oblivious and from the tone of his voice, bored with my company already. Through the thin cotton of our theatre pyjamas, I'm acutely aware of the warmth of his leg and struggle to concentrate on anything else. The only way this could get any worse is if I find myself developing a boner just from having his lean but muscular thigh pressed alongside mine. Um...okay, so it just got worse. Fuck. I hastily cover my lap with the patient's thick set of medical notes. I seem to have acquired a stutter as well as an inconvenient erection.

"Er...no. I...um...I live with my...er, ex-fiancée, Ellie? She's...um...a doctor too. She's training in the Emergency Department."

He raises one eyebrow and continues writing. "Fairly recent break-up, is it?"

I don't actually have to answer these questions if I don't want to. He's my educational supervisor, not my counsellor. But on the face of it, this is fairly standard anaesthetic chat when you have an operating list with someone new. Actually, it's harmless chat for any new acquaintance of the 'what's your name' and 'where do you come from' variety. Anyone listening would think nothing of it. But of course, anyone listening doesn't know that I sucked his knob eleven days ago. Not yet anyway. Christ, I've made a shitty mess of my life recently.

"Er...yeah. You could say that. We'd been together for about four years."

Another raise of a shapely pale eyebrow. I feel the need to clarify.

"It's complicated. I'd rather not explain. Sorry."

"Don't feel you have to explain yourself to me, Dr Sorrentino. Although it's always refreshing to meet someone even more fucked up than I am."

He pauses and sucks on his pen thoughtfully. "So I take it she found out about your extracurricular activities?"

I feel myself blushing. "I don't...I don't have any extracurricular activities. Generally. That was...er...a one-off. And no, she didn't. Find out, I mean. No one knows apart from you. I'm...um... Everyone thinks I'm straight."

He laughs; I glimpse those pointy teeth again. I'd probably find the whole situation funny, too, if I didn't play the starring role. He deliberately looks down at my lap and where the notes are strategically placed across it before bringing those knowing, languid blue eyes back up to me. Fuck, is he wearing mascara?

"Gosh, I hate to be the one to break it to you, sunshine. But you are not straight. There's definitely a wiggle in there. And I should know."

And then he's grilling me on the pharmacokinetic profile of fentanyl and its shorter acting derivatives, with barely a pause. To be fair, I don't think I do too badly, considering he's just frightened me half to death. And it certainly rectifies the trouser situation.

*

The afternoon eventually drags to a close. Conversation stays firmly away from the personal; indeed, Dr Avery becomes quieter and quieter, withdrawing into himself until we find ourselves sitting in total silence with about half an hour of surgery remaining. And it's not a particularly comfortable silence either.

"Dr Avery, I'm sure you have lots of things to do. I'm happy to finish this operation if you like," I suggest.

The patient is young and fit, and the surgery is progressing uneventfully. Thankfully, he acquiesces and disappears, whereupon the mood in the whole operating theatre immediately lightens. Someone puts on some music, and the surgeon and his assistant start discussing last night's football. Taking the vacated chair, Roger pats me on the back.

"You didn't do too badly, son," he pronounces sagely. "We've seen worse. At least I didn't have to get my box of tissues out. I think he likes you."

God help the ones he doesn't like. I've done a lot of operating lists with all sorts of different consultants over the last three years, and that was by far the most gruelling.

"Yes, well, I think maybe he needs to work on his interpersonal skills," I answer diplomatically, and Roger nods his agreement.

"If you ask me, I think the bloke's just lonely," he says. "He ain't got a partner or much family as far as anyone knows, and whether he's batting for the other side or not, everyone needs someone to go home to. But with his attitude, I'm not surprised he ain't got anyone—you would be a bloody fool to take him on."

*

After the operation finishes and the patient is awake and comfortable in the post-operative recovery area, I take a quick shower in the changing room before putting my civvies back on. Evan has texted, wanting to meet up/harangue me in the pub later. I delay replying—my nerves are too shredded to face a further bout of 'you're making a fucking monumental mistake, Jay'. As I'm walking through the operating suite on my way out, one of the nurses from Theatre Seven comes running up to me.

"Dr Sorrentino! Great, I caught you just in time! Either you or Dr Avery left your phone on top of the anaesthetic machine."

She hands me a slim, rose-gold iPhone, the little Apple logo in rainbow colours. Subtle and cute. Pressing the home button reveals a generic screen saver and a locked screen. Bloody marvellous, just what I need. I'm tempted to leave it on his desk in the department, but if he's anything like me he'd be lost without it, and the department isn't securely locked at night. On checking the rota, he's not due back at work for another couple of days, so with a heavy heart, I contact switchboard and request his home phone number and address. As I head out to my car, I text Ellie to warn her I may be a little late home. Not that she'll give a stuff, but it will give her more time to spit in my dinner. I ignore Evan, putting him off for a little longer.

After plugging the post code into the satnav, I set off. Estimated time of arrival is in twenty-five minutes, and the journey takes me south out of town, through some small villages, an unfamiliar route I don't travel very often. My parents live about an hour's drive north of

Allenmouth, and most of my friends are London or Midlands–based. I sit back, switch on the radio, and let the satnav do the work. I'll just go there, hand the phone over, and get straight back in the car.

Your destination is on the left.

Towns have turned into villages and villages have turned into hamlets. Even the hamlets have become progressively smaller, the houses replaced by fields, the roads replaced by winding semi-dirt tracks. I've officially reached the arse end of nowhere. As my precious baby, my beloved Audi, bounces over potholes, invisible in the growing darkness, I repeatedly curse Dr Lucien bloody Avery and his bloody phone. And the bloody warmth of his thigh against mine through cheap blue fabric.

There is no street lighting, and apart from what appears to be a group of shadowy buildings on the left, I can see bugger all. The address reads Rossingley Estate, so I was expecting a conglomeration of houses, not pitch-black sky and the stink of manure. There's nothing for it; I'm going to have to phone him.

He answers on about the eighth ring, just as I'm wondering if he's not home, with a curt "Rossingley", which is a bit weird. But, you know, everything about him is fairly weird, so I should stop being surprised by it. Picking up on the vibe he's not entirely thrilled to be hearing from me, I explain my mission and my current surroundings as best I can. He identifies my whereabouts from my description, effortlessly making me feel like a total imbecile for not locating his house.

"I suppose it could be slightly tricky in the dark," he concedes after I point out the lack of street lighting and signage. He goes on to explain that if I drive just a little farther down the road, past some stable buildings on my left, then I will see a set of wrought-iron gates with Rossingley Estate inscribed on a stone panel to one side. He tells me the three-digit code for the gates; I'm tempted to suggest he ought to change it to 666.

"Drive straight on until the floodlight sensor is activated. You'll find yourself in a courtyard, and I'll come out to meet you."

I surmise this must be one of those exclusive gated residences, one of those posh old houses converted into posh apartments for posh single people. And as I drive at a snail's pace through the gates, my suspicions are confirmed. Various unidentifiable buildings stand hidden in the shadows, and ahead of me is an elegant courtyard backing onto what is clearly part of the rear of a former stately home. There are very few cars parked, and even fewer lights on in the house for that matter. Fortunately, I spy Dr Avery stepping out of the back entrance to the apartments at the precise moment the floodlight sensor kicks into action.

Illuminated on the ground next to him is a small pile of chopped firewood, with a larger pile of bigger logs next to it, still waiting to be split. As I fiddle around nervously, parking up and generally delaying having to get out of the car, Dr Avery retrieves an axe from a nearby bench and resumes what I guess my phone call interrupted.

Jesus, what the fuck is he wearing? A kaftan or something?

It becomes blindingly clear the closer I get. On his top half, he's changed his work clothes for a ratty, baggy grey jumper, full of holes and perfectly appropriate for such a manual task. But on the bottom half, and also presumably on the top half but hidden under the jumper, he's sporting—and I'm not kidding—a cream satin negligee. A fucking slinky, satin negligee! Full length and most definitely clingy, it outlines every inch of his long slim thighs. On the upwards strokes of the axe, when the jumper rides up, it outlines pretty much every inch of his block and tackle too. A pair of old green wellies finish off the outfit beautifully.

Not sure what to do, I plump for doing what every well-brought-up boy has been taught and ignore it completely. My mother would be proud of me. Although less proud perhaps if she knew the effect the outline of his junk covered in a thin satin nightie is having on me. She'd just think that was peculiar.

"You really didn't have to bring my phone" is his super-grateful combined thanks and greeting as he continues swinging the axe. He seems different out here, not so intimidating, although that could be the nightie, I suppose. But he's evidently completely unfazed that I've caught him wearing it. He looks younger, too, more vulnerable. But looks can be deceptive, and before I get too carried away, I remind myself he's the one holding the axe.

"It was no bother, Dr Avery. I know how lost I'd be without mine."

"That's because you have people who probably want to get in touch with you, Jay," he drawls.

Yeah, right. "Not quite as many as I had about two weeks ago."

There's not a lot to say after that. Turning and getting straight back in the car feels a little abrupt. He's doing an okay job with the axe, but he's not really made much of a dent in the remaining pile of logs. And the autumn nights are becoming noticeably chillier.

"You're getting through those all right," I note after another downwards swing.

He nods. "Yeah, it's a good axe. You can take over if you like."

"All right."

Why the fuck did I say that? I could be back in the car by now. He hands the axe to me, then settles on the bench to watch, crossing his legs and lighting up a fag as he does so.

"That smoking won't do your sperm count any good," I observe. Christ, I must have a death wish. Sperm count? What the fuck? I could have gone with lung cancer or high blood pressure, one of the more obvious ones. And why should I care that he smokes anyway?

He smiles, showing those pointy canines, and carries on smoking, deliberately taking a huge drag. He's heart-stoppingly beautiful when he smiles; he should experiment with it more often.

It's strangely peaceful out here, and silent as the grave, apart from the rewarding *thwack* of the axe. My headache, a faithful companion these days, recedes a little. No traffic, no pavements, we could be hundreds of miles from any other civilisation. Maybe he's scared away the occupants of the other apartments. Or murdered them, then chopped them up into little pieces with the axe.

I've always enjoyed manual labour, and finding a rhythm, I get through quite a few logs and begin to build up a sweat. Pausing briefly, I remove my hoodie.

"Have you done this sort of thing before, Jay?"

For a second, I'm unsure what he's asking. Jilted a fiancée? Given a stranger a blow job?

"Chopping firewood, I mean. You're awfully good at it."

"Oh, no," I reply, although I wish I had. I'm finding splicing the dry timber extremely satisfying, particularly after my unbelievably stressful couple of weeks. Perhaps I should take some logs home with me and vent my frustration there, in our tiny backyard. With the added bonus of keeping out of Ellie's way.

"I grew up in a three-bedroomed semi with central heating. You should think about getting it installed, Dr Avery. It can be quite effective, saves doing this when you get home from a busy day at work."

"I do have central heating," he replies, eyeing me lazily. "It just seems pointless turning it on and heating the whole place when I'm in only one room. Anyway, my father always said that wood warms you twice. Once when you chop it and then again when you burn it."

So he's tight with money as well as grumpy. I'm not really surprised.

"You don't have to heat every room, Dr Avery. You can put thermostats on individual radiators and stuff. Timers that switch on and off. You can even control the heating via a phone app when you're at work."

Neither of us says anything; he quietly smokes, and I noisily chop.

"Why did you do it, Jay?" he asks suddenly, stubbing out his fag end. "You said that you'd never done it before. So why did you come to the club that night?"

I sigh deeply. "Dunno, really. Maybe I just got pissed and fancied something different."

Not the whole truth, obviously. It hadn't been completely spur of the moment—I'd been building up to it for a lot longer than that.

"Gosh! When most people get pissed and fancy something different, they have a kebab instead of a Chinese," he observes, showing me those pointy teeth again. I hide a smile; I didn't realise people still used the word 'gosh' without irony. And I bet he's never been drunk, then eaten a kebab in his life; he's way too posh.

I do need to offload my apparent meltdown onto someone though. My head is such a mess from thinking about it twenty-four seven. I can't remember the last time I slept for longer than five hours straight. He'd be as good a sounding board as anyone else, and he wouldn't sugar-coat his opinions, that's for sure. But not right now, it's still too raw. Having made a good dent in the pile of logs, I lay down the axe.

"This is weird, Dr Avery," I gesticulate vaguely. "You, this conversation, me being here. I think I need to go. I'll come back and finish the logs for you some other time soon, if you want."

He calls to me as I head back to the car. I carry on walking.

"I lied, by the way," he says, his clear, quiet tones carrying in the still air. Or that's what I think I heard. I stop and turn around.

"Huh?"

"I lied. About the cock sucking. It was good actually, really good."

Heat burns up my neck. I feel something approaching pleasure for the first time in many, many days.

"I know, Dr Avery. I lied about your name too. I like Lucien; I think it's very manly."

"Cocky little shit, aren't you?"

Chapter Five

LUCIEN

Action Man completed the task with twice my efficiency, and I was more than happy to conserve my energy and watch him. Granted, it was a pleasing spectacle; I'm beginning to see the point of all those rippling muscles. He's a rather big boy, at least two or three inches taller than me, not to mention significantly wider. Observing him at work, my slumbering cock had stirred without any manual assistance for the first time in months. And when he reached over his head to strip off his hoodie, he presented me with a wonderful flash of several inches of taut, olive-skinned six-pack, as if a Diet Coke advert was being filmed right in front of me. And if the good people at Lynx can so confidently declare that 'nothing beats an astronaut', then they clearly haven't witnessed Dr Jay Sorrentino chopping wood in a very snug-fitting grey T-shirt.

In his haste to leave, he'd left the pale-blue hoodie behind, and I bring the soft material to my nose, inhaling Fahrenheit combined with the delicious, unmistakeable aroma of fresh boy. Dr Jay Sorrentino is a bit of a puzzle, and he wasn't forthcoming with clues how to solve him tonight. I take the hoodie into the house and intermittently sniff it for the rest of the evening.

*

Every third week, I'm the consultant in charge of the ICU—the intensive care unit. Nearly all intensive care units are led by anaesthetists. Most members of the public have no idea what happens in an ICU, and they are the lucky ones because it means they've never had people they love admitted to one. Basically, an ICU is the specialist ward to which the sickest patients in the hospital are admitted after every other avenue of conventional hospital treatment has failed. Intensivists are not that interested in what disease the patient suffers from, or what sequence of events brought them to such a sorry state. For us, it's about seeing each patient as an amalgamation of organ failures—heart, liver, kidneys, lungs, brain—that need support until the illness is cured. So, if the illness has caused the lungs to stop working, we give an anaesthetic and support the patient on a breathing machine for days, weeks, or even months. If the heart is knackered, we give drugs to buff up the blood pressure, while the cardiologists figure out the best treatment. We dialyse kidneys. We deliver intravenous feed. And so on. We don't admit all desperately ill patients, just the salvageable ones, and unlike other healthcare systems, our wonderful NHS doesn't discriminate according to an individual's wealth. If treatment will ultimately prove futile, we don't treat, no matter how deep the patient's pockets. And if a patient is homeless on the streets, care will be equal to that of an earl. Like me.

Is it stressful playing God? Does it sap one's humanity? How to cope with all that death? Common questions with simple answers. Most doctors qualify at around the age of twenty-three, and as anybody in their thirties, forties, and fifties will tell you, that's desperately young. But youth is probably a good thing because young doctors become accustomed to bad things happening to older people, generally before they become that older person themselves and start panicking. Fortunately, young deaths are few and far between as they always hit hard, no matter how old and cynical the doctor.

We all have a private list of patients we can never forget. Mine is depressingly short, but if I grieved for every patient who died, I'd never get out of bed in the morning. None of the patients on my list would make an episode of a TV medical drama. There are no heroes on this list, neither the patients nor the doctors attending them. Still, they regularly drift into my thoughts in the small hours.

My first ever night on call as a junior doctor was in a sleepy hospital in Suffolk, and I attended my first-ever cardiac arrest. A stout old woman by the name of Nellie Blood, who'd probably already been dead for a couple of hours before the night staff checked on her. Never have I come across such a wonderful Dickensian moniker before or after. As much as I remember poor old Nellie Blood, I remember the anonymous, desperate, and emaciated old woman in the bed next to her, slumped in a pool of urine, gasping for breath after sixty years of smoking fifty fags a day. She died the next night. With irreparably damaged lungs like hers, admission to ICU would have been futile.

After that job, I worked on a neonatal ICU. Most of the babies were dreadfully premature. To my callous young eyes, they resembled hairless pink rats. We were only permitted to touch them with gloved hands through the holes in the transparent plastic walls of the incubator. Occasionally, we had babies who had been born after a normal nine months pregnancy but required surgery shortly afterwards—heart surgery or bowel surgery. Those babies were podgy lumps of gorgeousness. Perfect on the outside, yet all twisted guts on the inside. At night, if they were well enough, we would take them out of their cots and feed and cuddle them under the watchful eye of the nurse in charge. One of them, I grew fond of; I can still recall his sweet baby smell even now. He had young, hopeless parents, barely out of their teens. Returning to work after a weekend away, I discovered an empty cot and naïvely assumed he'd gone home. It was a few hours until I found out he'd gone to the big cot in the sky.

Another death, not long afterwards: I joined the ambulance crew on a call out to a girl the same age as me, who'd set fire to herself in her car. She lived for a few hours afterwards, reduced to a crispy piece of charcoal, incredibly still breathing in and out—there wasn't anything we could do for her. I could smell her for days afterwards. Even my parents noticed that I struggled with that one.

More recent times, at the start of my consultant career: A sick schoolkid with sepsis, diagnosed too late, silently dying on the end of my needle as I tried to stabilise him for transfer to the paediatric ICU. I beat myself up for months after that one. I still do from time to time in the wee small hours. Should've. Could've. Would've.

There are a few more on my list but thinking about them is depressing. And then there's my dead family, of course, but I'll never be able to talk about that.

And now we have Billy-Ray. He'll warrant a special list all of his own, the others relegated to the second tier. When I admitted him to the ICU three months ago, I knew without a shadow of doubt he wasn't long for this world, but we still have to try to save him first. Only nineteen, he lived with his mum and younger sisters in a shitty rental property owned by a shitty landlord who only cared about getting his money on time, not giving a fuck about tedious stuff like smoke alarms or condemned gas boilers. So, the flat burned down, mum and sisters perished, and Billy-Ray nearly died trying to get them out. Granted, he's still alive at the moment, but I wouldn't place any bets on him being here in a few weeks' time. Seventy per cent burns are not generally consistent with longevity.

Billy-Ray rarely receives visitors because his close family are all dead—I can relate to that—and the sort of friends he hung around with can't be arsed to trek over to the hospital to see him. He's off the breathing machine now, after the third attempt, and the burns are healing as well as expected. His guts are a different story; they're falling apart, so we can't get any nutrition into him, and he develops one infection after another that doesn't respond to treatment. Not unreasonably for someone in his unenviable position, he wants to die. He's in continual pain and practically everyone he's ever loved is dead. I can relate to that too. No amount of counselling by the well-meaning burns psychologist will ever bring them back.

The right side of Billy-Ray's face is fairly normal, his features pale and sharp, his light-brown eye bright. He was possibly quite good-looking once, in a sly, foxy sort of way. But a shocking Jackson Pollock canvas of purple now dominates the left half of his face, like wax dripping down the side of a red candle. And his torso, back, and left leg are a patchwork of angry skin grafts. If he had been much older, he'd have died weeks ago. He will die—I'd lay my entire inheritance on it—but modern medicine is ensuring that he suffers a slow, painful decline first.

The first time I enter Billy-Ray's room alone, after he's been off the ventilator for a few days, he pretends I'm not there. He fixes his gaze through the window and onto the view of an untidy cemetery (great town planning, guys), pretty much as he does when we have our daily team ward round to discuss his progress, or lack of, as if he's deaf as well as burned So I busy myself with his obs chart and calculate his fluid balance.

"You're gay, aren't you?" he says as I bend to measure his urine output in the catheter bag. His hoarse rasp reminds me to request the ENT surgeons to have another look at his burned vocal cords, an inevitable consequence of severe smoke inhalation.

"Yes, and so are you," I answer bluntly, deliberately not looking at him. From the corner of my eye, I can see his fingers worrying the frayed edge of his gown.

"How do you know?" he demands, letting go of the fabric and staring at me full on.

"Because I spotted you checking me out on Thursday when I came in with the dietician."

"Have you got a boyfriend?"

"Is it any of your business?"

He doesn't answer, and I think that's probably the end of the conversation. Pulling out volume three of his enormous set of notes, I begin writing.

"You're a twat to everyone who works with you."

I ignore him and continue writing.

"You are, you're a twat. A pasty, miserable twat. And you're old."

"You know, Billy-Ray," I say mildly, endeavouring not to laugh. "There is a big red sign on the door on the way into this hospital that advises, 'Abuse to members of staff from patients and relatives will not be tolerated'." I continue writing.

"Forgive me for not having read it, Doc. I was half dead at the time." He pauses. "Twat."

I stop writing and try to keep a straight face. "If you call me that again, I shall be forced to put you back on the ventilator. Without sedation and for a very long time."

A raspy, choking sound emanates from the bed, and I look up in alarm. I relax as I realise what it is. Through parched, scarred vocal cords, Billy-Ray is laughing.

*

Once a year, as part of my supervisor role, I am obliged to join a jolly band of enthusiastic educationalists throughout the region and accompany my assigned junior doctor on a course. There, we flatten hierarchical barriers, and he grows up to become a well-rounded, forward-thinking consultant. Like me. The course is named Lead and Be Led, although they should just save time and retitle it Do It Dr Avery's Way.

The venue for this ghastly meeting is a bland Hilton Hotel, *naturellement*, just off the M4 heading into Bristol. The programme lasts an entire dreary day, followed by an equally dreary celebratory course dinner to bring us all together as a united, happy educational family. I had no plans whatsoever to hang around for the course dinner, except that this year the whole shebang has been organised by Annabel and Emily. Not only have they informed me that if I don't turn up they will kick me out of the office and make me share with Dr Leitner, but they have also bought my ticket and paid for my meal. And thankfully booked me a hotel room so I can at least drink my way through it.

Fortunately, the precourse preparation is brief: Jot down on a scrap of paper, in no more than two sentences, a recent achievement which makes you proud. Before you get too carried away, please note that your comments may be anonymously shared with the other delegates.

Does managing to get out of bed and attend this bloody stupid course count as an achievement? Probably not. I decide to skip the homework.

The usual suspects are here, all bright-eyed and bushy-tailed. I recognise a few faces from Allenmouth, but there are many from other hospital training programmes I don't. Nevertheless, they are all carved from the same mould. Casually dressed, ambitious young professionals and a smattering of jaded-looking older consultants, who somewhere along the line found themselves having to endure this new world of self-discovery navel-gazing courses and Myers-Briggs personality analysis. I'm gratified when Jay grumpily slumps down in my eyeline. He looks knackered. Clearly not his scene either. Gosh, those manly thighs sure look good in a pair of jeans. Maybe he'll be amenable to slipping down to the bar at lunchtime. I idly wonder what he's put down as his proudest recent achievement. Ditching his bride at the altar? Sucking a bloke's knob for the first time? I'll be extremely impressed if he declares that one.

The room is filling up, already uncomfortably warm. I spy Dr Leitner manspreading in the front row, with sweat circles visible under his flabby armpits. Yuck. After hanging my Tom Ford jacket neatly on the back of my chair and loosely rolling up my shirt sleeves, I glance up to catch Jay giving me a once-over. I smirk, and he looks away, a slight pink flush to his cheeks.

Introductions over with, and having helpfully alerted us to the location of the nearest fire exits and toilets, Annabel moves on to the ice-breaking preliminary section of the programme, the part where we are all supposed to suddenly develop trust and openness amongst this group of relative strangers and feel sufficiently comfortable to discuss our deepest fears. Or some such dire nonsense like that.

"So, guys," she says brightly, her enthusiasm easily carrying around the room.

I loathe the term 'guys' and nearly head on out right then.

"You all hopefully filled out some 'proudest achievement notes.' I certainly did; I can't expect you to do your homework if I don't do mine!"

A few titters and I inwardly cringe. Annabel's proudest achievement is managing to strong-arm me into sitting here today. Only seven hours of purgatory to go.

"I'm going to read a sample of them shortly. The point of this exercise is to think about everyone's achievements as I read them out and focus on their diversity. Try to picture what success looks like to different people, yeah? Hopefully, anyway—this game has never let me down yet, guys, but there is always a first time!"

A ripple of polite laughter follows, and as Emily carries the box of papers over to Annabel, she continues earnestly rabbiting on.

"The diversity will demonstrate that not all leaders are cut from same cloth, that we are all different, from different backgrounds and cultures; we have different personalities and very differing ideas of what constitutes success."

There's a hell of a lot of 'differents' in that sentence. She pulls out the first piece of paper from the box and begins to read.

"My proudest achievement is when my wife gave birth to our gorgeous twin boys last year."

Annabel smiles, and there is a predictable collective 'aah' around the room. A thin, tired-looking Indian man sitting in the row in front of me smiles proudly. Achievement by proxy there, young fellow, I feel like saying. All you did was shag her. God, it's going to be a bloody long day.

"My biggest achievement is receiving the all-clear from breast cancer," continues Annabel, reading from another slip of paper. There is a smattering of applause.

"My biggest achievement is persuading my parents to buy me an Aston Martin on my thirtieth birthday."

Annabel rolls her eyes at this one, adding, "We always get one of those. I'll have worked out who you are by the end of the morning and will be sure to give you a hard time!"

I've already worked out who it is—it's the smug-looking blond idiot who was doing his best to smarm up to Dr Leitner on the way in.

"My biggest achievement is listening to my inner voice, then having the balls to act on it, even when I knew how hurtful it would be to people I loved. But it's something I should have done a long time ago."

Annabel raises her eyebrows thoughtfully. "Ooh, we seem to have a deep thinker amongst us," she comments pleasantly. "Such diversity on display already, guys!"

Jay is looking down at his feet, that cute pink flush in evidence again. Dr Leitner snorts derisively. God, that man's a twat.

"My biggest achievement is securing VIP tickets to see George Ezra play at the Isle of Wight Festival last year."

"My biggest achievement is rescuing my brother from a hospital in Ecuador after he broke both his arms skydiving."

And so it goes on, with my biggest achievement managing to stay awake and in my seat. Fortunately, my role in the day's events is as a passive, supportive listener. And as Dr Sorrentino and his rather scrummy thighs appear perfectly capable of negotiating the programme on their own, equally as passively, I can be even more of a bystander than I anticipated. The last few minutes of the morning session are set aside for us to have a quick one-to-one with our individual trainees before lunch. I'm disappointed to see that Jay has disappeared as I was planning on buying him a drink. I vaguely wonder if he's avoiding me. Thus, as minister without portfolio, I find myself surplus to requirements, and fearing I'll be assigned to someone else or, heaven forbid, have to make small talk during the lunch break, I make a sharp exit for my room and have a quick snifter from the minifridge.

Jay reappears for the afternoon session, and a whiff of a beery smell when I stroll past him confirms my suspicions that he fucked off to the bar without me. It hasn't escaped my notice that he seems a little short on friends himself today, which I'm guessing has something to do with the recent turmoil in his personal life. Slightly dozy after my liquid lunch, I decide his olive-skinned face with its stupidly long eyelashes and oh, so lovely mouth, is extremely handsome, and thus spend most of the afternoon daydreaming in the back row about a repeat performance of his lips round my cock. With a bit of luck, he's booked a room for the night here too.

A few hours later, at the mediocre Italian restaurant on the ground floor of the Hilton, I find myself wedged between Annabel, who I've already scolded for the infernal 'guys', and a semi-retired colleague called Geraldine, whom I know from past experience only ever talks about her cats and her Oxford-educated nephew. I push my tepid carbonara around my plate—the closest item on the menu to macaroni cheese—wishing I was tucked up in bed wearing my favourite nightie, with a glass of Campari and the day's *Telegraph* crossword for company. Sitting opposite me is Dr Leitner, his jowly face already as red as a beetroot from half a bottle of Rioja. Next to him, Jay Sorrentino looks devilishly handsome in a grey round-necked sweater. Actually, I'll ditch the Campari and the crossword; I'll just have him tucked into bed with me instead.

I generally tend towards a penchant for boys with physiques similar to my own, on the thin side of slender. More yin and yin, over yin and yang. Cool Loki, not muscle-bound Thor. But there is something about my Dr Sorrentino that draws me in. When I sniff his soft hoodie (granted, a bit needy and pathetic, but I'm not ready to return it yet), I imagine him wearing it while lounging on my sofa. And I'm resting my head on his broad chest, encircled by his brawny arms, and being, I don't know, cherished maybe? And maybe he'd be watching sport on the telly, a football match or something, perhaps sipping a beer. Every now and again, he'd lean down and kiss my lips, just an absent-minded peck, or ruffle my hair. It's not even a sexual fantasy, although his chest without the hoodie would be rather spiffy too. But as I've been such a dick to him, none of that's going to be happening any time soon. Billy-Ray was right to call me a twat. I'm astonished Jay's not put in a request to change his Ed Supervisor already.

Apart from the food being tasteless and the company tedious as hell, the evening is proving unexpectedly tolerable. Every time I look up, the heavenly Dr Jay Sorrentino is in my direct line of vision. He's knocking back a few beers, with red wine chasers, and I can't blame him. No doubt, Dr Leitner is boring the tits off him about the good old days of working seventy-two hours a week, and how this young lot have never had it so good. Although, aside from the attempt to drink his own body weight in beer, you'd never know how bored he is because he nods at all the right moments and laughs at the weak jokes. People are drawn to Dr Sorrentino, and it's easy to see why. With an easy, open smile and a cheerful confidence, he charms people, a natural social animal. I used to be like that once, believe it or not, but since the accident, well...not so much.

Geraldine is giving me a blow-by-blow account of her Siamese's latest bowel movements, and Annabel is determinedly not rescuing me. She thinks I need to socialise more and hasn't forgiven me for pulling her up on the 'guys' thing. Thanks a bunch, Annabel. Zoning out of Geraldine's ramblings, I focus on ogling Jay.

The newspapers over the last few days have been full of the death of a Russian gazillionaire, who somehow succeeded in ramming his superyacht into submerged rocks south of the island of Santorini. The whole thing sank rapidly (the yacht not the island), taking him and his poor, unfortunate harem with it. According to reports from one of the surviving crew members, this brainless oligarch insisted on taking the helm when he was pissed, showing off to the women, and none of the flunkies on board had the balls to stop him. The other side of the table are discussing it.

"Not a mode of death most of us are at risk of," observes Annabel drily. "I stand more chance of drowning in the bath than aboard a sinking superyacht."

"Rich people do have exclusive ways of dying," sneers Dr Leitner. "Even in death, they have to separate themselves from the rest of the great unwashed. Just as they insist on exclusive schools so that their darling Sebastian's and Saskia's don't have to mingle with everyone else's kids. Private hospitals. Invented illnesses! Heaven forbid they die of something as common as a stroke!"

Here he goes, well balanced, with a chip on each shoulder. He's partly doing it because he loves endlessly voicing his own opinions, but also partly because he's spotted that I'm listening. He doesn't know much about my background, but I never hide the fact that I'm obviously posh. Why should I? I couldn't influence into which family I was born. But he's just warming up; he'll no doubt move on to sly homophobic digs next. Christ, he's still bloody talking.

"Hah! Do you think they try to outdo one another by killing themselves on luxurious private jets, or helicopters that crash when they shouldn't even be flying? Much more exclusive, much more interesting than a simple old heart attack. There was that multimillionaire who owned that football club a couple of years ago, remember? Fell out the sky like a stone, took a load of other people with him, slap bang outside the stadium. And then there was that one last year—some aristos with more money than sense—the whole family wiped out in a helicopter, flying low in bad weather, the bloody fools. Actually, I recall they were from this neck of the woods, weren't they, Annabel?"

I'm vaguely aware of Annabel agreeing that she believed they were, and then Leitner chipping in with, "And no one remembers the poor pilot just doing his job in all of this, do they? Unless it's to blame him, of course. Oh no, just poor old Lord so-and-so and his precious heir to the bloody empire. Bloody deserve it, that's what I say. *Vive la révolution!*"

I knew there were solid reasons I avoided socialising. Ideally, I'd like to stand up and hit Dr Leitner really hard, pounding my fists into his fat red face, but I'm totally incapable. And I'd come up with a perfect rejoinder after I'd hit him so I could knock him down verbally too. While not prone to violence, I'm usually pretty good with my tongue. I'd humiliate him in front of everybody. But mostly, I think I just want to kill him.

Yet, for all of these grandiose, aggressive ideas, the only action of which I'm capable—and even that's hanging in the balance—is to rise from the table without crashing to the floor. My head and guts spin wildly, and I make for the gents. Knowing I'm not going to get there in time, I veer outside, banging through the fire exit next to the kitchens only seconds before my belly spews forth an arc of hot acid and lumps of carbonara. I manage to miss my shirt, with most of it spraying over a spiky bush behind the door.

Afterwards, when I'm all emptied out, I lean against a giant rubbish bin, panting and drooling saliva, my heart hammering in my chest and my eyes streaming. Eighteen months ago it all happened, that helicopter crash, but sometimes the phone call that followed feels like only yesterday.

My own private hell turned into idle dinner party entertainment.

With my breathing less panicky but my stomach still churning, I fish out a cigarette and light it with shaky hands. My whole body is shaking or shivering, I'm not sure which. Regardless that I'm probably over the legal alcohol limit, I'd like to get in my car and disappear. But this alley behind the building is a dead end, and I'd have to walk back through the restaurant to collect my belongings from my room. I'd have to face them all with some feeble excuse. They think I'm peculiar anyway, so it wouldn't matter too much. But then Annabel and Emily would ask if I'm okay; they'd fuss and be nice, and then...and then I might cry, and I couldn't bear them all to witness that.

The kitchen door bangs open. I quickly turn away, shielding my face, hoping I look like a chap who's come outside for a quick fag and taken a wrong turning. A big warm hand tentatively squeezes my shoulder.

"Dr Avery, are you okay?"

Jay's flattened vowels, full of concern. I don't trust myself to speak.

"Hey, Dr Avery...Lucien. What's wrong? One minute you were there, and the next, you looked like you'd seen a ghost or something."

That hand still rests on my shoulder. Humiliatingly, hot tears trickle down my cheeks and there's nothing I can do to squeeze them back in. That's the trouble when people are kind; it's so much easier when they aren't, when nobody knows you're suffering. I brush at the wetness with the back of my hand, then take a shaky drag on my cigarette, willing him to go away. If I pretend he's not there, then he'll give up and go back inside.

"Are you ill, Lucien? Maybe the food didn't agree with you? I chose the carbonara too. It was very stodgy."

He's persistent, I'll give him that. Keeping my back to him, in the iciest voice I can muster, I say, "I'm fine, Jay. Really. Go back inside."

He doesn't move. "I'm not going anywhere, Lucien, not until I can see that you're okay." That soft, kind voice again. Patient, determined.

I laugh, but it comes out as more of a sob, to be honest. "Gosh, then I hope you've brought a jacket because it's quite chilly. And if you are planning on waiting until I'm okay, then we'll be here a while."

"You're trembling like a leaf. Come on, Dr Avery. I'm worried about you. At least turn around and look at me."

When was the last time anyone declared themselves to be worried about me? I take a final drag and drop the butt onto the ground, squish it with my boot before slowly turning to face him. "There, now you see me. Satisfied? My humiliation is utterly complete."

The next thing I know, I'm crushed against that soft grey sweater, encircled in those huge muscly arms, his face buried somewhere in my hair. A faint waft of Fahrenheit mixed with Corona lager fills my nostrils. While the tears continue to flow, he carries on holding me as I let it all out, cocooning me against that warm expanse of chest, shielding me from the world.

I'm not sure how long we stand like that. I can't remember my last proper cuddle or hug from anyone. A year ago, at least? Or longer, maybe from my mother the very last time I ever saw her. No, it was my cousin Freddie in the immediate aftermath. This one with Jay probably only lasts a minute or so, but it's long enough for me to pull myself together. Gosh, this is horribly embarrassing.

"Lucien?" he whispers. "Tell me what's wrong. Let me help."

"I can't tell you what's wrong," I say against his chest, my voice weak and hoarse. "I'd like to, but I'm afraid I'm unable to formulate the words just now. Sometimes I wonder if I'll ever be able to. If you google Rossingley, the Rossingley Estate, then I daresay it will all make sense."

From somewhere in his jeans, he produces a crumpled, clean tissue and hands it to me. Averting his gaze, he pretends to study the bins while I wipe my eyes and blow my nose.

"How do I look?" I ask him, and he peers into my face.

"Beautiful," he replies, smiling, and I can't help myself by smiling back. He's a dreadful liar; my face will definitely be red and blotchy.

"Why are you so nice?" I ask.

"I'm not particularly." He shrugs. "At least, no one else shares your opinion at the moment. Perhaps I just seem that way compared to you."

He nudges my shoulder and clumsily, a little tipsily, in fact, puts an arm around me, pulling me close. "Whatever shit you've got going on, Lucien, we're going to go back in there, pretend we've just been out for a fag together, and get through it. Honestly, give it a few seconds more, take a couple of deep breaths, and no one will notice anything. Come on; you can do this!"

And so we do. And it's not that bad. Annabel throws me a curious look, but Geraldine is too busy explaining her nephew's scholarship at Harvard to the poor junior on her right, and probably didn't even notice I was ever missing anyway. Dr Leitner is haranguing the rushed waiter about the delay between the main course and dessert, and so I manage to sit quietly and relatively unnoticed, while all around me, people ooh and aah over synthetic chocolate puddings. A sudden firm pressure appears against my calf, and when I look up, Jay is smiling gently. It's been a while since a pretty boy played footsie with me under the table or smiled at me so kindly. I'm assuming it's him, of course. It could be Geraldine feeling unusually frisky, although if it is, then obviously, she's barking up the wrong tree.

The diehards carry the party on through to the bar, and I'm astonished to find myself amongst their number. Probably because the thought of going back to that characterless hotel room and lying awake for the next few hours doesn't appeal. Or it could be because a certain young doctor, who minutes ago had his foot curled around mine under the table, is also in the bar, sitting with a rowdy crowd of juniors. And he's definitely giving me the eye. Quite a bloodshot eye admittedly; he's knocking back pints of beer and Jack Daniels shots as if prohibition has been declared as of tomorrow morning. I can't blame him; he's had a shitty couple of weeks from the sound of things. One is permitted to drink oneself to oblivion when the world implodes. I speak from experience, recognising a fellow sufferer on a mission. Sipping my Campari and soda more sedately, I pretend to care that Annabel's oldest boy has narrowly missed out on being selected for the under-thirteen county cricket side.

A minor commotion at the juniors' table draws my attention a while later. A few of them are getting up to leave, Jay included, and in his state of inebriation, he's knocked over a pint glass, spilling its amber contents all over the floor. A sense of responsibility I never knew I possessed creeps up on me. It's time to return the favour.

"I think, Annabel, that I'm going to ensure young Dr Sorrentino safely makes it up to his room," I murmur, gathering up my jacket.

"Wow, you are taking your supervisor duties seriously," she drawls as we both watch Jay clumsily attempt to retrieve his phone from off the table. "It wouldn't by chance be because he's the finest specimen of manhood ever to grace Allenmouth Hospital, would it, Lucien darling?"

"Good gracious, no, Annabel. That would be dreadfully unprofessional of me."

The group spot me heading towards them.

"Hey, Jay," one of them shouts. "Watch out! The AA is coming for you! As if your life couldn't get any more shit!"

I take a mental note of the owner of the voice and store it away for the future. The smug blond one with the Aston Martin. That little twerp is going to wish he was never born. He need not bother applying for the ICU fellowship post, that's for sure. Or any other job within fifty miles of Allenmouth if I've got anything to do with it. I give him 'the look', and he visibly shrinks, suddenly finding the bottom of his pint glass infinitely more interesting than my face. Jay has no such qualms.

"Dr Avery!" he slurs happily. "You're still here! Come and join me! Last time I met you in a dark bar, we..."

"Right, Jay, show's over," I interrupt forcefully. "Part of my educational role is to see you safely to your room, according to Annabel, and so that's what I shall do."

Grabbing his arm, I steer him away before anything else spills out of his mouth that he might regret. Coming out of the closet in the middle of a Hilton Hotel bar on a Thursday night, in front of random colleagues and acquaintances, is probably not what sober Jay Sorrentino was planning. There is a chorus of "oohs" and whistles as we retreat, which I ignore and to which Jay is mercifully oblivious.

It's only when he starts walking, or rather stumbling, that I fully comprehend exactly how pissed he actually is. Manoeuvring roughly fourteen stones of solid man towards the exit is proving a challenge. I sling his arm around my shoulders, and he half walks as I half drag him into a lift.

"This is the last day of my honeymoon today," he slurs down at me as I prop him against the lift wall and press the button to take us up. "I should be on a beach in Cancun with my f...f...female wife. Did you know that, Dr Avery?"

"Yes, Jay, I did know that," I reply.

He giggles drunkenly. "Do you know why it's called a honeymoon, Dr Avery?"

I shake my head, and he giggles again. "It's because your wife is as sweet as honey, and she shows you her bum!"

I don't know why I find this funny, but I do, although not as funny as Jay, who is sniggering uncontrollably.

"You're very pretty, Dr Avery, has anyone ever told you that?"

"Yes, Jay, as a matter of fact, they have. But compliments are always appreciated."

He's looking at me strangely. "Are you still sad, Dr Avery?" he slurs. "I don't want you to be sad."

Gosh, am I still sad? Only every single bloody hour of every day. "Yes, Jay. But you are currently doing a very remarkable job of cheering me up."

It's like babysitting an oversized, naughty toddler. We leave the lift, and struggling to walk at all, he leans against the corridor wall, belches rather ungraciously, then slowly sinks down it, landing with a bump on the floor. His hysterical laughter after I bang my funny bone on the edge of the lift—his fault for leaning all that solid weight on me—has turned to sobs.

Great. This is so far out of my remit, although I can't for the life of me fathom why I'm smiling at the ridiculousness of my situation. Needless to say, a repeat of the blow job is definitely not on the cards. I hover in front of him, praying he doesn't fall sideways, as I'm not sure I'm strong enough to winch him up from a prone position.

"Fuck, Dr Avery. I should be in Cancun. Ellie hates me, my friends hate me, my family hate me. I've fucked everything up, haven't I?"

"Come on, Jay. Let's just get you to your room. Get some sleep. These things often seem better in the morning."

Now, this is an oft trotted out cliché that I know for a fact is a lie. Since my family were wiped out, the desolation of early dawn can often be the worst time of day. At least at night, it's socially acceptable to resort to booze or illicit substances to dull the pain. Jay will no doubt discover this fallacy for himself, but for the moment, he pushes himself away from the wall with a more urgent matter.

"I think I'm going to puke," he declares, and yeah, from the colour of his face, I think the doctor has self-diagnosed correctly. I haul him up and reach for my room key.

"Quick, get in here, my room's closest."

As I shove him through the door, his shoulders start to heave and a torrent of brown, fizzy liquid erupts forth. Like an idiot, I reflexively try to catch it in my hands, resulting in the bulk of it finding its way down the front my Battistoni shirt as he careers into the tiny bathroom. The second fountain of vomit mostly ends up in the bathtub, thank God. I'm nearly gagging myself as the sour stench of half-digested whisky, wine, and beer pervades my nostrils. The warm, half-digested contents of his stomach begin seeping through my shirt and onto the skin of my chest. Nowhere on the educational supervisor training course was this scenario mentioned as a possibility.

While I'm still coming to terms with this rather unexpected turn of events, Jay unbuttons his fly and charmingly proceeds to urinate into the bath, a gallon of steaming piss helping to wash some of the vomit down the plughole. Goodness, I seem to have become an honorary member of the university rugby club.

"It's that bloody carbonara, Dr Avery," Jay chortles as he sways over the bathtub. "It made you sick too. I'm going to have a pepperoni pizza next time. Shall we have the pepperoni pizza next time, Dr Avery? Fuck that, would you like to eat my pepperoni, Dr Avery?"

"Stay there!" I command, trying to sound stern and also trying not to let him see how amused I am. "Do not, I repeat, *do not* step away from the bath until you've finished!"

After wrenching off my ruined shirt, I dump it on the bathroom floor and wash the yuckiness off my hands. The vomiting and urinating behind me seem to have finally ceased. After wiping his face with a wet towel, I manhandle Jay onto the bed and put the wastepaper bin next to him for safety. Miraculously, his gorgeous grey sweater appears to have escaped the worst of it. I pull it off him—he's about as much use as a chocolate teapot.

"Are you undressing me, Dr Avery?" He giggles again. "That's very forwards of you. I'm not usually this easy."

His rather delicious chest is bare, apart from the rug of black hair blanketing it. It's been carefully manscaped but still oozes testosterone. No sign of hairy shoulders or a hairy back, though, so that's a blessing. I resist trailing my fingers along the grooves of his abs because that would be taking advantage of an inebriated man, and I'm so much better than that. Honestly, I really am, although my fingers do accidentally graze across his hip as I loosen his belt. Both hips actually. And pushing some of those soft black curls from out of his eyes is also very responsible of me. How the hell I'm going to get this half-naked man-mountain down the corridor to his own room, I've not yet worked out, especially as I don't imagine for a moment he'll be able to offer any assistance. I conclude he'll have to stay here, and we'll deal with the inevitable awkwardness in the morning.

"You've taken your shirt off, Dr Avery. Fuck me, Dr Avery, are those...?"

He's vaguely pointing to my nipples. "Are we going to bed together, Dr Avery?" he slurs, gazing up at me sleepily. "I've never been to bed with a man before. I think I want to though; you are so fucking pretty. Do you think I'll like going to bed with you, Dr Avery?"

"For goodness sake, Jay! I've removed my shirt because it is covered in your vomit! Let's just get your shoes off, shall we?"

Shoes and socks successfully negotiated. I decide to leave his jeans undone but in place, which, again, is very responsible of me because, ideally, I'd like to take this opportunity to completely check out every inch of him. The sour stink of sick seeping into the carpet is becoming hard to ignore, let alone the whiff emanating from my own body. Leaving Jay on the bed, I return to the bathroom to retrieve a towel, and the next fifteen minutes are taken up with me scrubbing at the floor and sluicing out the bath. Finally, I step under the shower and smother any lingering traces of Jay's vomit with the contents of every complimentary lotion on the shelf.

On my return to the bedroom, Jay is out cold in the middle of the bed, flat on his back and snoring blissfully. As I slip beneath the covers next to him, I discover that those big bulging muscles take up a lot of space. On the plus side, it's like having a personalised electric blanket. The aircon makes the room a bit chilly, and I haven't got much meat on my bones, so I can't help cuddling close to him. That's the excuse I'm sticking with anyway.

Smiling to myself at his ridiculous honeymoon joke and the memory of being wrapped in his arms against that soft grey sweater, I snuggle down. My final thought before I nod off is that I can't recall when I last had so much fun.

Chapter Six

JAY

The first thing I do when I wake up is get the fuck out of Dr Avery's room. Somehow during the night, I've managed to end up with him draped all over me, and I experience a moment of sheer panic. Not because I don't like the idea, far from it in fact, but the horror of him waking to the sensation of my morning glory pressed against his thigh doesn't bear contemplating. As I gingerly extricate myself, he murmurs slightly and shifts away. He's still sleeping, thank god, and I fumble around for my phone and room key, which he's considerately lined up next to each other on the bedside table.

I watch him for a few moments, ready to make a dash for the door if he stirs. He's moved so that he's lying on his back, with one arm raised above his head and the other resting across his taut belly. The covers are pulled down to just below his nipples. In disbelief, I stare at the diamond-tipped barbell gracing one nipple and the small silver ring in the other. Oh, my giddy aunt. Sexy. As. Fuck. With flawless alabaster skin and his features smoothed into a pale mask, he reminds me of a renaissance statue, like those found in cathedrals lying on top of tombs. Or a vampire maybe. Best not go there. He's immaculate regardless, even fast asleep, which is no surprise because he's exactly the type of person who doesn't snore, doesn't trip over stuff, never has food caught in his teeth, never has patients who vomit after anaesthesia, never vomits...fuck.

Back in the safety of my own room, I wonder whether I'm about to chunder again. And not because of my monumental hangover. Oh, no. It's much, much worse than that. Did I...could...did...his shirt...? Oh fuck.

*

I've been confused about my sexuality for a couple of years now. On some level, I think Ellie probably suspected, although we never talked about it. It's not something you really discuss with your fiancée. Not when there are so many other important topics of conversation, such as wedding venues, seating plans, bridesmaid dresses, and the like. And apart from that one time in the nightclub, I've never put it to the test.

We'd been officially together for coming up to four years, but had studied in the same year at med school, so we'd been on and off for a lot longer than that. And at first, it was good, really good. Looks-wise, she's hot, straight out of the top drawer. Tall, blonde, skinny, big blue eyes; she was the girl who all the blokes in our year lusted after from freshers' week, me included. And she's clever and funny; all our mates declared we were a perfect couple, and for a while, they were right. We were so perfect that we bought a place together.

Our relationship didn't sour immediately, and there was nothing specifically that I could put my finger on, but gradually we drifted apart. I tried to leave her a year or so ago, but the timing was wrong—she had exams, I had exams, and somehow it seemed easier to park our differences, concentrate on work, and pretend everything was okay. And when we met up with the gang, we could turn it on, do the golden couple thing, and maybe we even fooled each other for a while, as well as everyone else. So much so, that when Evan and his missus got engaged, we did, too. It was the logical next step. In bed, sex was infrequent—pretty ordinary and unadventurous—which on reflection, was probably a bit premature for two healthy adults in their twenties, yet we ignored that too.

But my newly discovered feelings for Dr Lucien Avery? Very hard to ignore. He's making me revise my confused fantasy therapy introduction that plays around in my head. Now it's a very unconfused: Hi, I'm Jay Sorrentino, and I'm totally, 100 per cent sure I'm gay. But is it okay to fancy a man in a satin negligee?

Back home. After several hours of oscillating between cringing in the foetal position on my bed and pacing up and down, repeating, "Oh God, oh God, oh God" over and over to myself at the hazy recollection of covering his shirt with sick and then weeing in the bath, I recall our conversation out by the kitchen bins before he realised I was an absolute piss artist. After firing up my laptop, I type in a single word: Rossingley. And then, three seconds and fifty-eight thousand Google hits later, all my personal problems—my aborted wedding, the suspicion that my parents are screening my calls, the knowledge that my friends all hate me, my closet gayness, my recent vomiting escapade—all fade into insignificance. Because no matter how many fancy titles and how much land you inherit, nor how much money has fallen into your lap, nor even how fucking drop-dead gorgeous you are, none of that comes close to compensating for the sudden loss of everyone you have ever loved in one fell swoop.

*

It's Saturday morning, Ellie is at work, and I'm restless. Even though we are no longer a united couple in the biblical sense, financially, we remain glued together and stuck in the same house. So, I do our laundry, the weekly supermarket shop, go to the gym, and then finally manage to touch base with my parents. It's a brief conversation; they are glad I'm still alive, but that's about as far as their happiness for me extends right now. In a word, unforgiven. My headache starts up again.

I spend a bit of time reading around burns injuries and the long-term sequelae, as we've got a young lad on the unit at the moment with severe burns following a house fire. Although the burns are doing okay, other bits of him are falling apart, and not having had experience of major burns patients before, it's new territory for me. I've noticed Lucien spends a lot of time with him, trying new meds, changing the treatment plans, but we all know he's slowly deteriorating regardless.

Evan drops by to say hello. On one level, I'm grateful to him for not following the herd and totally abandoning me. Yet once more, he pesters me; like everyone else, he's desperately trying to understand my unfathomable late change of heart. But I'm not ready to come out yet, and that's all there is to it really. I'll tell people when I'm good and ready. He's heard about my drunken performance after the course dinner and, naturally, finds the fact that Dr Avery took me off to bed in front of everyone bloody hilarious.

"Sounds like you've pulled there, mate," he jokes. "I bet he's got an arse like a cat flap. And I reckon he's predatory. I wouldn't want to find myself alone with him late at night in the theatre changing rooms. Hope you kept your back to the wall, mate."

You have no fucking idea.

Smiling weakly at his casual homophobia, I rapidly change the subject, hating myself for not picking him up on it. For not defending Lucien specifically, and gay men like myself generally. Did I used to laugh along with jibes like that? Probably. Will he still make the same derogatory comments when he finds out about me? Possibly. I'm relieved when he gets up to leave, promising beers at the pub later in the week.

All of this is displacement activity. What I really want is to drive to Rossingley, then apologise/grovel/curl into a ball and die. But, as I'm only too frequently reminded, Lucien's a prickly bugger, and even though he let me give him a hug, I could tell he hadn't wanted me to see him so distraught. He didn't have much of a choice; I was a bit pissed already at that point, and my arms seemed to move of their own accord. I wonder who he has to take care of him, if anybody at all. No immediate family, that's for sure. Perhaps he's surrounded by friends, perhaps even now, he has a house full of people—or maybe a lover who's supporting him in a way that I'd like to. Somehow, I doubt it. I sense that prickly, tense Lucien Avery is a very private and lonely man. But having looked after me when I didn't deserve it, and stopped me from embarrassing myself any more than I already had, he deserves thanks and an apology. And, at the very least, an offer to pay for his shirt to be dry-cleaned.

By lunchtime, I reach the conclusion that I've got the remainder of a pile of wood to chop. He might not be pleased to see me, but I can't get through the weekend without doing something about him. The wood chopping is a valid excuse to drop in, or that I left my hoodie behind. What's the worst that can happen? I go over there, he tells me it's not convenient, and I leave? Yes, I'll be embarrassed even further, but at least I'll be reassured. And then I can attempt to forget about him and concentrate on sorting out my own disastrous personal life.

The journey over to Rossingley is very different on a sunny Saturday afternoon, and as I get closer and the villages turn into fields, I realise how pretty the landscape around Allenmouth is. The Wikipedia article stated that Rossingley covers 6,000 acres. I've no idea what that amount of land looks like, but it sounds larger than your average back garden. As I approach, I wonder whether these are his fields and his estate cottages. Hah! Estate. I'm a working-class townie, and where I come from, an estate means a different thing entirely.

The stable block is easier to identify in daylight—the horses are a major clue—as are the sturdy gates just beyond. Recalling the passcode, I drive through, belatedly wondering whether I should have phoned first. Thanks to the miracle of the internet, I've pored over pictures of the main house, so I recognise this is the back entrance, as the front of it has an enormous long drive, preceded by a stunning avenue of oak trees. How bloody far was I wide of the mark, thinking he lived in an upmarket block of flats?

Parking up next to the courtyard, I spot Lucien sitting on the bench, smoking. He gives me a small wave as I step out of the car. Pleased or displeased? It's hard to tell. The pile of logs is untouched, the axe lying where I left it.

"I thought I'd finish what I started," I say with a cautious smile, my excuse for the visit at the ready. Once again, I pretend I haven't noticed the outfit, keeping my eyes resolutely fixed on his face. The same old jumper, although a string of fat pearls hangs down over the top of it. On this occasion, the accompanying negligee is black, not cream, but equally clingy. The smooth black satin matches his black eyeliner, and his light-pink lip gloss complements both. I swallow. Already, my dick is plumping up; even with the wellies, this extraordinary sight is turning me on. The conviction that I am way out of my depth doesn't even begin to cover it.

"Be my guest," he replies, unperturbed, and makes a space next to him on the bench. "And I should apologise for Thursday night at the dinner. I was caught on the hop and let myself down, I'm afraid, but you were very kind to me."

He doesn't meet my eye as he says this. I sense even raising the subject is an immense struggle. I'm not interested in pushing him; I want to see that sweet smile again, not the tears. And hell, he's the one apologising? Taking a seat sheepishly on the bench next to him, I briefly put my hand on his arm.

"Christ, Dr Avery, you have nothing to apologise for. I made a complete tit of myself!"

I'm rewarded with a diffident smile. "Yes, you did, but it was highly amusing, so I shan't hold it against you."

"You must let me pay for your shirt or something, though. Honestly, I'm mortified! I'm not usually like that, I promise you. I guess I was just feeling the strain and let my hair down for a night."

He gives my thigh a little rub. "Gosh, it's fine, Jay. I have plenty of shirts. And I think you should probably call me Lucien. Dr Avery feels a little formal now that we've spent the night together, don't you think?"

Heat rises up my neck at the image of him stretched out asleep and those fucking nipple piercings. A set of ancient binoculars is propped on the bench next to him, and I nod my head towards it, keen to change the subject. "I'd assume you were spying on the neighbours, but as you don't have any, what are you looking at?"

"That pair of lovers up there," he replies, pointing. "*Milvus milvus*. Red kites. We've had red kites nesting on the estate for hundreds of years. This land is as much theirs as it is mine."

He hands me the binoculars, and I scan the pale-blue sky until I spot them circling high above.

"They used to be a dying breed, but we've been part of a programme to increase their numbers in the UK. At one point, there were only three pairs left in the country— two pairs in Wales and a pair here. They are easily identifiable because of their forked tails. This particular husband and wife have been around for about fifteen years."

We track the graceful birds for a while, swapping the binoculars between us.

"So what do you do here all day, apart from watching birds and avoiding chopping wood?"

I'm rewarded with the shy smile again, and my stomach does a small flip.

"Oh, you know, the usual. Host gala balls, receive ladies for tea in the drawing room, alter the cut of my britches with my valet, terrorise the under footman. Swive the stable boy."

I don't know what swive means, but I can hazard a guess. "Very funny, Lucien. I'm a poor lad from a council estate in Wolverhampton. I haven't got a clue what someone like you does to run a place like this."

He sighs. "Nor did I until about eighteen months ago. I was just another weary junior doctor, with an ICU consultant job lined up at St George's."

He puts down the binoculars. "You've read up on me, I take it?"

I nod, slightly embarrassed. Wikipedia was very informative.

"Then you'll know that I'm the spare, not the heir. None of this was supposed to happen. But when it did, I took the job at Allenmouth and came back. I work at the hospital three days a week, and the rest of the time, I'm here, going through business with the estate manager. I'm gradually becoming better at being lord of the manor."

I'd wondered why he only worked part-time, and now I know. "Do our work colleagues know about this?"

He shrugs. "I don't think so, although it's not a deliberate secret. I can't believe even Dr Leitner would have been so...so cruel had he known. I've had the occasional older patient from this side of town give my name badge a strange look, but then, as you know, propofol is awfully good at rapidly closing down an undesirable line of conversation."

I grin at him. Propofol is the first-choice anaesthetic drug we administer to send patients to sleep. It's extremely powerful and works very quickly. Michael Jackson can vouch for that. Or maybe not. Lucien carries on.

"And Avery is a fairly unremarkable surname, so they wouldn't necessarily assume I was 'Duchamps-Avery'." Giving me a slightly apologetic look, he adds, "And I'm not exactly forthcoming with personal information at work. On balance, I'd rather you kept it to yourself."

I smile at him. "Even if they wondered, everyone would likely be too scared to ask you outright anyway."

He regards me slightly mischievously. Another flip of my stomach. "Are you scared of me, Jay?"

"God, yes! But perhaps not for the same reasons as everyone else."

I feel myself blushing and stand quickly, hefting the solid axe in my hand. "Why don't you sell up? You know, if you can't manage it all?"

Harrumphing, he replies, "Gosh! I'm not sure the fifteen earls who've gone before me would be very happy with that horrifying suggestion." He cups his ear with his hand. "In fact, listen! I can hear them all turning in their graves now."

"Yeah, but it's not as if you're going to be carrying on with the family line, are you? Seeing as you are batting for the other side and all that?"

His reply surprises me. "It's on my to-do list actually," he informs me. "The thirteenth earl managed it somehow, and he reportedly wore make-up and ball gowns and insisted the staff always addressed him as Lady Louisa."

I laugh. He's funny when he chooses. "What was his real name?"

"Lucien. As our American cousins are fond of saying, go figure."

*

I chop the wood for a while, and he stacks it neatly under a shelter at the edge of the courtyard. He doesn't talk much, but I don't mind. I'm surrounded by folk all day at work, and I grew up in a small house with three noisy sisters, so I'm always happy to have a bit of peace and quiet. After an hour or so, we break for a cup of tea, and he leads me into the house. He removes his wellies, and taking his lead, I slip out of my trainers. The only difference is that I'm wearing white towelling socks and his long slim feet are bare. His painted toenails match his lips perfectly.

I'm not sure what I was expecting as we enter the house—sweeping marble stairways, staff dressed in tailcoats, and Lucien ringing a silver bell to summon them before afternoon tea served in china cups. But he leads me through an ordinary solid back door and then along a fairly dark corridor, which opens out into a vast farmhouse kitchen, equipped with a dark-blue Aga at one end and a squashy, flowery sofa nestling at the other. A huge oak refectory table runs down the middle. Lining the walls are a hotchpotch of china plates, a couple of hunting watercolours, and dangling kitchen utensils. It's warm and homely. He fills a battered tin kettle with water and places it on the Aga.

"Do you have staff in the house, Lucien?" I'm quite self-conscious as I enquire, but in my defence, my mother is a huge fan of *Downton Abbey*. I'm still half expecting Carson, the head butler, to suddenly materialise. Lucien could probably do with a Carson in his life.

He shakes his head. "No, not since…no. I don't actually live in the main house these days. I use this kitchen and a service flat through those doors there."

I nod knowledgeably as if I fully understand the concept of a service flat.

As he reaches for the mugs, he carries on. "Before the…before…" He stops and swallows, then starts again. "We used to all live in the main house; I grew up in it. It was always full of people—my…my… parents were very sociable."

Voice breaking, he turns away from me, playing with the pearls around his neck, and I pretend to be busy with something on my phone while he composes himself again.

"You're the first person who's been in here for at least a year," he blurts. "Apart from my cousin, Freddie, who visits sometimes. I don't even invite Will, the estate manager, in—we meet at his office in one of the outbuildings. I haven't been inside the main house for nearly that long either. Nobody has, except for a cleaning company who go in every month. I should take a look at it, or Will should. I'm just finding it very hard. I can't explain it. I struggle to…to… I think…I don't like to…to let people in."

I realise he doesn't only mean into the house; he means into his life. Into his heart. He holds the mug out to me awkwardly with a trembling hand, tea threatening to spill over the rim. I take it from him.

"So you're the first, Jay. The first person I've let in. I don't know why."

"Well, clearly, after our intimate night together, it was the obvious next step!" I joke, and the shy smile puts in a brief appearance. "You could give me a tour now if you like? So you don't have to do it alone the first time? You can't put it off forever. You might have rats, or a big leak, or an escaped prisoner squatting in the east wing!"

Not for a moment did I think he'd say yes, but cradling his tea in one hand and fingering the pearls with the other, he beckons me over. We walk through what he referred to as the service flat. It's a little down at heel and very dark—narrow corridors, with sombre wood panelling. A section of the panelling has plastic sheeting stretched across it.

"Gosh, sorry about the mess," he says, indicating it. "There was a rotten section there, where I had some water escape last year. I haven't got around to having it repaired yet." He gives me a regretful look. "As I said, I don't feel up to having people in."

I take a peek under a corner of the sheeting. "It's not too bad under here, Lucien. Just needs the rotten bit of wood taking out and a new section put in. And then you'll have to sand and paint or varnish the whole lot, otherwise it will look mismatched."

Prodding the soft rotten bit, I then tap my fingers further along until the wood feels hard again. "I could do that with you; it's probably not even a day's work."

"I wouldn't know where to begin."

I gaze at him for a moment as he leans against the door frame, one hip cocked, drinking in his pale patrician features and elegant form. And the delicate negligee obviously. DIY and Lucien don't really go together.

"My dad's a builder, Luce. I worked for him for years on and off, spent all my med school holidays working for him. This bit of carpentry is pretty straightforward."

Bloody hell, did I just call him Luce? Apparently, I did. And my balls are still intact.

The sweeping staircases, marble pillars, fancy cornicing, and crystal chandeliers of my fertile imagination are on display in all their glory as we wander through the myriad of rooms. It reminds me of my mum's beloved period dramas, starring Colin Firth or Maggie Smith. These rooms would provide a perfect backdrop. Minus the butlers and footmen and whatever other underlings were once required to keep somewhere as grand as this shipshape.

"You could fit my parents' entire bloody house into here," I say incredulously as we enter what is evidently a library. All the furniture is covered in dust sheets, but the walls are lined with books from floor to ceiling, and they have those ladder things on wheels that sweep along the shelves. Under one dust sheet is the outline of a grand piano, or an oversized butternut squash, but my money is on the piano.

"So what's the proper term for a country pile like this, then, Luce? A manor? A stately home? A palace?"

I try the 'Luce' again on purpose, but he doesn't bite. In fact, he hasn't said much at all as we've wandered around his ancestral home, but he seems less trembly in this room. He's stopped fiddling with the pearls and has even pulled out a couple of books from the shelves and flicked through them. Returning one to a shelf, he looks up at me, smiling.

"My father used to say the definition of a stately home is when you can reach speeds over 60 mph on the driveway, which was obviously a red rag to a bull for me and my brother. When we were younger, we shared a beaten-up old Volkswagen Golf. Oliver once got it up to seventy-eight on the flat stretch before the lake. Draw your own conclusions."

It's the first time he's mentioned his brother. Wikipedia informed me that the difference in their ages was less than two years. His voice didn't waver either when he related this tale. I think he likes this room, he's comfortable in it, and even with the dust sheets it has a cosier feel than the other grand reception rooms. I have a fleeting mental image of the two of us ensconced side by side on the giant sofa in front of a roaring fire, surrounded by all these books. Crazy, I'm not sure he even likes me that much. I just don't think he wants to be alone.

We head off up that grand sweeping staircase. The first door opens onto a vast bedroom, dominated by a hefty oak four-poster, also mostly covered in dust sheets. From lying in the bed, one could take in the entire parkland as it falls away as far as the eye can see. I imagine waking with Lucien in this bed, looking out over the lush green lawns, with him wrapped in my arms. Christ, I need to pull myself together. I've never even kissed a bloke, and now I'm dreaming about cohabiting with a rather peculiar one.

He joins me at the enormous sash window.

"So, where does your front garden finish then?" I tease as we gaze over what seems to be miles and miles of immaculately mown grass. He smiles in gentle acknowledgement at my humour.

"You can't see the end of my *garden* from this window. Beyond the park is a woodland, where one of the tenants runs a clay pigeon shoot, and then the village cricket pitch is through those trees over here."

He points to a patch of woodland in the distance. "And beyond that is the village of Rossingley. Most of the smaller cottages in the village are tied to the estate too. And the pub. And...um...the tenant farm over there. And the...um...other two farms in that direction."

Putting a hand lightly at the small of my back, he turns me so I'm facing easterly. "This is the back *garden*. All of that farmland over in this direction. Arable mostly, but there is some livestock. A lot of the fields are rented out to other farms. Er...oh, and those four cottages on the far hill are mine too."

I burst out laughing. I can't help it. I've walked into a parallel universe, leaving the hospital and my little town house far behind. Or maybe not a parallel universe; perhaps I've just stepped back in time, back to the feudal system. *Downton Abbey* is positively slummy in comparison.

"Wikipedia says that you are one of the richest landowners in the UK," I state, turning to look at him. "I'm starting to believe it's true."

He shrugs and moves away from the window. "Probably. I've some land and commercial property in London too. And the house in Mayfair, of course."

"Oh, yeah, of course. Who doesn't have a house in Mayfair these days?"

I receive a sharp poke in the ribs for that comment, but he says nothing as we carry on through more sumptuous bedrooms and corridors. Up and down a lot of bloody stairs. I'm beginning to understand why posh people are so skinny—this house brings a new perspective to the phrase 'I'm just popping up to the bedroom to get an extra sweater'. I've lost my bearings completely; if he suddenly disappeared, I could spend days trying to find the right staircase out of here. We enter a room that is even bigger than all the others, not dissimilar in size to my old school's sports hall, but with a fancier parquet floor and a much nicer smell.

"The ballroom. Do you dance, Jay?"

"Only when I'm pissed, and not the sort of dancing that goes on in here. More of a lumbering, embarrassing shuffle."

He raises his eyebrows. "Gosh, it sounds fabulous, darling. If I'd known that, I'd have asked you to partner me the other evening!"

"Not when I'm that pissed, you idiot! But I'm betting fifty quid that you can dance properly."

He grins, a real grin that lights up his whole face. "What self-respecting earl doesn't? Maybe I should teach you sometime."

"You'd have your work cut out."

I have a fleeting vision of me in a dinner jacket and him in his negligee, foxtrotting arm in arm around the ballroom, like on *Strictly Come Dancing* but without Bruno's suggestive comments. I don't actually own a dinner jacket, but I reckon Lucien's got a few more of those slinky negligees tucked away.

"Come on though, you have to admit. Being an earl, it's sort of cool, isn't it? I mean, I can't imagine if I brought you home and introduced you to my mum and my nan as an earl—they'd be on the bloody ceiling. They'd be so stoked; they probably wouldn't notice me telling them I was gay."

He's looking at me curiously. "I didn't think you were sure that you were."

"No, nor did I. Or rather, I didn't know for certain."

"What, or who, helped you make up your mind?"

It's cool in these airy, uninhabited rooms, but for some reason I'm feeling very hot under the collar. "I think you probably know the answer to that, Lord Rossingley."

*

The next floor is darker, the rooms more dormitory-like and utilitarian, branching off narrow, twisty corridors.

"The old staff quarters," Lucien explains helpfully.

"Christ, you could have some wicked games of hide-and-seek in this place."

"We did." He laughs at the memory. "Oliver and I always won against everyone else, though, because we knew where all the hidey-holes were. There are a couple of secret passages too. Once, when we were small, Oliver and I took some food and hid for about six hours, and my mother had just about everyone who worked on the estate out looking for us. My father gave us an absolute bollocking for that."

I'm over at one of the windows again, taking in the view of the huge lake and the tiny chapel at the far end. "This place is incredible, it really is."

It takes me a few seconds to realise he's not answered or moved. Turning towards him, he has his back to me, shoulders hunched, head down. One hand is covering his face, the other grasping his pearls.

"Oh God, I'm so sorry. I shouldn't have persuaded you to do this. Don't cry. Please, I didn't mean to make you cry."

Christ, I'm a completely useless idiot. I feel absolutely wretched for initiating this trip down memory lane. Eventually, he speaks, his voice muffled into his hand.

"I think you should probably go now, Jay. Let me take you downstairs and show you out. There is a very high probability that I'm about to fall apart, and as you have already witnessed, it isn't particularly dignified or endearing, I'm afraid. Something I prefer to do in private."

His loneliness and his courage break my heart.

I've probably watched too much sci-fi, but he almost has a kind of forcefield surrounding him, radiating warning signs to keep out. He's no doubt built it up to protect himself, but it's gradually killing him from the inside.

"I don't think so, mate. What sort of friend would I be if I upset you and then walked away?"

I cross the room towards him and hover behind, unsure what to do. When he'd been upset outside the restaurant, putting my arms around him had seemed so natural that I hadn't given it a second's consideration.

And not only because I'd been three sheets to the wind. He'd needed a hug, and I'd delivered, exactly as I used to with my sisters when they had boyfriend trouble, or Ellie, the last time she failed her exam. A normal, natural human response to another person's distress. But this feels much harder; every cell of his body radiates 'keep off the grass!' loud and clear.

Fuck it. I touch him anyway, and nothing bad happens. I'm not electrocuted or turned into a pile of slime or anything. As I rest my fingers lightly on his upper arm, he leans back just a little into me, and his shoulders lower slightly. At least he's not pushing me away or falling apart like he'd warned me.

"Don't you have...er...I don't know...any old friends helping you, Lucien?"

He gives a shuddering sigh and shakes his head. "My friends are mostly in London, and I've pulled away from them somewhat since it all happened. All this misery becomes a bit tedious for them after a while. And they all have busy lives of their own. My oldest and best friend, Marcel, lives in France, and he has serious health issues, so we don't meet up as much as we'd like."

"What about relatives? You must have some of those."

Wearily, he rubs his face. "I have uncles and aunts, but I'm never sure of their motives, to be truthful. It would have been more convenient all round if I'd been in the crash too. The situation with my relatives is a little delicate. As you've spotted, I have inherited a substantial number of assets that various other people would probably like to own too."

He pauses then continues. "Death doesn't bring out the best in folks, as I have discovered to my cost. My dear friend Marcel meets up with me when he's well enough. I have a cousin, Freddie, of whom I'm very fond, but he's a lot younger than me and always jetting off somewhere exciting. I suppose that Will, the estate manager, keeps an eye on me—he'd notice if I didn't appear one morning."

And that's it? That's the entirety of his support network? A poorly mate in another country, a busy young cousin, and a loyal employee? Jesus wept.

"I'm just so sick and tired of feeling like this. Of feeling so dreadfully miserable. Like when everything is trotting along, and I'm coping and thinking that I'm back on my feet, then suddenly, wham! Out of nowhere, one careless comment over dinner and I'm back to square one."

I give his shoulder a gentle squeeze. He inhales deeply, getting himself under control again. I wonder how many times he's done this alone.

"Not long after the accident, I used to lie in bed and fantasise about all the different ways as an anaesthetist that I could painlessly kill myself. I'd mentally write a self-help guide, you know, *101 Easy Ways Out*, by Dr Lucien Avery."

He must feel me start back with shock, as he hurries on. "Gosh, don't worry. I've gone passed that stage. I realised that although I held the keys to the drugs cupboard, when push came to shove, I couldn't find the nerve to go through with it. Pathetic of me, really."

It's a well-known fact amongst the medical profession that male anaesthetists have higher suicide rates than average. Partly because of personality types—

we tend to be loners—but also because, rather like farmers and their shotguns, we have the ready means to execute it.

"I'm not sure a book like that would make it onto the Amazon bestseller lists," I murmur.

"Yes, but I suppose a lack of five-star reviews would be a very accurate measure of its success."

I laugh briefly, but even though he's joking about it now, he's clearly been to some fucking grim places in his head.

"I'm sick of lugging all this grief around with me. I want to dump it somewhere and feel normal again."

"Well, I can help you with that, Luce. I'm about as normal and ordinary as it gets."

"I'm not sure that's true at all, but carry on anyway. Let's talk about anything except me. Tell me something funny—you're the first person that's made me smile in months. I loved your honeymoon joke, by the way."

Christ, I must have been truly slaughtered; that's one of my dad's old favourites. I'll be producing a silver sixpence from behind his ear next. I ponder for a moment.

"Okay, I've got a story for you. Brace yourself; it's a tragedy worthy of William Shakespeare himself. I'm surprised Hollywood isn't clamouring for the film rights. They would cast Kit Harrington in the starring role."

I clear my throat theatrically and begin.

"A couple of years ago, I realised I might not be as altogether...um...into the girlies as much as I thought I was. I don't know why or how really, and I'm deliberately not thinking about it too much, probably because I'm not an introspective sort of person, and I don't want to tie myself up in knots analysing myself. There was no major event, no psychological drama that I've suppressed from my childhood. I just began to feel something was wrong or missing."

I don't know why I start telling him this now, but he's listening for sure, and he's leaned back into me even more. I cautiously slide both my arms around his middle, and he rests the back of his head on my shoulder. A tingling warmth spreads through me. The only sounds up here, at the top of this big old house, are my voice and his quiet breathing.

"Anyway, this feeling was sort of nagging at me. It was like an itch, and I couldn't get it out of my head. So I decided to scratch it for real and go along to a gay club, and just, I dunno, try and pull someone. I didn't really have a better plan, although I feel a bit stupid admitting that out loud."

He feels so nice like this, his body warm and lean against mine. He smells of fresh air and sort of outdoorsy, maybe it's the tatty sweater. The silky nightie underneath is slippery against my hands.

"So the first time, I waltzed straight into the club, sat at the bar for about thirty seconds, and then waltzed straight out again. It wasn't my scene at all. I felt really out of place, to be honest, surrounded by all these confident, flirty gay men. And none of them looked like me, you know, in my ordinary jeans and a polo shirt? They were cooler somehow. Anyway, after that minicrisis of confidence, I left it for a few months and then managed to talk myself into giving it another try."

I laugh softly to myself as I recall the second time. "So I went back to the same club—Spangles—and managed to actually sit at the bar and down three pints. I think I was the only beer drinker in the place; I'd never seen so many bloody cocktail umbrellas. A couple of blokes were giving me the eye, and the barman was definitely chatting me up. He was nice enough. Given time and a few more drinks, I could have been interested in him. Anyway, I went to the gents for a slash, and some guy basically tried to assault me in there while I was having a piss. Maybe it's normal behaviour for toilets in gay clubs, but it wasn't fucking normal for me."

"That was very brave of him," interrupts Lucien. It's the first time he's spoken, and at least my ridiculous tale has halted his imminent flow of tears. "Or very foolish. Had he not spotted your big bulging muscles?"

I give him a squeeze and press my nose momentarily into his soft hair, breathing him in. "Obviously not, but I panicked and clocked him one, then ran out the door."

The texture of the silky negligee against my hand and his taut abdomen underneath it, not to mention the summery scent of his soft hair, is giving me an inappropriate hard-on. Discreetly adjusting my stance, I pull away slightly so he doesn't feel it against his arse. I'm supposed to be comforting him, not rubbing my dick up against him.

"That little episode put me right off, and I left it for about six months after that. But then the itch came back again, and I built myself up to give it one last try. The timing wasn't great—it was a week before I was due to get married."

He unsuccessfully stifles a laugh at this.

"This is a very, very poignant story, Lucien, about an exceedingly troubled young man! I'd be grateful if you'd treat it with the gravitas it deserves!"

His shoulders jiggle again with silent laughter.

"Anyway," I continue, "The softly-softly approach hadn't been particularly successful the last time, so on my third trip to Spangles, I decided to get absolutely hammered *before* I went in, and then just find the most beautiful man in the room and ask him if I could suck his cock."

"And how did that work out for you?" Lucien asks softly, wriggling his arse up against me. Fuck, it feels insanely nice. So much for hiding my hard-on. I'm psyching myself up to kiss him when I finish my story. I've never kissed a man, but two nights ago, I vomited over this one, pissed in his hotel room bath, and he's still talking to me. So how hard can it be?

"Far too well, Lord Rossingley. I should have chosen the ugliest instead. My life would have been a hell of a lot simpler."

Somehow, I manage to disentangle myself, made easier by my stomach rumbling loudly, which sort of breaks the moment. The kiss will have to wait.

"I can offer you an apple or a slice of Battenberg cake." Lucien leads the way back downstairs. "Although the cake is well past it's sell-by date. And then I was wondering if...um...if you would like to come for a walk?" he adds shyly. "I usually force myself out at least once a day. But if you have better things to do than spend the remainder of the day with a depressive autocrat like me, then I'd completely understand."

The alternative is to return home and re-enter the shitstorm. It's an easy decision to make, and I'm becoming increasingly fond of this shy, lonely Lord Rossingley. He's sweet and quiet and brings out a macho protective side I didn't realise I had. I'm finding the reincarnation of Lady Louisa pretty hot too. She makes me blurt out things I never thought I would, and I haven't forgotten those bloody nipple decorations. Hell, I wanked in the shower this morning to images of those nipple piercings and the pale, smooth skin surrounding them. I'm not entirely convinced by spikey Dr Avery, but the other two alter ego's more than make up for him. Though, I conclude Dr Avery must be in charge of the food supplies because I reckon the other two would be much better hosts. An apple and a slice of stale cake don't touch the sides; I'm bloody starving.

A brisk promenade in the early evening sunshine will do me good. It will cool my ardour, or whatever phrase they use in Regency romance novels as, right now, it feels like I've stepped into one. And cool my ardour I must. It's only been a few weeks since I walked out on one long-term relationship, and me having the hots for my educational supervisor is not a complication I need to add to the mix. Especially as he's a bloke dressed in a negligee.

Wellies back on, and an old Barbour thrown over the sweater for warmth, Lucien lobs a second apple at me and leads the way. I half wondered if he'd change his outfit before stepping out, but no, he's quite content in his nightwear, and I've almost become used to it. We head across the front garden—sorry, park—to the woodland beyond and take a well-trodden path through it. Now I'm closer, the cricket pitch and smart-looking pavilion, with an adventure play area adjacent, are visible. Making the most of the unseasonably mild weather, several families mill around the play area, and dog walkers share the same route as us through the trees.

"Several public footpaths and bridleways cross the estate," Lucien explains, seeing my puzzled face. "The immediate parkland around the house is private, and the lake, the chapel, and some of the woods, but this bit is for all the villagers to use."

Which is fine, very generous of him and all that, but a middle-aged couple with a Labrador are walking towards us, and Lucien is, well...he's wearing a bloody nightie!

As the couple approach, we do that reassuring, very British dance.

"Afternoon! Lovely day for it, isn't it?" says Lucien expertly, nodding and smiling, and they return his comment, a familiar little ritual as we pass by.

"We need to make the most of the fine weather while it lasts!"

"Still a bit chilly for this time of year, though!"

From the plastic grins on their faces, it's obvious they've noticed his attire; Lucien, however, is totally unfazed. That's sixteen generations of aristocratic breeding for you.

"Er...did they know who you are, Lucien?"

"I have no idea." He shrugs, looking at me sideways, and I glimpse pointy canines as his mouth turns up wickedly. "I have a reputation for being a tad reclusive, to put it mildly. But I suspect they do now. If they're locals, they will have heard the rumours about me."

He waves an elegant hand, somehow managing to encompass his unusual attire, his make-up, and his striking hair.

"It will give them something to talk about at bellringing practice," I comment.

"Or at the Rotary meeting."

He steps ahead of me, then suddenly makes a graceful twirl in the middle of the path, which is quite a feat in a pair of wellies. Pirouetting ridiculously, he laughs.

"It will have made their day! They'll be able to confirm that I actually exist, that I'm not a figment of Will's imagination. They've finally seen gay, mad Lord Rossingley for themselves. The one they hear about but who never goes out, the crazy albino with the white hair. The recluse, the weirdo, the creature who wears dresses and is too scared to live in his own house. The ghost who only comes out at night and frightens small children!"

The walk has put him in a playful mood, the happiest I've ever seen him. We encounter more couples and families out strolling in the late afternoon sunshine, and Lucien greets them all cordially. At one point, he briefly takes hold of my hand. My palm is big and warm in his smaller, cool one as he points out the ruined stump of a tree and the frayed remains of a rope from when he and Oliver would dare each other to swing across the stream. I'm disappointed when he lets go.

*

I don't want our day together to end and sense with pleasure that the feeling is mutual. Back at the house, he peers inside the fridge. I'm still hungry; Lucien seems to survive on fresh air, fags, and Lapsang tea.

"I'm afraid I don't cater to healthy masculine appetites very well, Jay. I can offer you Waitrose macaroni cheese for one, or how about Waitrose macaroni cheese for one? And because you've made me laugh for the first time in aeons, I'll treat you to a glass of Campari."

I try not to make a face. I haven't got a problem with the macaroni cheese part, but Campari is bloody rank. And anyhow, I've already decided we can do much better than that. I want my sweet lord to carry on smiling shyly at me, I want Lady Louisa to carry on flirting with me, and I want Dr Avery to stay firmly locked in whichever room of this vast manor he's currently hiding in. Oh, and I want my dick to stop constantly reminding me of its presence, which is tricky in the presence of my other desires.

"Lucien?"

"Yes?" He turns, looking at me expectantly.

"Go and change into something less comfortable. Thanks for the very generous offer of Campari, but I'm taking you to dinner."

I'm sounding a lot more commanding and in control than I feel. And ashamed that, although I like the nightie, I'm not ready to accompany him to a restaurant while he's wearing it. I'm convinced any minute now, he's going to politely ask me to bugger off so he can be on his own and eat his macaroni in peace. Yet instead, he has a pleased, albeit slightly surprised, look on his face.

"Gosh, is this going to be a date, Dr Sorrentino?"

I pause for a second before answering. I don't know, is it? Do gay men take other gay men on dates? I'm completely clueless, but I'm guessing they do. The total extent of my gay lifestyle research up until now extends to locating a gay club in London averaging 4.5 stars on Tripadvisor. I've never even watched gay porn. But fuck it, yeah, why not?

"Yes, Lucien. I'm taking you on a date."

If thirty-four-year-old men could be described as scampering, then Dr Lucien Avery, sixteenth Earl of Rossingley scampers off in the direction of the flat.

"Oh, and Lucien? Keep the pearls on. I like them."

The more time I spend with him, watching him run them through his fingers, the more I'm convinced the pearls are a comfort blanket. He's not mentioned them, and I'm not going to ask.

Ten minutes later, he reappears, and it would seem that not only does he have three personas, but also three sets of clothing styles. Set number one is the Dr Avery, Consultant Anaesthetist ensemble—a more expensive, well-cut version of the smart casual chino/shirt combo popular with most male doctors. Set number two is apparently an array of female night attire, the extent of which I have a feeling I haven't been fully exposed to yet. Set of clothing number three is as individual as set number two, and way too cool for sleepy Allenmouth. I'm thinking Nick Rhodes from early eighties Duran Duran, with a hint of Regency dandy thrown in. The hair, the eyeliner, the lip gloss, not to mention the pearls. And I can't even see the nipple piercings, but just knowing they are underneath is sending my dick into overdrive.

I'm discovering a fetish for men in make-up I didn't know I had, or perhaps, it's just for one man in particular. Which is bizarre because I've always had a preference for girls who don't cake their faces in the stuff.

The old Barbour has been exchanged for a close-fitting vintage military greatcoat, complete with rows of gold buttons and tasselly epaulettes. His long legs are sheathed in impossibly tight black jeans. God knows what sartorial surprises await underneath the coat, but I'm finding this incarnation of Lucien Avery to be pretty damn perfect. Trying not to stare, I say the first thing I can think of.

"If we put you in a soldier's uniform, you'd be a poster boy for the Third Reich, Lucien."

"Gosh, you say the sweetest things, darling."

*

I drive us to a curry house on the southern edge of Allenmouth where Ellie and I and the rest of the gang have eaten a couple of times. I'm trying not to dwell too much on Ellie. While I was waiting for Lucien to change, I sent her a text, explaining I was helping my educational supervisor with some DIY, and that we were going to grab a bite to eat afterwards. Which is mostly the truth, except I omitted the bit about how my stomach turns somersaults every time I coax a smile out of him. But I still felt dirty sending the text. It all feels way too soon to be embroiled with someone else, however tempting that someone may be.

The curry house is busy, and we are given a table for two near the back. Lucien, with his shock of white hair, killer cheekbones, and tasteful make-up attracts attention, to which he appears utterly oblivious. I've decided to stop being so parochial when I'm out with him, so I try to be completely oblivious too. Acutely aware of every set of middle-class suburban eyes on us as we are led to our seats, I've still got some way to go to achieve his level of nonchalance. If Lucien weren't so striking, we'd look like any other gay couple having dinner together, and I'm a lot more comfortable with that notion than I thought I'd be. After ordering a couple of Cobra beers and a pile of poppadum crackers, we settle down.

"So, talk me through the girlfriend thing, Jay. Or should I say ex-fiancée?"

Well, that's a direct approach. "It's not good etiquette, Lucien, to discuss previous partners on a first date."

"I think that as a peer of the realm, I know a teensy bit about etiquette," he teases. "I have a whole page in *Debretts*, don't you know? But tell me about it anyway."

I need more than one bottle of beer to get through this conversation, but seeing that Lucien has witnessed me absolutely slaughtered twice now in the space of little more than a fortnight, I don't want him to get the impression I'm a raging alcoholic.

"After my little—what did you call it?—'extracurricular activity' in Spangles, I went home the next day and called the wedding off."

That made it sound a hell of a lot more straightforward than it was.

"Doing...what I did...with you in that club," I continued, "it clarified what deep inside I already knew but had been trying to ignore for years. There was no way I could go through with the wedding; just the thought of it made me feel ill. And equally as important, it wasn't fair on Ellie."

I swallowed down a mouthful of beer, reliving the hellish twenty-four hours that followed my encounter with Lucien in Spangles. Twice I'd stopped the car on the trip back to Allenmouth, convinced I would puke all over myself while I was driving. I'd parked in a layby for what felt like hours, desperately trying to work out how I'd break the news to Ellie.

"We were six days away from getting married, so as you can imagine, calling a halt to the wedding went down like a cup of cold sick. If I have to fucking apologise to everyone one more time, though, I think I shall scream."

Lucien was a good listener; he hadn't interrupted once. Another swig of beer. "Since then, my parents have virtually disowned me, her dad and brother have threatened to kill me, and all of my friends, apart from my best man, seem to have deleted me from their contacts. Ellie...well, Ellie is living at the other end of the house. And it's a very small house."

"Why are you both still living there? Can't you go somewhere else?"

It's a good question. "I'm still there because I can't afford to move out, rent another place, and manage to pay my half of the bills and mortgage. Ellie initially moved back to her parents' house for three days and then came back. 'You've done this, you fucker, and I'll be fucked if I'm the one who fucking moves out', I think, was her exact rationale."

"Oh. Gosh."

I'm getting into my stride now. "Gosh indeed. So, as the current situation stands, I'm a social leper. We've put the house on the market, and when it's sold, she'll have her share plus all of the money we lost on the wedding. Which is thousands, by the way. And typically, I chose to have my homosexual epiphany during a slump in the housing market, so it looks like we're stuck with each other for the foreseeable future."

I fiddle with the label on my beer bottle, and very soon it's a neat pile of paper strips on the white linen tablecloth. Lucien looks at me thoughtfully.

"Does she think you'll change your mind? Will she have you back?"

I nod my head resignedly. "Yes to both, I think. She's devastated. Both of our families are, too, particularly as I haven't come up with a good explanation for calling it off. They all think I've just got cold feet and will come around."

"Do you love her?" Lucien asked gently.

I shook my head immediately. "No, I don't. Not as much as I should. I love her as a friend. Which isn't enough to build the rest of our lives together, is it?"

He smiled, almost sadly. "The only marriage I've ever witnessed at close quarters was my parents. Looking back, I realise they were besotted with each other, even after all those years together. So, no, you're right, I don't think it is enough."

Our evening was taking a melancholy turn, which wasn't my aim at all. "My best man is convinced I'll come to my senses, that she'll forgive me, and we'll all find this episode absolutely hilarious in about twenty years' time."

"Jay, darling, you've mentioned your best man twice now, and it's beginning to hurt my feelings. I think you are going to have to start referring to him as your second-best man from now on, don't you think?"

As he coquettishly flutters his eyelashes at me, I find myself blushing.

"And?" he continues, "Is your second-best man correct? Do you think you will come to your senses?"

"No."

I shake my head. "My second-best man is not correct. Absolutely not. I'm gay, Lucien, maybe bisexual at a push. And at some point, I'm going to have to explain that to everybody. But not until I'm ready. I'm not ashamed of it or anything, or even wishing I was straight. I just want to come out on my terms, not anyone else's."

"Is there anything I can do to help?"

"You're doing it." I smile back at him. "Being with me. You're very...um...distracting. My life feels all a bit weird at the moment. Right now, I should be writing thank you letters for wedding presents, not having a prawn jalfrezi with my educational supervisor."

Lucien frowns slightly. "I'm curious that you've reached the grand old age of, what, nearly thirty? Before you've worked it out, I mean."

So we talk about that, too, but there isn't much to say, apart from that I've joined the party at least a decade late. My lack of ability to explain it is as frustrating for me as it will be for anyone to understand when I think the time is right to come out. I can tell he's quite pleased that my brief encounter with him in the club is the entire extent of my gay sexual experience. As he seeks clarification, I blush even more.

"What, no rumpy pumpy?"

Only Lucien could use the ridiculous euphemism rumpy pumpy and make it sound like the most seductive sexual act ever. Unfortunately, I'm not so silky-tongued.

"No, but I have shagged a couple of girls up the bum," I qualify unnecessarily.

He guffaws with laughter, splattering beer down his chin. It's the most inelegant thing I've ever seen him do, and it's a while before he can stop laughing enough to speak. "Gosh, you make it sound terribly romantic, darling."

"I'm making it sound a lot more romantic that it was."

He giggles again. "Well, thank you for insightfully establishing your gay credentials, Jay. You make a boy quite dizzy with anticipation."

Blushing once more, I'm rescued by the arrival of our poppadum crackers, and I make short work of mine while he breaks his carefully into smaller pieces.

"Have you ever, you know, done it with a girl, Lucien?"

"Gosh, yes, plenty of times," he replies, surprising me. "I had quite a few girlfriends when I was younger. I suppose I swung both ways for a while. I even had a vaguely serious relationship with one for a year when I was at university."

"Oh really? What happened?"

"She found me and her brother playing hide the soap in the shower one day. We sort of drifted apart after that."

He holds up a piece of his poppadum. "What shaped country is that?"

The cracker is broken into a sort of lumpy, squarish shape.

"I don't know, er...Germany?"

"No, silly, it's Spain." He dips it in the little pot of mango chutney and passes it to me. "You have to eat it if you get the answer wrong."

He concentrates on nibbling the edges of another piece before holding it up. "Which country?"

This piece is bigger and mostly triangular.

"Ooh, I know this one. It's India."

"Nope," he replies with satisfaction, dipping it again and putting it in my hand. "Eat up. It's clearly too narrow to be India; it's Argentina."

The third country is Venezuela, the next Chad. Kazakhstan is after that.

"I'm not going to get any of these right, am I?" I say, smiling at him. I've polished off most of the poppadums. I'm not sure he's eaten anything.

"Probably not." He grins mischievously and holds another piece up. It's tiny, but I'll be damned if it's not a perfect replica of Wales.

"Hah! I'm so right with this one. It's Wales," I say triumphantly.

"Don't be silly," he tuts. "It's way too small! Anyone can see that's Lichtenstein." After dipping it in the remainder of the chutney, he puts it in my hand, which is resting on the table between us. "Gosh, sorry, I've made your fingers all sticky."

And with that, he brings my hand to his mouth and sucks each sticky finger, one at a time, very gently. I'm utterly paralysed, unable to drag my eyes away from the wet tip of his pink tongue, licking and nibbling all the sweet gluey chutney off my bloody fingers. Compilers of anatomy textbooks have made a big error, a huge omission, as only now am I learning of the existence of a nerve travelling directly from the fingertips to the penis. A nerve I've never seen described, ever, but must exist, because him sucking on my fingers is making me rock hard under the table. If I'm still capable of coherent thought after this evening, I'll write it up in a medical journal: the lesser-known 'penodigital' nerve.

Naturally, I nearly die of embarrassment when the waiter comes over with our main courses. Thank god for long white tablecloths. Hardly pausing, and certainly not letting go of my fingers, Lucien only takes them out of his mouth for long enough to coolly ask for another couple of Cobras before he resumes sucking. Finally letting go, he puts my hand gently back on the table. I take a couple of deep swigs of my fresh beer and try to compose myself.

"So far," I say, "you've only eaten my fingers. We're not leaving here until your plate is empty. And if you do that, I'll show you my poppadum joke."

"Yes, Dad," he smirks. "So when you decided to call the wedding off, why didn't you just tell everyone the truth?"

I shake my head. It's really difficult to explain. I can't get it straight in my own mind a lot of the time. "Because...because I'm only just getting my head round being gay, let alone feeling up to telling everyone else. My dad and mum...they're old-fashioned, you know? Proper working class, I don't know how well they'd take it. It might have been different if I'd always been that way inclined, but it will come as a bloody shock to them now. They aren't homophobic exactly, just as long as it's someone else's son, if you know what I mean."

The curry tastes good—I went for something spicy; Lucien has chosen the world's mildest korma.

"And to be honest," I continue, "I feel like a bit of an idiot, too, to suddenly wake up one day and decide I'm gay—and that's what it will look like to them."

It's a crap answer really, but I'm out of any decent ones. "Come on, I'm still waiting for you to eat."

It takes him a while; he's obviously used to pushing food around his plate, but I'm not budging until he's eaten a goodly amount of curry. When I'm satisfied, I hold up two circular, whole poppadums, fanning them against each other in one hand, like a magician with a pack of cards.

"Tell me what you see."

"Er...two round poppadums?" he replies, humouring me.

"Very good. Now, how about this?"

This time, with a flourish, I hold them against my chest, one in each hand, like two fat pale breasts against my blue shirt. "Tell me, now what do you see?"

He raises an eyebrow, confused. "Er...still poppadums?"

I'm shaking my head. "Nope. Mommadums."

I've got him giggling now, the sweetest of sounds. We call for the bill, and his hand covers mine again.

"Thanks for bringing me on a date, Jay," he says shyly. "And for spending the day with me. It's been a while since I had such a nice time."

He's quiet on the drive back to his place; we both are. I pull into the courtyard, leaving the engine running. It's awkward; neither of us know what to do next.

"See you at work next week, Dr Avery," I venture eventually.

He reaches for my hand, interlinking his cool, slim fingers with mine. "I haven't done this for quite some time," he begins tentatively, those light-blue eyes gazing into mine. "I'm not sure what *Debretts* has to say about it, but as the etiquette expert, isn't it true that a date should end with a kiss?"

I say nothing for a moment, my face on fire. Then, "I've never kissed a bloke before."

"We can rectify that now, if you like," he responds softly.

I look down at our joined hands. I so want to. I really, really want to, more than anything else. All evening, I've fantasised about those soft lips, wrapped around his beer bottle, sucking on my fingers. But I have to sort out my life first; it's not fair on Lucien if I'm not ready to rush headlong into something else. Because it won't just end at a kiss, not the way my dick is throbbing. And there's the small matter of Ellie, the house, my family—all that fucking jazz to wade through.

"I'm sorry, but I can't," I say miserably. "If I do, then I don't know that I'll be able to stop at only a kiss."

He says nothing but doesn't pull his hand away. After a beat, he whispers, "That is the nicest turndown I think I've ever received."

"I can't believe you've been turned down very often. But will you ask me again sometime?"

Thankfully, he nods and, bringing my hand up to his mouth, gallantly kisses the back of it.

"You don't know what you want, do you?" he says kindly.

"That's the problem, Lucien. I'm fairly confident that I do."

Chapter Seven

LUCIEN

I'm mostly working on the ICU this week. I find myself sitting next to Billy-Ray's bed more and more, and sometimes, when no one is observing too closely and he's agitated, I hold his hand. Wearing nitrile gloves obviously; I'm really not one of life's natural hand-holders. It's more of a lingering squeeze, to let him know someone cares. Hardly anyone ever comes to visit him and thinking about someone else's loneliness instead of my own is a novel feeling.

I have Jay to thank for that. Every so often, I catch my underused facial muscles contorting themselves into what is almost recognisable as a smile. In the cold light of day, last Saturday's activities are fairly tame by most people's standards—a new friend dropped by, we took a country stroll together, and then popped out for a curry. No big deal, but for the first time since the accident, I'd willingly let someone into my house. I'd felt solid arms around me; I'd kissed a boy's fingers; I'd teased and flirted and eaten a square meal. I could replay the afternoon and evening a thousand times in my head and not tire of it, but right now, I'm racking my brain and wondering if there is any more we can do for Billy-Ray, something we've missed.

On paper, and from the end of the bed, he looks shocking. His guts are buggered beyond repair—that's a technical term for his condition, knowledge acquired after many, many years of study. His tissues leak protein faster than we're managing to replace it. One episode of severe sepsis follows another, each more protracted than the last, and the microbiologists agree we're running out of antibiotic options. He's a bag of bones—another technical term. All of us doctors know it, the nurses and physios know it, and Billy-Ray does, too, but no one is yet prepared to pull the plug. Apart from Billy-Ray himself, who wishes he'd died in the fire along with everyone else. I can relate to that feeling. I've had it myself for a long time, but for the last few days, it's faded somewhat. Years from now, I can almost dare to imagine myself carving out a semblance of a satisfactory life. And I have the existence of Jay Sorrentino to thank for that. Emily and Annabel take advantage of my good cheer and persuade me to help them on a teaching course sometime next year; they are staggered when I'm amenable to the idea.

Billy-Ray has begun calling me by my name, which is an improvement on 'twat' at least. Despite being physiologically worse, he's psychologically more buoyant than usual (all things are relative), because his nan came to visit. It took two buses and a painful walk across town on an arthritic knee and two hip replacements—a situation I'll be resolving immediately as from now on, she'll be calling a taxi with all invoices directed to me. But under the bright point of colour on his good cheek, he's pale, paler than usual.

"Had a rough few days," he admits gruffly when I begin my routine examination. It's easy to just look at the numbers on the obs chart and go through the blood test results, but sometimes it's more useful to go with a good old-fashioned hands-on examination to appreciate a real feel of the direction of travel.

"That nice doctor—much nicer than you—was in here last night. You know, the dark good-looking one? He's an Arsenal fan, but I'm not holding that against him."

Jay's worked a couple of night shifts this week—somehow, I have started tracking his rota. He's probably relieved that we won't bump into each other for a while, as our mentor-junior relationship has become unconventional, to say the least. I'm not sure who is mentoring whom any longer. I'm the mad Earl, the Androgenous Albino, everyone knows I'm a twisted mess. But Goldenballs? They only see what they want to see, the image he presents to the world. I'm the only one who's glimpsed the confusion, although maybe I wonder if Ellie has too. He gives good face, but he's exhausted by it all, buffeted by the cancelled wedding, Ellie, his friends and family, selling his house, new job, new man.

I hope the last item on that list buffets him for a while longer, whereas I'd like the other issues to all disappear. I trusted him enough to let him into my house, and I think I can let him into my life, too, most of it anyway. He rebuffed me gently in the car, but it's only a matter of time. And I'm still in possession of his soft blue hoodie. He'll have to come over and wrestle me for it if he wants that back.

"Oh yeah?" I respond, feigning disinterest. Billy-Ray gives me a withering look with the functioning side of his face.

"Hah! As if you haven't noticed him. He's dead fit. I'd like a man like that…"

"If you say so; I couldn't possibly comment. How's that tummy pain today? Better, worse, or about the same?"

He grunts and makes a so-so sort of noise.

"Bowels? Any more looseness?"

"I'm not surprised you haven't got yourself a man with chat-up lines like that, Dr Avery," he responds. "For your information, yes, very loose. They changed the sheets twice last night. I just can't keep it in."

He looks away out of the window, humiliated. My heart, the cold lump of ice that it usually is, bleeds for him. Watery diarrhoea, another sign of infection. Triggered by antibiotic treatment this time, which is ironic but to be expected. "We'll get a sample, Billy-Ray, and send it to be tested."

After writing some more notes and giving explicit instructions to the nurse for his care over the weekend, I make to leave. With my hand on the door handle, he rasps out my name, and I turn back.

"When are you going to let me die? Because I don't want any of this fucking shit anymore."

The young nurse regards me anxiously, making to intervene, but I hold my hand up to halt him.

"I'll take it from here, Sanjay. Just give us a minute, would you?"

Alone again, I sit back down beside him. "Your body will let you die when it's ready, Billy-Ray," I say firmly. "And if and when it happens, I'll make it as painless as possible. I promise."

"What if you're not there? What if it's not your week and I get one of the others?" He's tearful again, and I take hold of his pitifully bony hand.

"I'm always popping in and phoning up," I reassure him. "If anything happens to you, I'll hear about it."

We sit quietly. I should leave; I've got plenty of other things I should be doing. The other staff on the ward round have no doubt given up on me and are breaking for coffee. I'm just thinking about slipping away when Billy-Ray starts speaking again.

"Do you think he's gay?"

"Who?"

"You know, the buff doctor with the nice arse that I told you about. He doesn't look gay."

I smile. "What does gay look like?"

He stares at me as if I'm stupid. "I dunno. Like you, I suppose. Just...a bit...gay."

"There are gay rugby players, Billy. They don't look like me. Huge guys. And firemen and soldiers. When I lived in London, I had lots of gay friends. They came in all shapes and sizes."

He ponders this for a moment and closes his eyes. I don't think he's going to say anything else, and then very quietly, "If I get out of here, Dr Avery, will you take me to London to meet some of them?"

I swallow down an unexpected lump in my throat. "Gosh, yes, Billy-Ray. It would be my pleasure." I mean it, I really do. This poor boy tears me apart. I've made the stupidest beginner's error of becoming attached to a bloody patient, and it's too late to pull away.

"I can do better than that, Billy-Ray. I'll ask young Dr Sorrentino to come with us too. He's really nice; he'll definitely say yes. I'll take you both up The Shard."

Billy-Ray gives his choking, rasping laugh. I wait until he stops, gasping for breath.

"Is that a euphemism, Dr A? Because if it is, trust me, you wouldn't want to be going anywhere near my shard at the moment."

"No, you idiot, it's a really tall skyscraper! And right near the top, like fifty or so floors up, there is a bar, the highest bar in London. We'll dress up and go, all three of us. You can borrow something smart of mine to wear; I've got more clothes than I know what to do with. The cocktail menu in the bar is out of this world, except I suspect Dr Sorrentino will just stick to beer. But you and me, we could have a mai tai, or a margarita—they serve them in really beautiful glasses—and we'll get sloshed while looking out over the whole of the city and being entertained by Dr Sorrentino."

"I like the sound of that, Dr Avery." His eyes remain closed, his cool hand still tucked in mine. After a minute or so, I'm not sure if he's awake or not; he's much drowsier lately. I carefully disengage my fingers and pull away, still talking softly.

"And then, when we've finished there, we'll take Dr Sorrentino dancing. I love dancing, and apparently Dr Sorrentino can be persuaded when he's had a few drinks. And I know of lots of clubs where someone like you will fit in just fine. I'll introduce you to so many pretty boys, you won't know which way to look. We'll dance till dawn."

*

Men are like buses, or as Emily would say, like IVF treatment. None for ages, then two come along at once. She has twin boys, after many years of attempting to conceive. Jules Crawshaw, my ex, phones from his new home in Chicago, wanting to meet up when he visits the UK in a couple of weeks from now. He's a good-looking city hotshot, blond and sleek and confident. My brother introduced us at a charity function five years ago, and for three years, I imagined we were a perfect couple. Sure, he was overbearing, and sometimes it felt like he slotted fucking me into designated sections of his busy schedule, but he could be charming and generous when the mood took him. And frankly, I was so busy with work and exams that having any sort of life outside of the ICU felt like a massive achievement.

Not long after we started dating, Jules moved into my London house and all was good in the world until he had to choose between me and a job promotion in Chicago. Chicago won easily, which summed up exactly how much he loved me. Then two months later, my family died. Jules sent me a card, a big bunch of flowers, a couple of texts—too busy with the new job to make the trip over, he knew I'd understand—and that was that. It's only now, listening to his new faint American twang from across the Atlantic, as he insists how great it would be to catch up, that I realise I'm completely over him. Whereas I once thought I loved him to distraction. So yeah, we make vague plans; it's not like I have a full social diary or anything. Hopefully, he'll have scoffed lots of burgers and fries at cheap American diners and be flabby and balding.

The weekend rolls around, a mostly empty void, but I'm not dreading it quite as much as I did before Jay Sorrentino strolled into my life. Not that I'm expecting to see him. He's rostered for another night shift tonight, and I'm trying not to be disappointed. I know I joked that I'm his best man, but it's not as if we're a couple or anything. And I do actually have a few tasks to keep myself occupied.

I'm taking positive steps towards pulling myself together and begin with having Will, my estate manager, drop by early on Saturday for our weekly catch-up, instead of me going to his office. I'm proud of myself for inviting him to sit at the kitchen table with a cup of tea while we go through the paperwork. He's a nice chap, of indeterminate age but probably in his late fifties. His father was the estate manager before him. He's been as patient with me through the whole sorry saga as anyone could be; he managed the press in the aftermath of the accident as if he'd been dealing with them his whole life, which makes me eternally grateful to him, even if he never did anything else. Granted, having a trusted employee drinking tea in my kitchen and going through routine paperwork is not much to applaud. But it's a start, even if I do run my fingers over my pearls throughout the meeting, as though counting rosary beads. Will's seen me at my worst; he doesn't bat an eyelid. After he leaves, however, I collapse onto the kitchen sofa, exhausted, and soon enough, fall into a doze.

I'm woken by a warm hand lightly caressing my bare ankle. Jay is at the other end of the sofa, my feet nestled in his lap.

"Sorry to startle you," he says softly. "The door was open. And the back gates. You don't have much in the way of security around here, do you?"

I rub my face; I hope I haven't been dribbling. "The gates are usually closed—Will must be expecting someone." I smile at him. I can't help it; seeing him is such a nice surprise. "To what do I owe the pleasure?"

He holds up a bag of tools. "I've come to fix the panelling. I thought I'd take you on a date to B&Q first."

I've never been to B&Q or any other DIY store for that matter. My world is opening up!

Jay's so handsome, sprawled there on the end of my sofa. I wish it was my head in his lap and not my feet, and my face that he's stroking so tenderly instead of my instep.

"Surely you must have something better to do today—I commandeered you last Saturday. And don't you want a rest before going to work later?"

He shakes his head. "No, it's fine. I'd rather be here than trying to nap at home. Ellie...er...Ellie and I have had a bit of a row. To be honest, I think I need to give her some space."

"You haven't rowed because of me have you?" I ask politely. *Please say yes, please say yes.* I hope my question came out sounding more concerned than I feel.

He grins and tickles my foot. "Not everything is about you, Lord Rossingley."

I pull my foot away, squealing like a girl, but he's got a tight grip.

"Okay, partly about you," he confesses. "Although she doesn't know that. Last night, I told her we needed to drop the asking price on the house and get it sold so I can give her what she's due, plus all the money we lost on the wedding. Sharing the same small space is killing us both. But she failed her emergency medicine exams and said it was unfair for me to do all of this right now, particularly as she's so stressed and revising again. So I agreed we wouldn't, but I'm cross with myself for being so bloody weak because I really, really want to just get it over with for good."

"Anything...um...anything trigger this rush, Dr Sorrentino?" I ask innocently, trying to keep the pleasure out of my voice.

My other foot gets a tickling, and I wriggle as he mercilessly holds both my feet down. I don't stand a chance against those big strong hands.

"Come on, Lady Louisa, get your glad rags on. We're going on an adventure to B&Q."

Jay drives a souped-up Audi thing, with rich red leather covering every available interior surface. He drives it bloody fast too. I'm rigid in my seat. He doesn't say much, and although we made a joke of his row with his girl and he tickled my feet and we flirted, his mouth is set in a fairly grim line, and I suspect his brain is miles away.

"I'm sorry you're having such a tough time with everything," I say eventually and rub his arm with my free hand. My other hand is white knuckled and gripping the seat. Briefly, he turns to look at me, which is quite scary when we're travelling five million miles an hour, and he gives me a rueful smile.

"It's okay," he replies. "It's nothing compared to when I called the wedding off—I stayed awake all night just in case she decided to slice my balls off with a rusty cleaver. I'm making her out to be an ogre, but actually, she's a really, really nice girl, and she really, really did not deserve this."

"If I'd known sucking my knob was going to cause you so much trouble, I would have declined the offer," I say mildly, trying not to laugh. "Although I'm very glad that I didn't."

Gosh, I'm falling hard for young Dr Sorrentino. I realised that when he took me out for dinner last weekend and refused to kiss me afterwards, even though I knew he wanted to. Not many men of my acquaintance would have done that. Young, horny homosexuals aren't known for their sexual restraint. He's kind and honourable and trying to do the right thing by everyone, me included. And today when I woke up to find him stroking my feet, well, that was rather adorable too.

"Do you normally turn up at your consultant mentor's house offering to do DIY?" I ask after a silence when he's once more lost in his thoughts.

"No." He grins across at me and pauses. "But then I don't give most of them blow jobs in dodgy nightclubs either."

He takes my hand and holds it in his lap. Intermittently, he gives it a squeeze. When I said I wasn't one of life's natural hand-holders, I think I just hadn't found the right hand to hold. I feel the loss of his warm fingers when he lets go to change gear.

It's difficult to concentrate on wood primer after that, but Jay's a pro, masterfully negotiating our squeaky trolley up and down aisles and confidently selecting various unidentifiable bits of manly stuff. I follow him in a daze, in awe at the sheer volume and range of items on the shelves. How the hell I'd not discovered the joys of a DIY warehouse before this moment I have no idea. Jay even has a phone app to show him where to find everything.

Obviously, I couldn't resist adding a few bits and pieces of my own to the trolley. By the time we come to the checkout, it is groaning under the weight of two prickly pear cacti, a baby *monstera* in a pretty blue pot, eight outdoor cushions for my favourite bench (I couldn't decide on a colour so I bought two of each), a little stone elephant (because it looked lonely and cute), a wooden loofah (ethically sourced wood), three packets of cress seeds, and five Farrow & Ball tester pots. Oh, and his boring pile of bits and bobs for the wood panelling, obviously. Vowing never to take me there again, he somehow manages to cram it all into the pristine boot of his car.

Back home, I'm made to feel redundant fairly quickly as he gets to work, and apart from being the tea and Battenberg delivery service, I'm free to observe him do his manly thing.

"You don't have to stay with me, you know," Jay says, "if you have something better to do. You could arrange your new cushions or plant your cress seeds. Or put that ridiculous stone elephant where I'll never have to see it again. I'm not going to nick the silverware or anything."

"I like watching you. You're a very pretty boy."

He gives me a frown over his shoulder. "And you're an arse."

I indicate to the neatly cut hole in the wall. "It looks like warm work; you know you can take your top off if you're getting too hot."

He laughs and continues sanding down the edges of the new section of panelling. "I'll let you into a secret. The first time I clapped eyes on you, I thought you were the most beautiful person I'd ever seen in my life. Male or female. Then afterwards, I thought it was because I was so pissed—when you're wearing beer goggles, everyone's gorgeous."

"At work, they call me the androgynous albino," I protest modestly, but I'm secretly delighted. "They probably think I don't know everyone's nickname for me. But this pasty look isn't everyone's cup of tea."

"I didn't realise it was mine until I met you. And I think you know exactly how gorgeous you are. Lots of the women at work certainly do, and that gay nurse manager is always hanging around ICU on the days when you're in charge. If I didn't think it would make you big-headed, I'd tell you that your good looks are a favourite topic of conversation at night on the unit."

"Really?"

"Now don't give me that coy look, Lucien Avery," he teases. "You know they talk about you. To be fair though, most of them can't decide if they want to kill you or shag you. Killing usually wins."

"What about the second time you saw me, when we met in the anaesthetic department?"

He stops sanding and laughs, throwing his head back. "I thought you were as totally gorgeous as I'd remembered, but a complete and utter wanker."

"Gosh, how charming. And now?"

He sighs and resumes sanding, his back to me. "Well, I still think you're beautiful, but I also think I'm losing my marbles because for some reason, I want to spend every second with you. It's keeping me awake at night."

Why don't you then? I almost say. *Move in this minute, share my home, my life, my bed.* How the hell has this boy got himself into such a mess? Why is he so loyal, so…good? Why doesn't he just walk out tomorrow and come and stay with me?

I wonder if he's scared to do it. After all, he's been allegedly straight all his life. It's a big step. Maybe he's using sorting stuff out with his family and ex-fiancée as a way to slow us down a bit.

He puts down the sanding block and walks over to where I'm leaning against the opposite wall. Inhaling the scent of rich oak and Fahrenheit, I wish more than anything that he'd just kiss me, wrap his arms around me, take me to bed. The other shit he can sort later. He stands very close. If I reached up, just a tiny bit, I'd get my wish.

He gently smiles at me and steps back again, then softly strokes my cheek with the pad of his thumb. I slowly let out the breath I hadn't realised I was holding.

"Fuck, you make this hard, Lucien. Give me time, I'm going to get this sorted, and I'll be here for you. I just need some time."

After the work is done, I heat up two portions of macaroni cheese, both for him. He rejects my offer of a tiny tot of Campari, citing work, and I make a mental note to buy some beer next time I visit Waitrose.

"Do you have plans for the rest of the weekend?" he asks after he's hoovered up his dinner and gets ready to leave.

I make a pretence of looking at my watch. "Goodness yes, I should get ready," I reply sarcastically. "My twenty-one-year-old toy boy should be arriving any minute now."

Rolling his shoulders back, Jay stretches to his full height and winks at me. "Tell him his services will no longer be required, sweetheart. There's a new man in your life."

*

Jules phones me as I walk into the office on Tuesday, after collecting my pager from theatre reception. Assigned to the emergency list, I deducted a long time ago that it is easier to wait until the nurse in charge contacts me with details of the first patient rather than trying to fathom the list order myself. I put Jules on speakerphone so I can simultaneously fire up the laptop and flick through my work emails as he talks. He's back in the UK and seems to be labouring under the misapprehension that I'm desperate to meet up. A year or so ago, this phone call would have commanded my full attention, but now, it doesn't. Not because my emails are riveting, but because Jay Sorrentino has wandered into my office, fresh from his post nightshift shower, his thick black curls still damp. Hardly able to draw my eyes away from this vision of masculine perfection, I motion to him to sit, mouthing an apology.

"How about Thursday? Or Friday? I can do Friday," Jules says. "Friday would be excellent! Say yay, Lucien! Is it a deal? Shall I pencil you in?"

That new American twang is grating on me, as is his insistence on pinning me down for an evening this week. I roll my eyes at Jay, who's watching me curiously.

"Okay, Jules, yes, I can do Friday," I sigh, drumming my fingers on the desk.

He lets out a whoop. Yes, it's definitely an American whoop, and Jay and I both cringe simultaneously. I rattle through agreeing on a time and a location—I'd have agreed to a bacon sandwich in the hospital canteen if it would have got him off the phone—and then finally, I can turn to Jay.

"Morning," I say, smiling at him. Grinning inanely actually, which is very un-Dr Avery-like. Jay's going home to bed, and I wish I was joining him because, right now, perched on Annabel's desk, all tired-looking and snuggly and warm in yet another soft blue hoodie, he's absolutely delicious.

"Who was that?" he asks without preamble, nodding towards the phone.

"Nobody special." I get up and reach around him for the pile of research papers I was planning on perusing during the operating list. "Well, not anymore. His name is Jules. He's an old boyfriend, back in the UK for a while. He wants to...well, you heard the rest of it."

"Mmmm, I did," he replies, frowning. "Was it a serious thing?"

Well now, this is very interesting. Jay seems rather perturbed. "We did cohabit for a few years, so I guess that qualifies as serious."

"And you're meeting up with him for, what? Drinks? Dinner? Sex?"

I'm amused, and it shows. "Definitely the first two, and he'll no doubt be expecting the third, if he's anything like he used to be."

Scowling at me, and not moving from his seat on Annabel's desk, Jay leans across, deliberately closes the office door, and flicks the lock with an audible *click*. Then he turns back to me and, taking hold of my wrist, tugs me towards him so we're inches apart. With his legs comfortably spread, I'm somehow manoeuvred between them.

"I'm not very happy about your Friday night plans, Dr Avery," he murmurs with a frown, not letting go of my wrist. His determined gaze flickers between my mouth and my eyes. "Really not happy at all."

"And why would that be, Dr Sorrentino?" I ask, rather breathlessly as he's caged me between his solid thighs. His big hands have somehow found themselves cupping both my arse cheeks, pulling me even closer towards him. Lots of reasons to feel breathless, just one of them would have sufficed. His voice drops lower, a little gravelly.

"Let me put it simply, Dr Avery. I don't like to share."

Okay, so at this, I could point out to him that we aren't exactly a thing, that we are merely friends and colleagues, that he lives with his ex-fiancée, that he's firmly in the closet, that I haven't had sex for like, ever, and that... But I don't because his mouth captures mine, and at this precise moment, all words are totally superfluous to requirement.

Eight o'clock in the morning in my cramped, impersonal office is not exactly the time or the romantic location I had envisaged when Jay would finally make his move. Maybe I saw him pinning me up against a shady oak tree on the grounds of Rossingley, following a stroll in the wintry sunshine, or across the front seats of his Audi after a trip to the cinema, snogging like horny teenagers, the car smelling of popcorn. But we've pussyfooted around for a while now, and suddenly, *bang*, just like that, here in the hospital, he kisses me. It's a firm kiss, close-mouthed, yet inarguably possessive. And as he pulls away, unquestionably not enough.

"I thought you wanted to have 'everything sorted' before we did this?" I suggest, reaching in for another.

"Seems like a touch of jealously is the only prod I need," he responds, his mouth briefly against mine again. Frustratingly briefly.

I giggle. "There are so many inappropriate comments I could make right now."

"You need a shave, Luce," he declares, studying my smooth chin, a small frown creasing his tanned brow.

Now, I can confidently declare that I'm the least hairy man I know. Perhaps my cousin Freddie comes a close second. Back in the day, I snogged women with more facial hair than me.

"I've had a shave!" I counter, miffed. "About an hour ago! This is just what kissing a man feels like!"

"Oh."

He looks like he's considering this, and then closing his eyes, he leans in for another, softer this time, deeper. I taste mint toothpaste and inhale coconut shampoo. My tongue touches his, tentatively exploring. And, Christ on a broomstick, if he doesn't bloody pull away again.

"It's just a wispy scratch against my chin really," he pronounces. "I can probably live with it. Must be worse for you, Luce, because I'm hairy as fuck."

"Darling, can we discuss shaving routines later? I'm trying to bloody enjoy this!"

Goodness, he knows how to kill a moment. Or, for all his outward confidence, I wonder if he's stalling, unsure where to take this. After all, from what he says, I'm a willing participant in his first-ever man-on-man kiss. However chaste.

"It's okay to be nervous, Jay. I get it; I'm nervous, too, a little. It's...well, it's been a while for me too."

He grins at me with that generous easy smile, his hands gently massaging my bum. "This isn't me nervous, this is me exceedingly jealous and horny as fuck."

And then he's up and pushing me backwards, effectively pinning me between his massive body and my desk. Trapping me, with both of his hands in my hair, he leans in again, ferociously claiming my mouth. He might never have kissed a man before, but he's not scared of taking the plunge. The kiss is sloppy, messy, needy. He lets out a low moan, more of a growl, really, as he fucks my mouth with his tongue, wedging his thigh in between mine, nudging up into my balls. Yes, his stubble is scratchy, but who gives a fuck; his arms slide around my waist and then down further still, squeezing my arse again. The length of his hard, muscular body presses against mine; his equally hard cock also presses against mine, and not for the first time do I appreciate there is something rather lovely about being crushed against a warm hoodie and an unyielding wall of muscle. Loki can go to hell; I've become Thor's biggest fan.

I rub up against him, revelling in the friction until he eventually lets me come up for air and eyes me hungrily.

"What about marmite?" he breathes, the tip of his tongue running maddeningly along his lush bottom lip as if he's still tasting me. "Is that a kissing-a-bloke thing too?"

I can't recall the last time I was kissed so thoroughly; my cock can't either. As my balls tighten, I give myself a rough squeeze through my trousers to relieve the ache. "No, that was my breakfast."

He regards me thoughtfully, his lips pursed. Those long-lashed hazel eyes travel down to my hand at my groin and back up again. He plants a whisper of a kiss on my chin, then on my left cheek, my right cheek, and finally on the tip of my nose before moving to the side of my neck and burrowing in. It's tender and cute and funny all at the same time.

"I haven't got a fucking clue what I'm doing here, Dr Avery," he says, his words muffled into my neck. "It's all bravado. I bet your Jules bloke knows what he's doing."

I tilt slightly so I'm kissing the top of his damp head. Not entirely as confident as he pretends then. "Yes, he does. He was always quick to tell me what a wonderful lover he was, and how lucky I was to have him. But trust me, you're the only person who's made me smile so far this morning. And, incidentally, made me nearly ejaculate into my boxers, which would have made for an uncomfortable day in the operating theatre."

He lifts his head, grinning shyly, and I lean in for another kiss. And maybe more because, hell, he's locked the office door, and my cock is very keen to get in on the action. Slipping a hand down between our bodies, it would appear that his is, too, and I palm its long, hard length, eliciting a gasp of surprise from my gorgeous man. With my other hand, I start undoing his belt so I can unleash him from the tight confines of his jeans. Impromptu sexy games in my office at eight a.m. on a Tuesday? Gosh, yes please, bring it on.

My pager, however, has other ideas, barking out a curt message and vibrating angrily across the desk behind me, desperately vying for my attention.

"Adult trauma call in ED. ETA six minutes. Adult trauma call in ED. ETA six minutes."

How dreadfully inconsiderate. Surely the world should have stopped spinning on its axis, or at least the population of Allenmouth should have had the good grace to take extra special care with its health and safety during the last phenomenal few minutes. Groaning with frustration, I take one final lingering kiss before regretfully stepping out of his hold and silencing the persistent vibrating. I pick up my keys and my badge.

"Sleep well, Jay." I cup his cheek and lightly stroke his lips.

"How I'm going to sleep after this, I don't know," he grumbles, rearranging himself. My eyes travel down to the obvious bulge in his jeans, and he blushes delightfully.

"You will," I determine. "I'm going to be picturing you sorting that out when you get home. Will you promise you'll think of me while you do it?"

"Fuck, yes, Luce," he breathes with a quick squeeze.

Reaching down, I cover his hand with mine as he holds his cock through his jeans. I press into him.

"When you're jerking off, imagine how I'll look when you fuck me. Right on this desk here."

I'm so close; his breath is hot against my face. "When you are back at home and touching yourself, imagine me here, spread open for you, my legs wrapped around you. Think about how it will feel when you come deep inside me and I cry out your name."

Reluctantly, I step back. With my hand on the door handle, I take one last glance down at his groin and grin.

"But maybe don't leave the office quite yet, we don't want you scaring the secretaries."

*

The trauma call turns out to be an overreaction to a middle-aged man in Lycra fancying himself as Bradley Wiggins. But overreactions are much safer than underreactions, even if they do scupper my sex life. My day continues as anticipated, delivering anaesthesia for a couple of appendicectomies, followed by an impressively large bottom abscess on an impressively large bottom, and a screaming toddler who sustained a lip laceration after being pushed over by his older sibling because he wouldn't share his chocolate digestive. Oh, the glamour.

I steal a few moments to myself mid-afternoon and hide in my office. It's a bonus that nothing challenging is scheduled on the emergency operating list, as a certain junior doctor is exclusively occupying my thoughts. When Emily wanders through, I'm unaware that I'm grinning like an idiot to myself.

"There's definitely something odd about you at the moment, Lucien," she begins, settling herself down for a natter. "You seem...well, cheerful may be putting it too strongly, but you have certainly shifted several adjectives away from morose."

I groan inwardly, recognising the tone of voice. Fishing.

"You haven't had a new haircut, so it's not that. You haven't wound up Dr Leitner yet today, so it's not that either. New shirt?" She pretends to search for another spurious reason for her earlier statement before smiling at me naughtily.

"If I didn't know any better, I'd say that it is somebody, not something that's caused the sudden change."

Annabel and Emily are forever trying to coax information from me regarding my love life. As probably their only gay friend, I suspect they like to imagine I maintain a small harem of well-oiled, willing young men chained up in the cellar. The truth would be a huge disappointment to them. Until now perhaps. The collective department jaws would be skimming the floor if they had an inkling about Jay and me. Stories of his aborted wedding have probably reached their gossip-hungry ears by now, but from what I've overheard myself in theatre, the rumour mill is short on detail.

I escape, on the pretext of an important visit to intensive care, but the urge to share my excitement with someone is overwhelming. The change in my demeanour must be blindingly obvious to everyone since even Billy-Ray notices I'm less surly than normal.

"So, has he shagged you, then?" he begins as I wash my hands prior to examining him. He looks absolutely awful this afternoon, even worse than a few days ago. I decide we need to recheck his infection markers. We restarted his nasogastric feeding two days ago, and from his overnight spike in temperature, I wonder if he's aspirated some feed and is brewing yet another chest infection.

"Who?"

"The mystery guy you've been mooning after the last couple of weeks?"

I stand up straighter. "I have no idea what you are talking about, Billy-Ray. And I do not moon," I declare haughtily, in full Lord Rossingley mode.

He smirks. "Twat. You've had a daft grin on your face every time I've seen you. Or perhaps it's you shagging him?"

I retrieve a stethoscope, feeling uncharacteristically flustered, and listen carefully to his chest. He mercifully cooperates, leaning forwards obediently so I can focus at the lung bases. Sometimes he tries to hold his breath or makes squeaky noises so I can't hear properly, just to exasperate me. His ribcage stands out against thin, bluish skin; he's pitifully thin. With a sudden pang, I realise how much I'm going to miss him when he's gone, and deliberately push the thought away. After I lay him gently back down, he watches me expectantly, waiting for an answer.

"Can you keep a secret, Billy-Ray?" I ask, settling into the chair next to him. For the sake of appearances to the nursing staff possibly watching through the glass, I pick up his obs chart. God forbid they think I'm going soft. I *am* going soft though—crazy too—confessing my innermost thoughts to a bloody patient. Billy-Ray nods without expression. Curiously, I think he can probably keep a secret better than anyone.

"I've met a boy," I begin softly. "A really nice one, much nicer than me."

"That's not hard," he butts in. "Carry on anyway."

"He's someone I don't deserve. I...I...I think I'm in love."

I look away from him, embarrassed, wishing I could take the words back. But treacherously, even more of them continue to spill out of me. "He kissed me this morning."

I'm expecting that raspy hoarse laugh again; if ever anyone knows how to burst a bubble, it's Billy-Ray. I wonder what he was like before the injury. Caustic and funny, I'm guessing. Brave too; after all, he did run into a burning building to try to save his sisters. I think I'd have liked him.

But when I look up again, there are only silent tears trickling freely out of his one good eye. I take his bony, thin hand in my ungloved one, not caring anymore if I'm spotted from the nurses' station.

"Describe him to me," he whispers.

And so, I do. "He's got a body like Thor, but he's dark, olive-skinned with curly hair. Like that handsome actor from *Game of Thrones*. He goes to the gym a lot; you'd definitely appreciate his body. He eats a lot too; he's forever hungry, and he's good with his hands."

I get a squeeze for that comment.

"Not in that way, Billy! I mean he's good at mending things, DIY type things. He's kind and gentle and a little bit sad at the moment, but he hides it well."

"More importantly, has he got a nice arse?" Billy-Ray's voice is hoarse and sleepy; his eyes are closed.

"He's got an amazing arse, Billy-Ray."

"If I'm not mistaken, he sounds a bit like that doc who comes here at night sometimes. You know, the Arsenal fan."

I laugh softly. "Yes, he does, doesn't he? Now you mention it, I've described him exactly."

Billy-Ray is silent for a moment, then, "Yeah, you're right, Dr Avery. Sounds like you don't deserve him."

I squeeze his hand gently. "You're a twat, too, Billy-Ray. A nice one, though."

"Takes one to know one, Dr A."

*

Leaving work at lunchtime on Friday, I drive up to the townhouse in Mayfair, where I spend an inordinate amount of time making myself look good for the dinner, without knowing why. Not because I want him back—that ship sailed long ago. Perhaps it's to show him that, despite everything, my horrific family tragedies haven't turned me into a jabbering wreck, although it was a close-run thing, no thanks to him abandoning me at a time when I needed him the most.

I don't mind coming up to London every now and again. Mostly for the purpose of a clothes shopping splurge a couple of times a year. This house doesn't hold any particularly upsetting memories for me. We never lived here as a family. My father much preferred the country life, so time spent here was more as a young man about town than with my parents and Oliver. The vast rooms still feel empty, though, especially when my cousin Freddie isn't around to divert my attention.

Dinner with Jules starts badly and ends even worse. We meet at an old familiar haunt, a seafood restaurant we favoured in the early days when I thought the sun shone out of his bottom and I erroneously believed he felt the same about me. I'm gratified to observe he's gained a few pounds, and his thick blond hair slightly recedes from his suspiciously smooth, tanned forehead, but if anything, it only enhances his suave, controlling manner. Which he always had, even in bed. Especially in bed—controlling, precise, and, well, metronomic in his desires and the predictable way he set about them. I always bottomed. The alternative was never up for discussion, another aspect of his domineering nature. And afterwards, without ever cleaning up, he would roll away from me and sleep, leaving me feeling used and unloved.

Even as Jules greets me with a firm bear hug and a wet kiss to my cheek, my mind drifts back to Jay and the light touch of his lips against the same cheek. The youthful scent of Fahrenheit and coconut-scented shampoo, instead of an eye-watering spray of a stupidly expensive, leathery Tom Ford something or other, mixed with stale whisky. I vaguely wonder how Jay's night shift is going.

"I rather thought you'd have grown out of all that by now," he drawls, that artificial transatlantic twang even more grating in person than down a phone line. He indicates my discrete eyeliner and lip gloss. "Now that you're the lord of the manor and everything."

I choose not to rise to it. "Come on, let's order, I'm famished."

If he was paying the least bit of attention to me, he'd know this for the diversional ruse it is. I'm never famished; my appetite was even smaller towards the end of our relationship than it is now. But he doesn't care or notice because he's caught the eye of a twinky, dark-haired young waiter, who's only too happy to talk him through the wine list.

And so, the course for the evening is set with Jules expounding at great length on his marvellously thrilling new life in Chicago and me picking at a probably delicious seafood risotto and fervently wishing I was at home with

Waitrose macaroni cheese and a glass of Campari. And Jay Sorrentino.

I didn't think he would get around to it, but he does, eventually, as we're halfway down the second bottle of Romanée-Saint-Vivant, a Chablis vintage probably costing more than Jay's monthly mortgage repayments. Jules attacks the cheeseboard with gusto.

"So, how are you coping, Lucien darling? I can only imagine how dreadful this entire ghastly business must have been for you."

Yes, you can only imagine because you couldn't be bothered to find out at the time.

He raises a shoulder in a what-can-one-do sort of way. "I'd have grabbed the first flight over, but as you know, that huge contract with Sacharet wouldn't wait for man nor beast. The New York office would have had my guts for garters if I'd missed the deadline."

His face is unpleasantly flushed; white wine always did have that effect on him. His heavy-lidded eyes watch me lazily. Pulling my shoulders back and sitting up straighter, I inhale deeply, determined to deny him the pleasure of seeing me squirm.

"I'm great, Jules, really great. Things were tough for a while, obviously..." I take a swallow of my wine, allowing myself a second before soldiering on. "But the estate is all on track, and the job at the hospital is working out...and so..."

"I'd have thought you'd have knocked that doctoring thing on the head now that you are *lord of the manor.* It's not like you need the money, is it darling?"

Lord of the manor. That phrase is beginning to grate on me. I wish he'd stop using it, especially as I detect a mocking tone whenever he says it. And most definitely, I'm no longer his darling.

"Well, I enjoy my work, and for the moment, I feel I'm able to combine both."

It's weak response, and I should stand up for myself more robustly, but he's always had this effect on me, somehow managing to make me feel slightly inadequate, slightly not quite up to the job.

"And I've met someone at the hospital recently. It's very early days and, well, a bit complicated, but I'm hoping our...our friendship will turn into something more."

Jules's eyes light up at this bit of gossip, so I tell him about Jay and the wedding, or lack of it. I gloss over how we unconventionally met—that's private and just for me and Jay. After I've finished, Jules leans across the table, patting my hand rather patronisingly.

"Falling for a straight man? How foolish of you, although you always were a sucker for a sad story. But come on, sounds like he's stringing you along, isn't he? I thought even you knew better than that."

I'm affronted. "He's not straight, Jules. He's coming out when the hoo-ha has calmed down a bit and he's sold the house and everything. He's just trying to do the right thing by everybody, that's all. He's incredibly loyal and thoughtful. So if it means I have to wait for him, then I'll wait, because I think he's going to be worth it."

Jules regards me pityingly. "Oh, darling, you and your big heart. Always determined to see the best in people. Think of me and my wise words when he's continually making excuses as to why he still hasn't left her six months from now."

Right, I'm so more than ready to bring this tedious evening to a close. I should never have agreed to it in the first place. It's bringing back far too many unhappy memories of other evenings when Jules slyly picked apart my apparent defects. Eventually, we call for the bill, and he makes a show of paying for me, which is slightly ridiculous given my circumstances. From his detailed bragging regarding his obscene Christmas bonus, he's rather flush with cash himself, but even so, it's no match for my crazy, undeserved good fortune, and we both know it. I let him pay anyway, not wishing to cause a scene. It's not me he's trying to impress, it's the strangers around us. The two bottles of wine had been followed with a couple of hefty tumblers of brandy, and thus his mood is bullish. I prepare my goodbyes outside the restaurant, but predictably, Jules has alternative plans.

"My hotel is around the corner, darling. I have a suite at the Dorchester. Fancy a fuck, for old times' sake?"

The question was inevitable, anticipated since he'd phoned to arrange the dinner, to be honest, but he could have handled it with a little more panache. I shake my head in apology.

"I don't think so, Jules. No need to tread over old ground is there?"

My response is nearly as gentle as Jay declining to kiss me after dinner in another restaurant not so long ago, but I accepted that rejection with a lot more grace than Jules is accepting this one.

"Christ, Lucien! Who swiped the jam out of your donut? There was a time when you couldn't get enough of my prick up your arse. Think you're too fucking high and mighty now, is that it, *Lord* Rossingley?"

Jules is quite drunk and quite loud. And his hand is quite tight around my wrist.

"Ow! That hurts!" I try to pull away, but he's always been stronger than me, and he just tightens his grip, twisting hard.

"Fucking prick-tease, that's what you are, *Lord* fucking Rossingley. I know you want it. Really, you're a fucking slut most of the time."

If he twists any more, he'll break my wrist.

"Jules, stop it, for God's sake! You're hurting me!" Hot tears of humiliation threaten at my eyelids.

A few other patrons leaving the restaurant turn to look at us.

"You all right, mate?" A sizeable young bloke and his girlfriend are looking in our direction, and the man's narrowed assessing gaze is enough for Jules to relax his grip and enable me to pull away.

"Fucking cunt," he snarls, and turning his back, he stomps off.

The guy and his girl are still there. "Are you okay?"

I nod dumbly, mortified, wishing they would take their kindness and concern somewhere else.

"There's a taxi rank down the road. We're heading that way." The man hesitates. "You can walk with us if you like."

I nod miserably again, and we silently fall into step. I wonder what I must look like. A cheap pickup probably, in my skinny jeans and vintage McQueen blazer. Okay, perhaps an expensive pickup. And goodness knows the state of my mascara. I'm too old for this, and even though I'll never see these Good Samaritans again, I want to explain that this isn't the real me; I'm not the sort of man they think I am. But I don't, of course, and mumbling my thanks to them both, I step into a cab and give the driver my address, settling back relieved.

As if sensing my misery, my phone pings a text message from Jay. His timing couldn't be better.

I was just wondering what colour my best man had painted his toenails tonight.

All thought of Jules and the ugly scene on the pavement vanish. A little squeak of delight escapes my mouth. Christ, I'm thirty-four, I need to get a grip. Jules is so wrong about Jay leading me on. I know he is. Nothing could be further from the truth. He's just giving it some time, that's all.

Luscious Pink Velvet, I respond, tapping quickly.

A pause. Then:

I'd like to see your luscious pink velvet.

I'd like to see yours too.

My cock stirs at thoughts of Jay, naked on my bed, and me above him with my lips pressed around...well, around his luscious pink velvet. A longer pause, the taxi turns into Berkeley Square, and I indicate my house to the driver. Then:

I'd like to lick your luscious pink velvet.

Crikey, my hand involuntarily moves to my hardening cock, and I squeeze myself through the tight denim.

Are we still talking about my toenails? I type with a shaky thumb. Gosh, I wish he was here with me, more than anything.

No, Lucien, we're most definitely not, although I'd be happy to lick those too.

*

I drive back to Allenmouth early next morning, glad to put distance between myself and the unpleasant evening. Jules hasn't been in touch, and hopefully he won't, but if he's true to form, he'll sober up and apologise. There will probably be extravagant flowers, and then he'll attempt to repeat the whole performance again sometime in the distant future. Over my dead body.

My route takes me past the hospital turn off, and on a whim, I decide to pop in and check up on Billy-Ray. I've had a vague anxiety about him for the last couple of days; if my hunch that he is developing an aspiration pneumonia is correct, then I want to check whether anyone has chased the blood culture results, and Monday morning seems too far away.

His bed is empty on my pass through the unit. I'm not concerned; it's a nice sunny day. When the unit is quiet and Billy-Ray's well enough, Kevin, the technician, sometimes bundles him up under a pile of blankets and, accompanied by one of the nurses, takes him outside for some fresh air. Looking at the staffing notice board, I establish that Kevin is scheduled to be working today, so thinking nothing of it, I head to my office to catch up on some paperwork.

I might not be a closet gay, but I'm a fully signed up closet nerd, and I spend a happy hour immersed in a fascinating clinical review of the long-term sequelae of rising D-dimers in CMV positive patients with ulcerative colitis in Korea. I even take out my multicoloured pens and highlight a couple of points to raise with my colleagues at our next morbidity meeting. They'll be on the edge of their seats. With my mind occasionally drifting to thoughts of Jay, I even hum to myself as I leave the office, startling Kevin, the technician, as he saunters past. He's wheeling a ventilator machine along in front of him.

"Morning, Dr Avery," he nods cheerfully. Inclining my head in his direction, continuing with my current buoyant mood, I startle him by initiating conversation.

"You look busy," I remark, indicating to the equipment. Okay, so I'm a bit out of practice with small talk, but at least I'm trying. He sighs and pats the top of the ventilator as if it's an old friend.

"Yeah, taking this ancient thing down to the workshop to get it stripped and serviced. It's been due for a couple of months, but we had to wait until he died to take it out of the room. We're a bit short at the moment, what with the other two being mended. We had to keep this old one handy because we never knew when he was suddenly going to need it, did we?"

A cold sweat breaks out on my forehead, the leather strap of my bag feels slippery in my hand. And from a distance, Kevin's gruff voice: "He's not going to need it now, though is he, poor kid? Bless him, at least it was quick at the end, but he'd have been better off dying in the house fire with the rest of them, I reckon."

Occasionally, when driving alone, especially through quiet streets, or if I'm stuck behind a slow lorry for an interminable length of time, my mind wanders off to somewhere else. And then, with a jolt of alarm, I land back in the present and realise that if a ten-tonne truck had crossed the path of my car during that brief interlude, I probably wouldn't have seen it until it was too late to avoid it. Well, that was me all the way home from the hospital.

I have no memory of walking to my car. I have no memory of driving back to Rossingley. A screaming voice in my head is telling me that he was just a patient, a boy I hardly knew, a sick, scared boy, and I should pull myself together. Patients die all the time. Every day. Plenty of my patients die, not because I'm an appalling doctor, but because they just do. Billy-Ray is merely another name on the list.

But this patient dying hurts more than the others and god how it hurts. A thousand times more. Because Billy-Ray is like me. I'm still a scared boy, too, even though I'm much older, my face isn't disfigured, and I'm not lying in a hospital bed. But perhaps I should have been. Perhaps it should have been me burned to a crisp and now dead because... Why the hell wasn't I in the helicopter with them? Why did I have to be the one left behind? What did the likes of Billy-Ray and I do that was so terrible we had to be punished like this? Every time I looked at him was a reminder that it could have been even worse for me, that I could have been like him. He didn't have a chance at living without everyone else, and at least I was given that, even though I haven't wanted it most of the time. Now I do want it, and Billy-Ray dies; he'll never have that chance, and it all takes me back to square one. I've escaped again, I'm the lucky survivor. And I'm confusing myself and not making any sense anymore, and all these jumbled, screeching thoughts are whirring around my head, and I can't block them out, not even if I put my hands over my ears and scream, not even if I stick my fingers down my throat and spew bile everywhere. I don't deserve to eat. I don't deserve to live.

My pearls. I need my pearls. Pearls and vodka.

Chapter Eight

JAY

"Jay-Jay, it's me, Evan. I phoned loads and then remembered you were working nights. My bad. Just calling to arrange that beer session. Give me a bell when you wake up. Oh, by the way, someone on the ward reckoned they saw you in B&Q with Dr fucking Avery last week! How funny is that? You must have a body double walking around."

My sleep-deprived, post-night shift, addled brain may have been responsible, but on finding out Lucien was arranging a meetup with an ex-boyfriend, an absurd level of jealousy I never knew I possessed threatened to overwhelm me. And so I kissed him since alternative methods of marking my territory, like cocking my leg and pissing on him, are socially unacceptable for many, many good reasons.

Even though the depth of my desire petrified me, from the moment I put my lips to his, burying myself in his wonderful scent and his wonderful taste, I was poised to wrestle him to the floor and claim him in another way—

also deemed socially unacceptable in the anaesthetic department office at eight a.m. on a Tuesday morning.

So I had to settle for doing exactly as he'd instructed, hardly reaching the privacy of my bedroom before pulling out my dick and wanking into my hand to the picture he'd so eloquently painted. I haven't come as quickly or as copiously since I was about fourteen. I'm thrilled, regardless, as for the first time in all my twenty-nine years, I kissed a man on the lips. And not just any man. No, for me it had to be the most confounding, scariest, hottest man alive. And fifty-eighth in line to the throne to boot. Not that I've been reading up on him or anything.

The night shifts were a distraction at least, and a busy distraction at that. In addition to a pile up on the M4—resulting in three casualties, each requiring an operating theatre and admission to intensive care—the poor young lad in the side room, with the horrendous burns, finally dropped off his perch on Friday night.

His condition had deteriorated by degrees throughout the week, and each night had found me spending time in his room, whether inserting new intravenous lines or making small adjustments to his treatment strategy on the advice of the microbiologists. In some ways, I'd always found him quite intimidating to talk to. What the hell do you say to someone who has had his family wiped out and has horrendous, ugly, life-threatening injuries that he knows he's unlikely to survive? With his aura of anger, the lad was easier to avoid than to befriend. Once I cast my own inadequacies aside and got over the obvious disfigurement, breaking through his spiky defences, I discovered he was clever and sharp and not angry at all, just scared, grieving, and lonely. A bit like someone else with spiky defences that I know. In fact, although worlds apart in so many ways, the parallels between Billy-Ray and Lucien are hard to ignore.

Billy-Ray and I had established a bond over him taking the piss out of my love of the Gunners, and in turn, I'd mocked his preference of the Chelsea nancy boys. In another situation, although my gaydar is nowhere near up to full strength, I'd have wondered if he was flirting with me. But as the week progressed and he got sicker, he'd become quieter and withdrawn.

In the end, it was mercifully quick and mostly painless, thank God. Billy-Ray departed this world with scarcely a whimper. A very brief episode of acute shortness of breath, a loss of blood pressure swiftly followed by a virtual loss of cardiac output, and all assembled agreed that jumping up and down on his poor thin chest was not in his best interests, honouring a decision made during a formal discussion with him a few weeks before.

Earlier that evening, he'd been agitated, already struggling with his breathing, so I'd found a moment to sit with him to work out if I could do anything to make it better. He'd asked repeatedly after Lucien, wanting—no insisting—I find him between gulps for air. Why Lucien, I'd asked him, but he was probably becoming confused at that point—a lack of oxygen has that effect. He kept on repeating that Lucien was taking him for cocktails, that I was on the trip, too, that Lucien had said he loved me, that I was his Italian Stallion or some such craziness. In the end, I held his hand and let him ramble on until exhaustion took over, before creeping out of the door. He didn't properly wake up again.

Later, after he'd died, a few of us took a minute to compose ourselves. It's hard for the nursing staff when they lose long-term patients. They spend all day every day with them, whereas us doctors can avoid emotional ties by just popping in and out. Through his tears and over a cup of tea, the nurse on the night shift, Sanjay, explained that Lucien had visited Billy-Ray a lot, that he'd arranged transport for the lad's granny, and he'd even bought him a mobile phone after his was lost in the fire.

Everyone had been surprised by this, but I'd thought of the gentle, soft Lucien that I knew, hidden behind an impenetrable wall a little like Billy-Ray's, and more than ever had wanted to be with him. Knowing he was on his date in London, I'd texted him with a message as sexy and light-hearted as I could dream up because no one wants needy and possessive. Neither was it a good moment to offload to my educational supervisor the horror of not resuscitating a young lad and spoiling his evening out.

The remainder of the weekend passes trying to avoid conflict with Ellie, catching up on sleep, and sternly telling myself not to contact Lucien. Of course, I can't stop torturing myself with images of him in his fancy Mayfair townhouse with some faceless gorgeous man, convincing myself that even now he's sprawled in bed with this Jules character and the Sunday newspapers, having enjoyed mutually satisfying, rampant morning sex. By Sunday lunchtime, my fertile imagination has them planning their happy future together and choosing matching wedding rings.

I escape the horror that is living in a cramped house with someone who hates your guts because you've ruined their life, and meet Evan for a couple of beers in town. He's staggered when I don't deny the trip to B&Q.

"Okay, so I helped Lucien with a bit of DIY? What's the big deal? You know I enjoy that sort of thing."

"Fuck, it's *Lucien* now is it? You'll be invited for an intimate supper, darling, and a trip to the opera next!"

He says this in a hoity-toity sort of voice, mimicking Lucien's upper crust accent. His attitude towards Lucien is starting to piss me off. I don't know about Evan being my second-best man. I'm thinking of relegating him to about twentieth.

"If you knew him, you'd think he was okay too. He's different outside of work."

"Yeah? I know you're open minded about stuff, Jay, but come on! Don't start hanging about with Dr fucking Avery! He's a bloody nightmare!"

"No, he's not. It's just that he's wary of letting people get close to him," I reply rather sniffly. "He's a very private person, but actually, he's been really kind and nice to me."

"Jesus!" Evan rolls his eyes with disgust. "So presumably you went to his house as well? What's that like—coffin-shaped?"

I roll my eyes back at him wearily. "Yes, Evan. I went to his coffin-shaped house and I helped him with some carpentry. Building more coffin-shaped things. And then we drank a bottle of blood each and watched Dracula on the telly."

He laughs and downs some of his pint. "I bet his house is full of whips and chains. I bet he has a dungeon!"

"Don't be an arse. It's a very nice house actually." There's a fucking understatement. "The carpentry job was quite straightforward, to be honest. Once I'd removed the old wooden panelling and worked out the right thickness of ..."

"What, was there just the two of you? Did he try to jump you?"

I shake my head, somewhat incredulous. I guess casual homophobia has been there all along; I've just never noticed how prevalent it is before. "Since when did we decide that being alone with a gay bloke was a bad thing, Evan? They're not all lying in wait to pounce on every willy that wanders past, you know! You wouldn't have made that assumption if I'd been alone with a heterosexual woman."

Okay, so I'm not exactly waving a banner at London Pride dressed in a tight rainbow T-shirt, but, baby steps. Lucien would be proud of me. We drink our beer in silence for a few minutes. Evan watches me sadly.

"I don't know what's bloody got into you. It's like you've changed, like something's happened to you. If you tell me what it is, I'll help you however I can. Ellie will help you. We'll get through it. It won't be easy, but she'll have you back, I know she will."

I rest my head in my hands with frustration. "I'm not going back. It's over. I don't know how many times I've got to tell you. I did the right thing for both of us by pulling out. Because it wasn't right. I don't love her as much as she deserves. There is nothing else to discuss, apart from that I shouldn't have left it so late in the day. Trust me; I'll never forgive myself for that."

Evan has enough sense to drop it and let the conversation drift to other things. He's getting married in five months himself and definitely won't be calling it off— Paula and he are besotted with each other and are planning on kids already. I don't want to fall out with him as he means well and has stood by me, but if he's any indicator, my family are going to struggle just as much when they all find out the truth.

*

I manage to make it all the way through until Monday without contacting Lucien, hopefully giving the impression that I'm supercool and not a pathetic, lovesick puppy. Despite having a few scheduled days off following my night shifts, after checking with the rota, I decide to wander into the hospital on Monday afternoon anyway, on the off-chance of conveniently bumping into him. By that I mean walking past his office door every five minutes until he spots me.

But he's nowhere to be found. I recheck the rota. Maybe he's off sick? Or perhaps he was having such a marvellous time with his former lover (who by now, in my mind, has turned into a very young, impossibly gorgeous Brad Pitt circa his brief cameo in *Thelma and Louise*) that he decided to extend his stay. Even now, Lucien's at the embassy sorting out a visa and booking flights for his new life in Chicago. Okay, perhaps I'm overthinking it, but I wander down to ICU hopefully anyway, just in case I've somehow missed him.

Glancing through the window, I see that Billy-Ray's bed is now occupied by a woman who looks older than God, peacefully lying in her drug-induced coma as the breathing machine does its thing. Kevin is tinkering with a blood gas analyser in the corridor, and we exchange a greeting. I enquire as to whether he's seen Dr Avery, but he shakes his head.

"Not seen him since Saturday morning. Quite chipper he was for him, even stopped to chat. Mind you, not quite so chipper when I told him the lad in room three had finally kicked the bucket. Looked like he'd seen a ghost, to be honest. I was in half a mind to go after him he was so upset, but you know Dr Avery, he would have been as likely to tell me to bugger off as admit he had a heart."

He turns back to the complicated piece of machinery and starts dismantling the filter. "He spent a lot of time with that lad, more than anyone else. I've never seen him care so much about anyone."

*

I'm so blinded by him and becoming so comfortable around him, that I don't notice the warning signs until it's too late. On my arrival at Rossingley, I find the back door is unlocked as usual, and after knocking a few times with no response, I let myself in.

He's in the kitchen as normal, lounging on the squishy sofa, with his feet propped up on a low stool and a book in his hand. Thank god he's not got the bloke from London cuddled up next to him. On initial impressions, Billy-Ray's death doesn't appear to have hit him too badly. Not if he can sit there, cool as a cucumber, reading a novel. I'm so enthralled, it takes me a moment to notice the ashtray overflowing with cigarette butts, the empty vodka bottles stacked in a careless heap next to the bin, or the mess in the sink. I just grin like a village idiot at him, and he regards me coolly back, his eyes glassy. And I still don't bloody catch on.

"Hello, Lady Louisa. You look nice."

He puts the book down, saying nothing, so I feel the need to qualify. Having never really made a direct reference to his unusual attire before, I hope I haven't offended him.

"You know I like you in a dress. You should have worked that out by now."

"It's not a dress," he corrects waspishly. "It's a dressing gown."

"And very fetching it looks, too, Dr Avery."

I chance a grin. The memory of our fucking amazing kiss and his dirty talk in the office has my dick swelling, and perhaps whatever mood he's in, I can charm him out of it so I get a repeat performance, and maybe more.

"Feel free to fuck off, Dr Sorrentino," he responds coolly.

He's speaking in a very clipped, precise way, as though every word is an effort. His eyes are pale blue chips of ice as he silently appraises me. He hardly ever swears, unlike me. Fuck, this conversation isn't going how I planned at all. Perhaps he is really upset by Billy-Ray dying, although it was a few days ago now, and it's a sad occupational hazard that patients come and patients go, even unusual, interesting ones. I try again.

"No, I really mean it. The nightie also. It's...it's kind of hot." And bizarrely, I truly mean it.

The dressing gown is rose-pink and fluffy, possibly cashmere. I've never seen him wear it before; it's a very expensive-looking version of something my nan would buy. Underneath, he's sporting a full-length white cotton nightie with fancy lace detailing around the neckline and little pale-pink satiny ribbons weaving in and out of the lacework. Both items of clothing chastely reach down to his ankles. Just visible through the gap at his sternum is the ubiquitous rope of pearls, and he fingers them almost constantly. Not that I noticed that either, until it was too late. His narrow feet are bare, his toenails painted midnight-blue. Oh, and he's wearing black eyeliner and a pearly-pink lip gloss. The diamond earring glints at me.

Why the hell am I finding this whole eccentric package so bloody enticing? When this is all over, when he's clocked that I'm a confused idiot and moves on, I'm going to need to book myself in for counselling or something because this stuff is way too deep for me.

"Are you... um... trans?" I ask, pretty bravely, actually, considering this is Dr Avery. "And, like, you're not out at work? Because it's okay if you are, you know, I'm... um... cool with...with that."

He says nothing, just tilts his head and examines me in that way he has, with those glittery eyes. Oh, God. I've overstepped, asking questions when they aren't invited.

But at least I've finally caught on. He's not in the best of moods, to put it mildly. Perhaps his night out went badly. Lady Louisa is in hiding, and the sweet, shy sixteenth earl has definitely gone AWOL somewhere on the vast estate. My best option would be to have a quick cup of tea, offer consolation over the death of Billy-Ray, make my excuses, and go, leaving him to his grump. Suddenly sitting forwards, he glares at me, trying to decipher if I'm laughing at him. I'm not, far from it. He's the most beautiful man I've ever encountered, whatever he wears.

"No, Jay. I just like putting on a nightie every now and again. I'd rather you didn't label me."

That clipped, deliberate voice once more, every word dripping ice. And still, I don't give up, even though something is clearly wrong. Maybe that Jules geezer is upstairs, maybe they've had a row, maybe he's being odd because he wants me to go, maybe...

"Does wearing a nightie turn you on?"

Christ, what has got into me today? It's like I'm on my knees and begging for the firing squad to point every single gun at me, whereas right now, I should be running for my life. I'm on the cusp of apologising for asking such an intrusive, embarrassing question, before banging my head against the nearest brick wall, when he responds.

"Do you want to find out?"

Do I want to put my head in the lion's mouth? Run, Jay, run, and don't look back.

He leans back into the sofa again, seemingly challenging me, although his eyes are a little unfocussed. With one hand, he carelessly fondles himself through the white cotton. Fuck. I want Lady Louisa; I want the sixteenth earl. I'm not sure I'm man enough to handle Dr Avery. My dick is thinking independently of my brain, however, and I make an effort to take control of the situation.

"Yeah, all right then. Come and join me over here."

For a second I think that he might; it appears as though he's about to lift himself up off the sofa. But then he sighs heavily, as if even the effort of that simple movement is beyond him. Without warning, his face suddenly crumples, and covering it with his hands, he emits a wild, anguished sound, somewhere between a sob and a hiccough, a hopeless, animalistic cry of despair as he rocks on the sofa.

"He's dead, Jay," he moans, his face hidden in his hands. "He's fucking dead, and I wasn't there. I promised him I'd be there, Jay."

The clipped voice has gone and in its place are slurred words, rolling into one another, and tears—hopeless, despairing tears—run freely down his beautiful face. I'm over on the sofa with him in two strides and sweep him into my arms. He clutches at me desperately, and even though he stinks of booze and fags and stale sweat, I kiss his hair, his eyes, his wet mouth, rocking him, whispering that everything will be okay because I really want to make it okay for him.

Lucien even cries elegantly; after that initial outburst, there are no more ugly sobs, no snotty nose. Just glittering tears endlessly falling down those pale cheeks, and if licking them off wouldn't freak him out, then I would, because I'm so desperate to taste him, all of him. Eventually, he falls into an exhausted, restless sleep, still cradled in my arms. Typically, he doesn't snore either.

He wakes about four hours later, his head nestled in my lap, and blinks up at me blearily. I've not sat there gazing at him the whole time, although it would have been easy to do so. Instead, I cleaned up the mess, stripped his bed sheets, and nipped out for some food.

"You smell like a camel's arse," I say when he's fully awake. I pet his hair anyway.

Smiling sadly, he closes his eyes with a heavy sigh. "I suppose a shag's out of the question then?"

I persuade him to take a shower, hovering anxiously behind as he wobbles into the bathroom on legs that threaten to collapse beneath him. We establish that he last ate solid food in London on Friday evening and has existed on a diet of fags and vodka since. As I adjust the shower controls, he slips out of his dressing gown, and I avert my eyes as I help him lift the nightie above his head and off. Ensuring the door remains unlocked, I leave him to it and lay out an almost replica clean set of soft nightwear I found in a drawer. As far as I can see, he has an endless supply.

Clean and dressed, he pleases me by obediently swallowing down two slices of toast with marmite and a glass of orange juice. Watching him chew, working the pearls with his fingers the whole time, I decide that now is not a good moment to discuss his food issues. Or nag him that he should have called me the minute he found out about Billy-Ray. Or ask him about his night in London. Or tell him how much I think I love him. Instead, I lead him back to the sofa.

Chapter Nine

LUCIEN

I wake for the second time with my head in Jay's lap and pretend I'm asleep for a while longer, savouring it all. Now he's appreciated I'm an utter fruitcake, he'll politely withdraw, and memories of little stolen moments like this will be all I have left.

"I know you're awake," he says softly, and I sense the smile in his voice.

"No, I'm not. I'm dreaming about a gorgeous junior doctor I met recently and what I'd like to do with him."

"Your skin is flawless; has anyone ever told you that?" he murmurs, leaning down and pressing his silky lips gently on mine. A wave of something approaching peace wafts over me. Maybe he won't leave yet after all.

"Yes, my mother. She used to stroke my forehead with her thumb and say that my skin was even softer than hers." I find that my throat is closing, and I keep my eyes firmly shut, willing those bloody tears not to breach the barrier.

"What, you mean like this?"

Last Friday evening, I dined opposite someone who once knew me inside and out, but who never in five years said anything or did anything as sweet as this boy is doing now, the pad of his thumb so warm and tender across my brow.

"It won't bring them back, Lucien," he says carefully. "You know, the drinking, the not eating thing, the hiding yourself away from everyone. It won't bring any of them back, not Billy-Ray, not your parents, and not Oliver."

My voice wavers as I reply. "Oliver was going to be a father. His wife, Isobel, was lovely, so perfect for him. They were childhood sweethearts. She had just discovered she was pregnant, and they were so excited about it. We all were. They would have been wonderful parents."

The tears breach the barrier, and he dabs at them gently with his sleeve. I have not felt so cherished since my mother died. It's a while before I can speak again.

"I should have been with them in the helicopter. Me, instead of Oliver and Isobel. I should be dead too. But at the last minute, someone called in sick at work, and I agreed to stay on and cover a shift for a few hours and take the next flight out. Why did I get to live when everyone else died? I should have been in that helicopter. I feel guilty that I wasn't. I feel guilty that I'm living, when they died and Billy-Ray died."

"You did everything you could for Billy-Ray," he says. "All the ICU staff did, and he was comfortable at the end. I was there, I saw him and held his hand just a few minutes before. He was ready to die. And if you'd died in that helicopter, then patients like him wouldn't have had the benefit of you caring for them—the world would have been worse off."

I'm lost in the sincerity of those brown eyes gazing down at me, the slight quirk of his upper lip, the beginnings of a smile.

"And you dying would have made my world much worse, too, because then I wouldn't have had this."

He kisses me lightly again, melding his generous mouth to mine, and I lose myself in his fresh, honest taste, in his strength and warmth. If I'm brave enough to just hold it all together and trust his words, then I can kid myself that I can taste the tiniest edges of happiness too— me with him, feeling cherished, feeling loved. And not long after that profound thought, like the insatiable sex god that I am, I fall fast asleep again.

*

At some point during the night, he half carries, half manhandles me into bed. I'm sleepily aware of his warm bulk settling in next to me and laying my head on his chest, encircled in his arms. Waking at dawn several hours later, the room still dark, I lie quietly, listening to Jay's regular breathing. My first thoughts are that I haven't felt so calm and refreshed for as long as I can remember. My feet haven't been so warm either, which has everything to do with the human hot-water bottle lightly snoring alongside me.

My libido is also feeling refreshed, and suddenly, the few centimetres distance between me and that broad expanse of naked boy are too much. I could lie here for ages and watch him as he peacefully sleeps, and when he wakes, I could gently seduce him, with teasing caresses and nibbling kisses, until he's begging me for more. He's never been with a man before; I could take it easy and slow.

But as my libido has sprung awake for the first time in aeons, I have a much better plan in mind. After quickly stripping off my nightie, it would not be stretching the realms of exaggeration to say that I launch myself at him. Thus, in the sleepy half-light of early morning, Jay wakes with a jolt of incomprehension to find the length of his huge firm body covered in mine. I snuggle closer, relishing every point where our bodies touch, my face nestled into the warm crook of his neck, breathing him in. As his hands automatically slide around my waist, he shifts slightly, sleepily spreading his legs so I can settle myself comfortably between them. I hum contentedly.

"Are you purring, Lucien?" He chuckles softly in the dark.

The memory of our amazing kisses against the desk in my office has my cock stirring. I hum again, feeling his chest rumbling with laughter, and my cock swells even more. Wriggling it gently against his, he gasps with shock and pleasure as our hard shafts greet each other.

"Christ, that feels so nice," he groans softly into my ear as I do it again, a more deliberate roll of my hips this time, relishing the scratchiness of his pubes against my groin. Very slowly, very gently, we find a rhythm, and for the first time in his life, he learns to love the delicious, lazy bump and slide of a simple cock rub as our bodies slicken with sweat and leaking pre-come.

"Gosh, you like that, don't you, Jay?"

"Yeah, God, yeah. Remind me why I waited twenty-nine years for this?"

You waited for me, I want to say, so I would be the only man who ever had you this way.

His big hands explore lower over the swell of my hips, easily covering my arse cheeks. As his hips rock up to meet mine, I bury my face further into the shadowy groove of his neck and collarbone, nibbling and sucking as I go, tasting his fresh salty skin. I slide my mouth lower, down to the flat brown disc of a nipple, and he cries out with shock when I tug it into my mouth.

"Lucien, fuck. Luce," he moans, and I wonder if he can sense me grinning with delight against his skin. I move back up his body again and find his mouth. Gradually, our rhythm becomes faster and more ragged as he lifts his hips higher, our cocks battling against each other. A familiar delicious tingling in my spine tells me I'm close to release.

"I'm going to come," warns Jay, and I'm not sure if he's surprised, panicked, ecstatic, or semaphoring a mixture of all three.

"That is generally the idea," I pant, and as I bite down firmly onto his nipple again, gorgeous waves of liquid heat spurt between our bellies, accompanied by his gasp and curse of pleasure. That cry is all it takes for my own orgasm to erupt, mingling with his, both of us jerking out every drop until I settle gently back on top of him, our bodies stilling once more, the only sound the slowing thump of his heart in my ear.

"Fuck," he says eventually. "Just...wow...fuck."

With his strong arms wrapped around me in the dark, I could lie cocooned in this wet, sticky mess for the rest of the day. He makes a wonderful pillow, and whoever declared a Midlands accent wasn't sexy has never heard my boy Jay calling their name in the midst of orgasm. I think I nod off again; there is something about this solid boy that makes me want to curl up against him and never let go.

As the sky brightens and my room lightens, I reluctantly lift up onto my elbows and look down at him more clearly.

"Good morning, my darling," I murmur, and he blushes beautifully.

"I think we're going to be glued together forever now," he remarks, shifting his weight experimentally. Yep, he may be correct. It's fairly crusty down there.

"It's odd being in this position," he carries on, shyly looking up at me. "You know, lying here underneath and not on top. I mean, I've obviously had a girl on top, but you're, like, bigger and...um...it feels like you're in charge up there, you know? You're stronger than you look, Lucien." He smiles self-consciously. "I like it, though. I didn't think I would. In my head I sort of always imagined me up there and you down here. But I like it a lot."

"I like it too, Jay. And I like you a lot."

I lean down and kiss him, my tongue exploring. We've both probably got stale morning breath, but neither of us notices or cares. He breaks away and looks up at me self-consciously.

"Are you okay?" I ask.

He's about to say something but changes his mind and nods instead before stretching his neck up for more and then breaking off again.

"...Do you, I mean, are you always on top?"

I shake my head, smiling, and just to demonstrate, I roll off him, taking him with me so that our positions are reversed. Blimey, he's heavy. Fortunately, he quickly realises I'm squashed and takes some of his weight on his elbows.

"Don't you dare tell anyone, because it will spoil my image," I whisper in a conspiratorial fashion, "But Dr Avery is very, very easy to please. He's extremely versatile. He likes it top ways, bottom ways, sideways, diagonal ways, um...on seaways, leeways, motorways, on bridleways..." I giggle. "And in alleyways, pathways, doorways, archways...anyways probably, as long as it is with you."

My silliness is rewarded with his beautiful easy smile, beaming down at me, followed by a loud tummy rumble.

"Gosh, I've been a dreadful host." I pout up at him girlishly. "In pursuit of my own pleasure, I forgot that all those well-honed muscles need regular feeding."

"Puny aristocratic ones do too," he replies, manoeuvring off me and climbing out of bed. "And you need to eat more before you waste away. Which is why I'm going to make you a proper breakfast."

*

I luxuriate in bed with a warm, fuzzy glow for a while before quickly showering, then follow the delicious aroma of frying bacon into the kitchen. As much as I could have lazed around under a duvet with him for the rest of the day—because, basically, I'm aching to have him inside me—I appreciate that this is all a bit new for him, and he may need time to adjust. And some protein and carbohydrates. So I'm going to be generous and allow him at least half an hour to regroup before I launch myself on him again. And who said we need to be in bed to fuck? I've been fantasising about him taking me over my kitchen table for weeks.

Having anticipated a couple of rashers of bacon between two slices of bread, the full English being dished out onto my delicate white china plates is quite impressive. As is the vision of my new man, filling out a long-sleeved white T-shirt, a pair of grey sweatpants hanging low from his hips.

"Which rugby team have you invited to join us for breakfast?" I enquire, eyeing the mounds of food. "I'm not saying I'm not up for a challenge now I've acquired a taste for the larger physique, but I'm not certain I could manage all fifteen of you."

"You won't grow big and strong, Dr Avery, if you don't eat a proper breakfast. It's the most important meal of the day. Now sit."

I do what I'm told and accept a plate laden with more calories than I've consumed all week. I'm actually vaguely hungry, and he watches me eat like a proud father with a recalcitrant toddler.

I chew a mouthful of black pudding. I should ask him to photograph it, my cousin Freddie will never believe me otherwise. I swallow. "The most important meal of the day is the one you have before a big night out drinking in dodgy nightclubs. If anyone should heed that advice it would be you."

He looks at me amused through his lashes before lasciviously licking a blob of stray ketchup from his upper lip. "But if I'd heeded that advice, then I wouldn't have gone to Spangles, and I wouldn't be here with you, would I?"

Chapter Ten

JAY

I virtually fled down to the kitchen this morning. I needed space away from him, a moment of calm to sense check my emotions. I'd actually done it. A night in bed with a man. Waking this morning to him lying on top of me, rubbing his bare dick against mine, making love in the dark, was fucking beyond unbelievable. And making love was exactly what it had felt like to me. Even though the light had been too dim to see him properly, I'd felt every perfect inch of that smooth long body covering mine, the pleasure-pain pinch of his teeth on my nipples, the velvet hardness of his dick. I'd only just managed to last as long as I did, coming with a surge of need I've never experienced before. Any lingering doubts about my sexuality had been comprehensively annihilated at dawn.

And the having him on top part, that was a shock to the system, too, understanding how much I'd enjoyed being held underneath his firm, masculine body. All my sexual fantasies up until this morning had always culminated with me on top, with my cock in another bloke's arse. But Lucien has blown my mind because now

I think I fancy a bit of the other. I want to be taken by a bloke, to have a man inside me.

But it's not just any man; it's him. It's Lucien Avery making me feel chaotically adrift. All my life, I've been steady, dependable, reliable, sensible. Son, brother, doctor, boyfriend. Following an unwavering path down the middle of the road, without checking left or right, so certain of my place and role on this earth. Until something changed, until out of all the homosexual men I could have picked for my last-ditch experimental flutter before locking those feelings safely back in their sealed box forever, I selected him.

Watching him now, delicately picking his way through his breakfast to please me, every glimpse of his sharp little teeth, every bob of that long white throat as he swallows, every blink of those knowing pale-blue eyes, has my dick as hard as a fence post.

With a final forkful successfully swallowed down, I push my plate aside and pull him upright. I'm rewarded with an amused smile; he's feeling it too. We were almost racing each other through the last few mouthfuls.

First things first.

"As much as they turn me on," I breathe, "this granny dressing gown and *Wee Willie Winkie* nightie have to come off."

The reason being, from the odd peeks I've stolen, and from the outline of him in the dawn light, what's hiding underneath is awesome. I throw myself at him, no chat, no deliberation, no opportunity to change my mind. It's all or nothing, and it has to be all, otherwise my balls will explode.

The lacy garments are left in a pile on the kitchen floor, then I push myself up against him. I'm broad, and he's slender; he's only a couple of inches or so shorter than me, but much lighter and barefoot. I easily scoop him up in my arms as our mouths clash together, all teeth and tongues. I hear myself groan, and I swear with pleasure. He giggles delightfully against my open mouth at the ridiculous noises I'm producing. I squeeze his taut bare arse, so smooth and hairless, while his hands are wrapped in my hair. The desperate neediness isn't all one-sided; he eats my mouth with equal abandon, exploring every dark corner of it, although minus the sound effects I'm unable to control. If I make noises like this just kissing him, god knows what I'll be like when we actually do anything more.

I move across his jaw and onto his long, elegant neck, sucking and biting around the rope of pearls. Lucien stretches his throat up and away, allowing me more, allowing me the whole length of that narrow pale expanse. It's not enough; I close my eyes and drift lower, down to his nipples and bite around something hard and metallic, sucking and kissing and biting again. And then the other side, and I know he likes it, even though he hardly makes a sound, because he thrusts up into me, pushing my head closer still, wanting more. And then I'm back up at his lips, and he wants that again, too, his tongue as eager as mine.

Wiping his mouth with the back of his hand, Lucien breaks away first. He eyes me like prey, hardly out of breath, whereas I'm panting like a dog on heat.

"Only one of us is naked," he indicates vaguely in the direction of my body. "Seems a little unfair."

My brain is slow to catch up with his words when he leans with one hip hitched casually against the sink as if he's fully dressed and contemplating whether to have a cup of Earl Grey or Lapsang, as though his beautiful raging hard-on belongs to somebody else entirely. Standing back, I see his body properly for the first time in broad daylight. It surely is something to behold. Long and lean, on the thin side of slender because he hardly fucking eats anything, his smooth skin is as flawless and white as alabaster. His chest is hairless, by design not a razor. His nipples are...well, difficult to see actually, because both have stuff hanging from them—one has the diamond encrusted bar through the middle of it and the other a feathery thing. Who cares what it is? It's hot as hell. No scars, no moles, no blemishes, he's Adonis brought to life, and that dick...fuck. I've seen it once before, but I was pissed then, in a dark corner of a dark nightclub. Now I'm sober as a nun's tit, and the sun is streaming brightly through the kitchen window. In its full glory, it's long and pale, hard as granite, curving upwards out of its neat, cosy bed of pale hair towards his navel. A fat bead of pre-come, mimicking one of the pearls around his neck, gleams at the pinkish tip.

"Matching collar and cuffs. Nice," I blurt idiotically as I wriggle out of my joggers, so I'm just in my long-sleeved tee. Not cool, Jay. Taking off the top half first is a much more attractive striptease. I seem to have temporarily mislaid the rational part of my brain.

"Did you think that I dyed my hair this insane colour?" he asks, icily amused.

Finally, my clothes are off and I'm in front of him once more, fists clenched at my sides. "I'm thinking nothing sensible at the moment. As you can probably tell."

He gives his dick a couple of lazy strokes, as if I'm not even in the room, openly appraising my body. The tip of that pink tongue flicks over his lower lip. "Tell me what you want to do with me now, Jay. I'm all yours."

I want to make you smile properly again. I want to hear that sweet giggling more often. I want to cook you decent meals and watch you eat them. I want to make slow gentle love to you; I want you to show me how gay men do it properly. I have a suspicion I want your cock up my arse. I want to lie in bed next to you all night and every night, with my arms all around you, holding you tight as you sleep, keeping you safe.

But I can't say all that. I don't have the nerve, and I'll scare him off. More than that, my brain is being totally dominated by my inner caveman, my vocabulary has shrunk to words of two syllables max. "Um...I want to bend you over this table and fuck you. I want you to show me how."

More evidence of my silky tongue, but he's unfazed, just more slow stroking. Christ, I swear I could come just watching him do that.

"I think you probably know how, Jay."

He reaches into what looks like an ancient flowery tea caddy next to the sink, retrieves a condom packet, and tosses it to me. Well, I suppose that's one place to keep them.

"We don't need that," I inform him, preferring not to use it. "Ellie and me...we...neither of us ever cheated or anything. I haven't been checked for years, but I don't need it. I don't want to use it, Luce. I want to feel you properly, although I know that gay men do use them and it's safer and we should be careful and responsible and, okay then, I'll use it, and..."

My hands are shaking. I'm babbling like a fucking idiot. Of course I should use the bloody condom; it's only a bloody condom after all. But when I state I don't want to use it, I swear his breathing becomes just that little bit faster, the tip of his tongue darts out again, wetting his upper lip. He deliberates slowly.

"Since Jules and I parted ways, I've been in the sexual equivalent of the Sahara. I didn't totally trust him and arranged to be tested after he left. And nothing. So, in that case...do you trust me?"

I nod; at this point I'll agree to anything, to be honest. The mood's been killed for sure. I wouldn't blame him if he regrets his haste in agreeing to let such an inexperienced guy fuck him.

Coming to a decision, he takes the condom back, drops it in the tea caddy, and carefully replaces the lid.

I am so out of my depth as Lucien strolls past me to the table. He slides our breakfast plates and a copy of the *Telegraph* to one side, presumably to avoid getting newsprint on his face. With increasing awe and incredulity, I watch as he then arranges himself over one end of the solid oak, long legs spread and arse in the air, before settling his chest against the tabletop and lightly gripping the edge of the opposite side to brace himself.

"Is this what you want, Jay?" he asks coolly, his voice a low whispery flutter.

Of course, deep down I know it shouldn't be like this. His protective Dr Avery shield has made a reappearance, and it's not how I wanted it to be the first time. In bed earlier, I experienced the joys of sweet, loving Lady Louisa. For this, I imagined the shy earl, all soft and flirty, hand-holding and gentle kisses. A bit like when I've done it with girls for the first time, starting slow and patiently building up, half expecting them to put the brakes on if I go too far. Not like now; his Dr Avery persona is too cold, too emotionally stunted.

The sunlight in the kitchen is too bright, the objects around us too ordinary. Sex should be like what we had in bed this morning, a loving union between two consenting adults, the culmination of a gradual crescendo of foreplay, teasing, nibbling, touching, kissing. I know it's not always like that, not for everyone, and not for me either on occasion in my drunken randy youth when any shag was the holy grail. Maybe tender sex is not what gay men generally do, maybe our rubbing off on each other in bed this morning was just a fabulous anomaly, never to be repeated.

But fuck, he's here and giving it to me, just like that, and he's confusing and beautiful, and I don't always understand what's going on in his head. I've waited so fucking long for this, not just with him, but to experience it with any bloke. My dick is telling my brain that he's a willing participant, that he wants it as much as I do. And bloody hell, his arse is so fucking peachy perfect, two smooth white globes spread wide, with a tantalising hairless pink bullseye twitching up at me, desperately trying to win my attention. It has my attention, my full fucking attention, completely and utterly. Nothing else could possibly compete, not an Arsenal hat-trick in an FA Cup Final, not a drowning man, not a herd of zebras barging through the kitchen door. Because I have to—I just have to get my dick in that teeny tiny hole right now. And there lies the problem.

"Luce...er...Luce, I haven't got any...um...stuff, you know, to like..."

"Use this," he commands, talking into the tabletop, and he nudges the butter dish with his left elbow. "Open me up with your fingers first. I suggest you avoid double-dipping if you fancy a slice of toast later."

I shall never look at Lurpak butter in quite the same way. Scooping up a massive handful, I smear most of it over my dick and the rest over his hole. In retrospect, I could have done it in a more careful, seductive fashion, but there isn't time because if the phrase 'open me up with your fingers' isn't designed to get me almost coming over his back before my dick is fucking anywhere near him, then I don't know what is.

With one hand squeezing the base of my knob to stop it from exploding, I gently insert one finger. Christ, the sensation as it gets swallowed up, he's tight in there. I pause, getting myself back under control, then bend over him and trail my tongue over the long line of his spine, my body covering his. He pushes back on my finger, signalling his need for more, so I add another, twisting experimentally.

"Gosh, that's...gosh, that's very good, Jay," he breathes. "Just there...gosh, oh gosh."

I like gosh; gosh is good. His whispery, fluttery gosh is more than I can take, and grasping my dick in one hand and his hip in the other, I press myself against that rosy-pink star for all I'm worth. The pink star pushes back, resisting, and then I'm in, eliciting more swearing and groaning from somewhere deep in my throat, and merely a slight hiss through his teeth from Lucien.

"Oh my god, oh my god, fuck, that's so tight," I gasp, petrified to move any further in or out. I'm embarrassingly close to coming.

Lucien, the sexy fucker, isn't helping matters by pushing his amazing arse up against me, wriggling and goading me into action. "Get on with it and fuck me, Jay. Hard. Now."

His words, his movements, are excruciatingly unbearable. Keeping my hand firmly on his hip and leaning forwards, placing the other around his shoulder, I take him at face value, or rather arse value, and bloody go for it. I'm conscious of my balls slapping against the backs of his thighs, and some animalistic grunts I've never made before, and the rattling of a teaspoon in a mug on the table. Or rather, off the table because I'm really shaking it now, and he's holding on for dear life as the table inches across the wooden kitchen floorboards, making a scraping noise with every forwards thrust. The mug goes flying onto the floor, followed by a splintering crash as the butter dish joins it, and Christ, this feels like nothing I've ever experienced. And when I said tight, bloody hell, is it fucking tight. I look down, mesmerised by my glistening, swollen dick disappearing and reappearing, squeezed in a vice of warm velvet, and he pushes back with my every thrust.

"I said. Fucking. Hard. Harder," he hisses.

Christ, I thought I was, but I'm a big strong lad. I'm beyond the point of no return, and if he wants it, he can fucking have it because I've got plenty to give. Gripping him even more tightly, I ram into him as though my life depends on it, as if I'm trying to climb inside him. Finally, finally, I hear him, desperate gasps, or are they sobs? Neither pleasure nor pain, but something. I've fucking elicited something out of him that makes my balls clench and my spine set on fire. As I minutely adjust my angle to get a better purchase, I sense it—he's really loving it now; whatever spot I've hit, it's really working for him; he's almost screaming out with every push and pull. I know the precise moment when he comes because his arse spasms around my dick, and I'm only a second behind him with what feels like litres of spunk spurting into his narrow channel, my hips jacking on and on. When I'm finally done, every drop squeezed out, I flop down over him almost sobbing myself, my mouth at his neck, my sweat-drenched body no doubt squashing him ever further onto the wooden surface. But it's only to support my weight because, otherwise, I think I'd be on the floor.

I lie like that forever, getting my breath back. Even after my exhausted, flaccid dick slithers its way out of his hole, I still lie there, coating him with my body, smelling the sex, smelling our sweat, loving the feel of his ragged breathing under me. And admiring the rather beautiful discreet tattoo on his left shoulder that I hadn't noticed before. Two red kites, soaring together, gracefully swooping over his scapula down towards the elegant nobbles of his thoracic spine.

"Feel free to get off me any time you like," he suggests quietly, and reluctantly, I totter back on wobbly legs and reach for my sweatpants, immediately feeling very exposed with my limp dick hanging out in the middle of the massive kitchen. Lucien remains motionless. I secure the ties of my sweatpants and grab my T-shirt. Still not moving. Still lying exposed across the table. My spunk dribbles out of his reddened arse and down his left leg.

Fuck, this is awkward. I'm not sure of the etiquette. Is he waiting for a repeat performance? If so, he may be lying there awhile because I am so, so drained.

"Gosh, I think I may need a hand getting up, Jay," he murmurs once I'm fully dressed. "I appear to have deposited my brain and my motor skills, along with the entire contents of my balls, on the kitchen table."

*

Good lord, I've broken my educational supervisor.

I guide him to the sofa, pretty much totally supporting his weight, and he gingerly sinks into it, lying down on his side. Curling into a foetal position, he shuts his eyes. Tears trickle from under his closed lids. Oh my God, what have I done? I know people cry after good sex— I've come close to it myself once or twice—but are these tears of joy? Tears of oh-my-gosh, Jay, you were wonderful and sex with you is fantastic? Or tears of oh-my-gosh, I'm never letting that animal anywhere near me ever again. Fuck if I know.

He's white as a sheet, even whiter than usual. Hovering above, unsure what to do, I take a proper inventory of him, starting at the top. His soft yellow/white hair is sweat darkened and sticking up at all angles. Disarrayed hair. Flustered hair. Just-fucked hair. Nice. His usually immaculate eyeliner is fairly smudged—to put it mildly—like when my sisters get pissed and sleep in their make-up all night. His chin and cheeks are inflamed from repeatedly being grated on my coarse stubble back at the start of the proceedings. His mouth, Christ, his fabulous, lax mouth. Red, swollen, debauched, fucked. Moving on down, I count two enormous love bites on his neck, one near the front, covering his beautiful white stretch of throat and another in the region of his left carotid pulse. I don't even recall doing that one, but it's a corker.

His shivery body is covered in a sheen of sweat, some areas a lot shinier than others where I was probably excessively enthusiastic with the Lurpak. Smeared with blobs of dried semen, some parts of his torso and chest are less shiny. Both nipples look raw from the repeated friction of being rubbed against the tabletop and from my sharp teeth. Oh fuck. I reckon they will hurt like buggery later, if not already. The elbow visible from this angle is rubbed raw, too, for the same reason (the tabletop, not my teeth).

Moving lower to his hips, the right side boasts four perfect imprints of my fingertips from where I rode him hard, four angry reddish ovals which will very soon turn distressing shades of purple and grey. Both hips display a purplish band across them from being repeatedly ground into the edge of the table. His dick remains delicious, long and pale, nestled in its light feathery bed, resting limply against his left thigh. Actually, his legs are okay, too, although they're trembling slightly, but as long and slim as ever. His toe polish has also escaped damage, although he has a small cut on the sole of his left foot from the shards of the butter dish. Oh, and one over his right big toe too.

So, in summary? Bloody gorgeous.

"Luce...Lucien...are you okay?" I ask tentatively, still not sure what to do with my enormous clodhopping body. Do I lie with him? Cuddle him? Check for other injuries?

The flawless white skin of his arms is covered in goosebumps, and I reach for the throw on the back of the sofa and carefully arrange it over him before tucking him in. Covering up the damage I've inflicted. I try again.

"Have I hurt you, Lucien?"

Still nothing, although his chest is slowly rising and falling and a few tears keep on appearing, so I know he's still alive. Great doctoring skills, Jay.

"And I'm sorry about your butter dish. Please don't tell me it's from the seventeenth century or something."

Finally, he opens his eyes, his gaze gently falling on me. I breathe a sigh of relief.

"No, that one was just a gift from Queen Victoria to the twelfth earl, in around 1857, I believe. Part of a very large, unique dinner service. Thanking him for his support in the Crimea."

Fuck.

"Of course you haven't hurt me, Jay," he begins softly. "I may look like I'm made of porcelain, but you don't have to treat me as if I am. I like being fucked hard sometimes." He looks hesitant, "I'm crying because...I'm...because every intense emotion makes me tearful these days. If we'd done it carefully and nicely in bed, like we did this morning, then I think I'd be crying a lot more. And I don't want to cry, I really don't."

Fuck, I want to treasure this beautiful man so much; I want to crush him to my chest and not let him go. Falling to my knees in front of him, I stroke his hair. "I don't want to make you cry either. I want to make you happy."

He indicates to me to join him on the sofa. Once more, his head is in my lap, and I stroke his brow, planting ridiculous soppy kisses all over his face. "I loved it, Luce. But Christ, that was...well, not what I was expecting, not like...um...so well...rough. What I mean to say is I'm not doing it like that ever again, not as rough as that, even if you ask me to."

Taking my hand, he brings it to his lips. "You are very sweet, did anyone ever tell you that? Jules...was...he was very cold. I think I've probably forgotten that sex doesn't have to be like that. Next time, we'll smooch and cuddle and make it perfect."

Next time. I like the sound of next time. He winces as he makes himself more comfortable.

"I have hurt you. Shit, I'm sorry; I'm a bloody idiot."

"I'm fine, honestly, just out of practice maybe. As my father used to say, there's no point having a sword if you don't draw a little blood every now and again, darling."

Grinning mischievously at my reddening cheeks, he reaches up for a deeper kiss. "And maybe I'd failed to fully appreciate that your sword is impressively large..."

If ever a comment was designed to put a man in a stellar mood, that's it. "So, what's the plan for the rest of the day? Unless you want to just stay here and let me kiss you all afternoon because that would be a good plan too."

He wriggles with delight. "I'm saving that for later. But I do have an idea for the afternoon actually."

I raise my brows with interest.

"I'm moving house."

He registers my look of confusion. "It's time I stopped hiding. I'm emptying the flat and moving my belongings back into the main house properly. We'll open it up and turn it back into a home. My home."

*

Yesterday morning, which seems light years away now, because of all the crazy fucking-over-the kitchen-table stuff that happened afterwards, I woke to the unbelievable sensation of Lucien's elegant naked body draped over mine and our hard dicks pressed together. This morning is almost as good; I'm sleepily aware of his lips tracing a route up my left arm and then something cool and hard pleasantly slithering around my wrist. I stretch lazily, and my dick stiffens as he moves onto my right arm, bringing it up higher with each delightful press of his mouth so it's resting with the left one above my head, and then something cool slithers over that wrist too.

Wanting to pull him into my arms, I immediately discover that I can't. Now I'm properly awake.

"Um...Luce, what the fuck?"

"Shhh, it's only my pearls, just relax."

Only my pearls.

Oh, my giddy aunt. He's only gone and handcuffed me with his precious string of pearls to the bloody wrought-iron bedframe I was so admiring of yesterday. Looped several times around each wrist, a crossover in the middle binds my wrists together, and a final loop over an iron curlicue neatly pins me to the bed.

"Stop tugging or you'll break them, darling! They're priceless! Another gift from Queen Victoria."

I look up to see him now straddling my thighs, naked. With his tousled pale hair and a wickedly impish grin on his perfectly symmetrical face, he looks about twenty years old. I have no idea whether to believe him or not.

"Morning, Jay, darling."

"Morning, you." I tilt my chin up to assess the wrist situation. "Don't we have jobs to go to? Patients to see?"

He nods. "Yes, that's why I woke you up extra early, so I could do *this* first."

"Um...what does *this* entail?" I ask suspiciously, still eyeing the pearls above my head. "This doesn't look like the promised smooching and cuddling."

"*This* is my plan to give you something to think about over the next few days," he replies. "So that you don't forget about me."

"Hah! No chance of that happening. Not after yesterday's little escapade over the kitchen table."

While we've been talking, he's been caressing and flicking my nipples, which apparently also have a nerve directly linking them to my dick. Another glaring error in my anatomy textbooks. They're already throbbing painfully, and I have a wary suspicion he's only just starting. He swaps his hands at my nipples for his mouth, causing me to arch my hips up off the bed.

"Careful," he tuts, looking up through his golden lashes. "My pearls, remember?"

"You do know that I am going to kill you for tying me up without asking my permission first. I'm going to...aaah, fuck that's nice, so fucking nice."

"You are beautifully groomed, Jay," he remarks carelessly, turning his attentions to the sensitive skin of my inner thigh.

"It's to make my dick look bigger," I growl, trying not to struggle against the exquisite torture of his tongue working its way up towards the crease between my hip and my groin. I'm half Italian; if I didn't pay attention to my body hair with regular manscaping, I'd be mistaken for a gorilla. His hands at my hips pin me down.

"Gosh, your dick doesn't need any help to look big," Lucien observes, and he's instantly forgiven for tying me up.

As if aware of being the topic of conversation, my dick starts dribbling wetness, and Lucien dabs at it, almost daintily, with the tip of his tongue, causing me all sorts of anguish.

"Fuck, Lucien, you've had your fun, now untie me so that I can touch you."

I pointlessly flex my wrists, which only results in the soft click of pearls sliding against one another.

"No."

His own dick stands tall and straight, and leaning back on his heels, he lazily fists himself, long slow strokes with his thumb circling the slit each time, the sight of which has me leaking even more.

"You enjoy watching me do this, don't you?" he breathes, caressing his balls with his other hand. A shaft of early morning light catches him through the thin curtains, bathing him in a silvery glow. A more beautiful sight I'm not certain I've ever beheld.

"Yes," I gasp, canting my hips, uselessly fucking thin air. I try pleading with him. "I need you to touch me; bloody touch me."

"Say please."

"Oh, for Christ's sake, *please* bloody touch me, Lucien, otherwise your pearls will be scattered all over the floor. Please."

Lucien would clearly rather me dissolve into a pile of frustrated goo than damage his precious pearls, and he curls his lean body forwards. With both hands steadying my hips, preventing my involuntary upwards thrusts, he firmly licks the underside of my dick before enveloping it in one easy motion into the back of his hot wet mouth. He's all the way to the hilt, effortlessly it would seem, and I gasp as he begins suckling, his wet slurps and my moans the only sound in the still of morning. He swallows me even further into his throat, his mouth tightly stretched around my shaft. Fuck. My balls clench, my spine tingles, and sensing I'm close, he pulls away wetly, his lips red and swollen.

"Don't stop, that's not fair, please don't stop." I'm begging, all attempts at any dignity gone.

Releasing his grip on my hips, he generously allows me a couple of pointless thrusts, and I spread my legs wider, digging my heels into the mattress as I uselessly chase something to rub my dick against for relief. Settling himself lower, every nerve fibre fizzes, and I shout out with shock as his clever tongue licks a path from the underside of my balls to...fuck, he's licking my arse.

"Luce, oh my god, you can't do that. Stop...oh...fuck, Luce, no...it's too...oh...fuck. Don't stop...don't ever stop... oh..."

It's too much and not enough all at the same time, his tongue lapping and sucking all around my hole. My dick is going to explode off the bed. I'm slick with sweat from the effort of remaining still while he licks me in that most intimate of places and from wretched, hot embarrassment. He's got his mouth *there*, and it feels so fucking unbelievable. I groan and babble complete shit because it's fucking agony. I want to lift my arse up to his face and shamelessly beg for more while simultaneously wriggling away. It feels wrong to want something so much, to be so open to him in this most private of ways.

"I'm going to come, I'm going to come," I pant, writhing on the bed. Lightning shoots down my spine and there's nothing I can do to stop it, and fuck, I don't want to stop it. My dick is screaming for release even louder than I am. I have never, ever been even remotely this turned on.

And like the utter wanker that he is, Lucien stops, squeezing the base of my dick so hard that I cry out with surprise and pain, before he sucks off the juice leaking copiously from the end. Nearly sobbing with need and frustration, I fuck the air with my bare wet knob, while he leans across and grabs something from the bedside table.

"You're going to come inside me, Jay. I want this big cock inside me again; I want to feel all of you inside me."

That voice, that maddening, fey, whispery flutter, the voice that screams sex, sex, and more sex, and fucking hell, I'm lost to him; I want to be inside him again so badly it hurts. Surely now, he'll loosen my hands. I need to have my hands on him.

But no, my hands stay exactly where he's tied them, and I whimper as he takes all the fucking time in the world to warm some lube between his palms before kneeling up tall astride me. And oh, fuck, he reaches behind to leisurely, fucking *leisurely* prepare his arse with his fingers. His dick leaks, too, as he finger-fucks himself, the gorgeous red tip impossibly swollen, wet and shiny as he palms it with his free hand.

"It's too late, I'm going to come," I wail, not caring that I've lost complete control. "I'm going to come just watching you do that."

"No, you're not," he warns, shaking his head. "You're going to hold on and wait until I'm riding your cock."

Nothing could tear my gaze away from Lucien, his eyes briefly closing, biting his lower lip in concentration as he crouches over me and spears himself on my dick. His neck and throat still bear the bruises from my claiming of him yesterday, his nipples still reddened from our rough rutting. His breath hitches, and he briefly grimaces as my whole shaft disappears inside him. He must be sore there too. Stilling, he catching his breath for a few seconds before resting his hands on the tops of my thighs and leaning back.

"You fill me completely," he breathes, closing his eyes again and inhaling deeply.

Then he begins to move, gradually at first, and I lift my head, hypnotised by the hot, impossibly tight glide of my dick in and out of his stretched pink hole. Opening his eyes wide, they meet mine, and we stare at each other in wonder as our mutual pleasuring reaches a crescendo, my hips rising up to join his downwards press in perfect union.

"I'm close," he moans as he throws his head back.

His hips jerk suddenly as ropes of creamy, hot jizz spatter my chest and face. Finally given permission, my own orgasm barrels through me, powerful and unstoppable, as his arse spasms around my dick; even when I think I've finished, another spasm wrings even more from my empty balls.

Reaching for my wrists while I'm still inside him, he unties me. I throw my arms around him as he comes down on top of me, licking up his own release from my face before sloppily kissing me. I taste myself and his come as our tongues frantically join, and I crush the length of him against me, smelling us, tasting us, joining us.

*

"You're bloody amazing, Luce," I pronounce while I'm still reeling in a shattered post-coital haze. "Did anyone ever tell you that? Absolutely unhinged, too. So far, in the two days that we've, that you…"

"That I've been your best man?" he interrupts mischievously.

"Yes. In the two days that you have been my *very* best man, I've shagged you over the kitchen table, which I loved but am going to do so much more nicely next time, and you've tied me up and licked my arse. On a school day too!"

"Heteronormative ideals are terribly overrated, darling." He giggles, nestling in closer.

Bloody hell, have we really got to get up and go to work? I never want to move again. I'm not sure I've the energy to move again.

"Don't laugh," I begin. "But it feels like I've been watching the snooker in black-and-white and then gone out and bought myself a colour telly."

I say it with a degree of wonder and feel his happy laugh against me. He's still sprawled on top, his head tucked into my neck. We're sweaty and sticky and the bedroom stinks of sex, but neither of us care a jot.

"If you don't start making lewd jokes about potting the brown, then I can probably live with that analogy, darling. Don't mention cue extensions either; I may get queasy."

"I mean it, Luce," I persist, pressing a kiss to the top of his head. "It's...it's...everything I've been looking for."

"Is it me particularly, or just having a man in general?"

I pretend to give it some thought. "Well, I'm going to have a crack at old Roger in theatres later today, and Dr Leitner looks pretty hot rocking that red tweed jacket which matches the colour of his cheeks...and now I think about it, Sanjay is..."

I yelp as he bites down hard on my shoulder and then softens it with a kiss.

"Of course it's you, you bloody drama queen; you had me in Spangles."

Chapter Eleven

LUCIEN

I'm smiling to myself as I plough through my ECT sedation list on autopilot, my thoughts dominated by images of Jay with my pearls tight around his wrists and my spunk coating his face. I'm regularly rostered for this psychiatry list because my colleagues hope I accidentally receive the treatment instead of the patient, but definitely no ECT required for me this morning. The twinge in my arse is a reminder of him every time I sit down. I'm so upbeat, they'll be wondering if the usually spiky Dr Avery has been replaced by a friendly alien.

Replaying the whole of the last twenty-four hours is an utter delight. Jay had left me recovering on the sofa after our kitchen table exertions, and I'd been woken from my boneless haze by shouts of "You bastard, Lucien, you absolute sod!" from the direction of the scullery. Shuffling through, I'd solemnly stood next to him at the kitchen bin as he'd held together some pieces of my broken butter dish, the writing on the underside clearly visible.

"I don't think Ikea were making dinner services in the 1850s, Lucien." He'd glared at me, and I'd laughed, slipping my arm around his waist as naturally as if we'd been teasing each other for years.

And we'd spent the rest of the day moving my stuff from the flat and back into the east wing of the main house, which took forever, not because I have lots of belongings, but because every few minutes, I had the pressing desire to be kissing him. He seemed to understand and indulged me clambering all over him, seeming to crave it just as badly as I did.

As we'd thrown off dust sheets, opened curtains, and lugged my clobber up and down the stairs, we'd talked about Billy-Ray, which had been tough, and Oliver, which had been much, much tougher. And he'd taken the piss out of the ridiculous number of lotions and potions lining the bathroom cabinet, had been flummoxed by my extensive collection of haute couture, and hugged me and pretended he didn't think I was completely bonkers at all as I explained about my pearls.

I'd pinch them out of my mother's jewellery box as a toddler and taken a shine to wearing them everywhere, which, when I look back, was a horrific strangulation accident just waiting to happen. But my parents had indulged me, as was their wont, and the long string of cool, gleaming pearls became a kind of comfort blanket for me to run my hands through and rub against my face whenever solace was required. They became a family joke. Scraped knee—pearls; overtired—pearls; spat with a school friend—pearls. And so on, until I went to boarding school, when they remained behind at home, curled around my bedstead, abandoned but not forgotten. In the school holidays, I'd finger them absently and occasionally slip them on if Oliver wasn't around to take the piss.

Unsure about my sexuality as a young teen, I'd sometimes wear them under my clothes, a reassuring comfort as I navigated the tricky path towards adulthood. Until my family died, I'd not needed them for a while, but I've worn them since, not only for comfort but as a reminder perhaps of simpler times.

Yesterday evening, Jay had cooked for me, a plain dinner of cheese omelette and salad, and we'd shared a couple of beers while cuddling on the kitchen sofa. I'd not been sure if he would stay the night and was too scared to ask, but he did. When we tumbled into bed, into my huge four-poster back in my old room, it felt natural that I should cover his body with mine, ending the day as it had begun, with a lazy, sleepy cock rubbing. Wrapping both of our shafts in my hand, we'd fucked together gently. Afterwards, I'd fallen asleep where I lay, with my head resting on his broad hairy chest.

Towards lunchtime, my ECT sedation list finished, Annabel bustles into the office.

"Goodness me, you're the talk of the department this morning, Lucien."

I raise my eyebrows with interest. "Really, Annabel? Why's that then?"

"Well, there is a rumour doing the rounds that you were seen smiling this morning and...good grief! How on God's earth did you acquire those?"

She's staring hard at me, or to be more precise, she's staring at my neck. Her eyes widen. The love bites are evidently big news. In collarless theatre pyjamas, they are difficult to hide and I've made very little effort to try. If everyone has nothing else occupying their small lives, it's not a concern of mine.

"The conventional way," I reply drily.

"There is nothing conventional about a man of your age and status sporting those! No wonder you are the only topic of conversation this morning. I'm surprised there isn't a queue forming outside this office of people wanting to see if it's true for themselves!"

Movement in the corridor behind Annabel distracts her, and we both turn to see Jay approaching.

Annabel whispers to me, "Here's one of them!"

A ridiculous sizzle of excitement thrums through me. In the presence of Annabel, however, I endeavour to give Jay my usual chilly Dr Avery appraisal.

"Dr Sorrentino, Annabel was just asking me about my neck. Apparently, it's a hot topic today. She's been sent to find out how I acquired these rather shocking purple marks."

"From a fellow vampire, by the looks of things," he replies, equally coolly, making a show of studying them.

I stifle a giggle. Annabel's mouth literally hangs open in awe, staggered that anyone, let alone a junior, would have the balls to address me in such a fashion. Another little titbit of gossip to fly round the department by the end of lunchbreak.

She stares at Jay with newfound admiration, and then, pulling herself together, shakes her head with despair at me. "Aren't you even the tiniest bit embarrassed?"

"Nope. Should I be?"

She signs with annoyance. "He's all yours, Jay. Good luck."

She's spot on; I'm totally all his.

Jay takes her seat when she leaves after locking the door behind her. It's only been a few hours, but I sink into his lap and kiss him hungrily, devouring him as if I truly am a vampire. He allows me a moment. I feel the beginning of his erection through the thin cotton of his theatre blues as I squirm into him, trying to relieve my own needy cock. With a groan, he gently stills me, a firm hand at my hip.

"Not here, Luce. It's too risky in the middle of the day. And..." He shifts back from me slightly. "And...nothing. It's...it's just too risky."

He's pulling away, I sense it from his averted gaze. Awkwardly, and suddenly nauseous, I clamber off and take my own chair. I've come on too strong. I'm scaring him off. The rough sex on the kitchen table—I knew it wasn't really his thing; I just hadn't felt I had the emotional bandwidth for proper lovemaking, so I slipped into what I knew. Jules had enjoyed taking me like that, he never wanted to see my face when we fucked. But I've since realised that I'm a fool because Jay has the emotional bandwidth to carry the both of us. Everything I am—the nightdresses, my dietary idiosyncrasies, the make-up and pearls, Rossingley even—he just takes in his stride. Except believing he'd hurt me; he hated thinking he'd done that. I told Billy-Ray I didn't deserve Jay, and I meant it. Inhaling deeply, I steel myself for rejection.

"Is there anything you came for in particular?" I ask. "I don't believe our formal appraisal is due for another couple of weeks."

"Don't be like that with me," he responds in an irritated manner. "You know it would be crazy to try anything here in the middle of the day. Annabel will be back in a minute."

He rubs his stubbly chin, blowing out a sigh. "Sorry, but the last two days have been fucking insane. Added to the last few weeks and my head's bloody imploding at the moment. I don't feel like I have the space to think or breathe."

He rubs my thigh briefly. "I meant all the things I said in bed this morning, Luce. I really did. Being with you, it's the best thing that's happened to me in a hell of a long time. But my problems are still there, you know? They haven't vanished just because I've hidden away at Rossingley and pretended they don't exist for forty-eight hours."

My mouth is dry; my heart beats faster as I try to stay calm. This is it. He's ending it before it's scarcely begun. I put my hand up to my neck, feeling for pearls that aren't there.

"There are so many layers to my life at the moment. I can scarcely tell if I'm coming or going. And after I left your place this morning, I felt like a dead weight had been thrown around my neck once more because all the other stuff just hit me again as soon as I got back to my own house. Ellie was leaving for work, so I had to make some bullshit excuse up about how I'd been out for an early morning drive to clear my head."

"I thought you called the wedding off," I point out icily. "I'm not entirely sure why you feel the need to dissemble."

Jules's spiteful voice echoes in my head. *Falling for the straight man, Lucien?*

Jay pushes a hand through his thick curls in frustration.

"Of course I've bloody called the wedding off! Our relationship is totally over! Since I walked out of Spangles, I've been kipping on a shitty camp bed in the spare room! But as much as I want to, Luce, I can't rush headlong into another relationship with you. Not without sorting all this other shit out first. For one thing, Ellie and my family and friends will think I jilted her because I'd been with someone else all along. They'll never believe otherwise if you and I start parading around."

"Perhaps you care too much about what other people think," I bite out angrily.

"No, I fucking don't! Most people can go to hell! But my family do matter to me, and so does Ellie. I don't want them believing I cheated on her, and she deserves me to behave decently. Throw into the mix that you're a bloke, and they'll think I've lost my fucking marbles. It isn't how I want it to play out, and you know it."

Deep down, I know he's right. I should pull back. I'm going at him like a bull in a china shop. I'm too much—me and my baggage are too much for him. And niggling inside is the worry that maybe he'll decide he's making a mistake, that I'm a homosexual experiment, and now that he's satisfied his curiosity, he'll realise what he's throwing away is worth more... *Falling for the straight man, Lucien?*

And the sex, for god's sake, the sex was amazing. But why hadn't I just played it steady? Stuck to a bit of frottage, a straightforward blow job maybe? Instead of throwing the whole smorgasbord at him. The rough stuff over the kitchen table frightened him half to death. No wonder he's having second thoughts; he's realised he's chucked in his lot with a complete nutter.

I stand up to go, and the movement reminds me of the ache in my arse, that and the marks on my neck are all that remain of his gift to me. "I get it, Jay. I understand. I'll leave you alone."

He stands, too, and grabs my wrist, pulling me close. The scent of clean, healthy boy washes over me; what I'd give to dive into his warm, welcoming chest.

"Listen, Luce. That's not what I want. You're not listening to me, or perhaps I'm not explaining very well. I've got a lot on this week, stuff to sort out as well as a shift here every day. I've only just started this new job, for god's sake—I should be concentrating on expanding my experience and making a good impression. Yet at this rate, I'm going to cock up monumentally because I can't focus properly. I can't even remember the last time I opened a textbook."

Five hours ago—only five hours ago, I had him tucked up naked in my bed, with the distinct impression he was more than happy to be there. And now I'm preparing for the brush off. He'll leave it open, of course, a vague plan to meet up sometime. He'll let me down gently because he's so damned nice. But incredibly, the brush off doesn't come.

"You can say no if you like, and I don't blame you if you do, but..."

He looks up at me shyly through his thick black lashes, and I feel a pathetic spark of hope. Whatever he asks, the answer will be yes.

"I'm working a shift on Saturday, and I promised to go to my folks for Sunday lunch. I'm not anybody's favourite person right now; the lunch thing is an olive branch. I don't want to turn it down. I haven't seen them since I cancelled the wedding. But I'm going to need some moral support. So...um...I was wondering if...if you would come with me?"

He turns pink under his olive skin and quickly clarifies. "You know, just as a friend or whatever. I'll tell them you're my boss from work—I've taken people home before, you know, other doctors working a weekend away from family or whatever. It won't seem weird or anything. And it will mean that they can't have a go at me because you can't have a blazing family row when you've got guests, can you?"

Meet the parents? Gosh, so I wasn't expecting that request, but hell, why not? I've nothing else planned, apart from painting my toenails and rearranging the bookshelves, and it would mean I get to spend even more time with this boy, who has given me something approaching happiness. Even if I can't have him all to myself. And if it's not happiness, and if happiness and sadness are opposing points on a straight line, then he's definitely edged me further away from the sadness end.

So we arrange a pickup time, and as he gets up to leave, we have an awkward shall-we-shan't-we kissing moment. I think we should, he thinks we should, too, but we just end up with a brief hug. I'm favoured with a whiff of Fahrenheit, which reminds me that his blue hoodie is still neatly folded on the kitchen sofa. Oh well, he can pick it up next time.

Chapter Twelve

JAY

"What the fuck, Jay-Jay? Your sister told Ellie, who told Paula, who told me, that you took Lucien Avery home to meet your parents on Sunday??!!! WTF? I am seriously concerned re your mental health at the moment. CALL ME!"

*

My parents live on the edge of a little town about an hour's drive north of Allenmouth. They moved there from Wolverhampton a couple of years ago to be nearer my eldest sister, who has kids, and to be closer to the static caravan they keep on the Welsh coast.

We're both fairly subdued in the car, content to mostly listen to the radio. Lucien's trying not to show it, but I'd hurt him earlier in the week when I'd backed off in his office. My feelings for him are spiralling out of control. I thought having a few days space might help me work out whether it's the newness of a male relationship or the fact that it's Lucien making my stomach churn and my head spin. Seeing him today after a few days break, seeing his cautious pointy smile and hearing his fluttery voice, I have my answer.

"I like your tattoo of the red kites," I say after a while. Pleasant daydreams about his bare chest have led to, well, even pleasanter daydreams about the sexy stuff. I'm half hard as usual in his presence and adjust myself discreetly. "I forgot to tell you at the weekend. It's cute."

"Thank you," he replies, genuinely pleased. "Oliver and I had matching one's done when I was about eighteen. We were on holiday in Greece. Our mother was absolutely furious when she spotted them, but my father just laughed. Next thing we knew, he went and got himself one too. Talk about world war three kicking off."

He smiles to himself at the happy memories. It's a real step forwards that he can reminisce without the telltale catch in his voice, or the pauses, the swallows. I take hold of his hand and keep it in my lap.

I'm cross with myself that I should care but secretly relieved Lucien has settled for one of his conservative Dr Avery outfits, and his face is bare of make-up. It shouldn't matter what he wears, but somehow it does. Yet even like this, he's extraordinary—ethereal and unworldly. The pearls are tucked away on the inside. I spot the outline of them under his soft shirt. Part of me wants to stop the car, undo the buttons on that shirt, and see them against his pale skin, run my hand over his smooth chest and... I need to get a grip.

"So let me get this straight," he says out of nothing. "You fancied men for a while, and then when you finally plucked up the nerve to do something about it, you chose the week before your wedding."

I nod, slightly irritated. I've told him this already. The problem with car conversations is the captive audience. Unless I hurl myself through the door at seventy miles per hour, killing myself and most likely Lucien, too, there is no escape.

"Thanks, Lucien, for bringing up my disastrous last couple of months. I was just thinking how pleasant this journey was."

Ignoring me, he carries on, happily covering old ground. "After sucking my cock, your suspicions that you'd changed teams were confirmed, so you did the right thing and called off the wedding, alienating your friends, family, and your bride." He pauses. "Yet you still haven't given anyone a reason as to why you suddenly developed cold feet."

I nod again.

"So, when *are* you going to tell them?" he asks, not unreasonably.

"Not today," I reply firmly. "Look, I hadn't expected to meet you, had I? After the episode in the club, I cancelled the wedding and assumed I'd have months, years even, to sort it through myself, and when all the furore had died down, maybe find someone. Perhaps a shy, naïve gay bloke like me, with a flat in town and a cat, and we'd gently bond over our shared love of Arsenal or something. Instead, I bloody walk into you and your fabulous craziness, scarcely a week later!"

A glance over and he's looking directly ahead and stifling a laugh. We're only ten minutes from my parents' house, a three-bedroom semi on a neat suburban housing estate. Why the hell did I invite him again? A spur-of-the-moment impulse I hope I don't regret.

"By the way," I say, "my granny will be there too. She has been diagnosed with early dementia and is very sweet, but don't let her make you a cup of tea. The last one I had, she put Gaviscon in instead of milk."

"I like peppermint-flavoured tea."

"God, don't tell my dad that. He's a red-blooded, unreconstructed male."

I'm obviously tensing up the closer we get because Lucien gives my hand a reassuring squeeze.

"Just relax, darling," he says. "I'm a well-brought-up boy, and I'm looking forward to meeting your family. And if conversation veers towards you being nagged about the wedding, then I'll do something distracting."

Oh fuck, that could be anything. I hardly know this man, not really. What if he calls me darling in front of my dad? Yep, that would be distracting. And what if they ask him personal questions, just making conversation about his background and things? He related the tattoo story quite happily, but what if something triggers him, and he becomes upset?

"And my folks, well, um...we're very ordinary, very working class. My dad's a builder, and my mum's a school dinner lady."

Lucien leans across, far enough to give me a peck on the cheek. "Believe it or not my family were pretty ordinary too. No, don't scoff, they were! Obviously, we were stinking rich and had the estate and everything, but I'd describe the four of us as pretty normal when we were alone. It wasn't all cream teas on the lawn and croquet, you know. My parents argued sometimes, Oliver and I bickered a lot when we were bored. We had family holidays where we played Monopoly if it rained, albeit in a very swanky location, and during term time, my mum nagged us about schoolwork. We occasionally ran out of milk and teabags; I got told off when I left my dirty rugby boots lying around, or if I forgot my please and thank-yous. You know, normal life stuff."

He stops abruptly and looks out of the window. I say nothing and squeeze his hand a little tighter.

I'd prewarned everyone I was bringing a friend, so Lucien isn't a surprise, and I was right surmising his presence would provide a useful foil. My parents and I haven't been face to face since my unhappy phone call announcing the wedding was off. Most of our communication since has been perfunctory. My mum is convinced I've temporarily developed cold feet, and by the time I've sold the house will regret it forever and will want Ellie back. As well as being extremely fond of Ellie, they're out of pocket financially, too, as they contributed to the cost of the wedding reception. It's money they can ill afford to lose, although I'll pay them back out of my share after we sell the house.

A complete fuck up all round, to be honest, so thank heavens for my muddled granny, oblivious to the whole fiasco. With open arms and a whiskery kiss, she greets me like the prodigal son. As does my two-year-old niece, who is here with one of my sisters and has taken a shine to Lucien. They say babies naturally gravitate towards pretty things.

My dad is quiet and seems to be the only one not gravitating towards Lucien. He's a good, decent, family man. My grandad came over from Italy after the war, with barely a penny to his name, and between him and his brother, they built up a little family building business which my dad took over when he left school. Having had their financial ups and downs, as they head towards retirement, my folks are proud to own their own house and see four kids grown and financially independent.

As the first family member to go to university, a big deal at the time, I've made my dad very happy over the years. Less so recently, for obvious reasons. With three older sisters, I was the golden boy he always wanted. Throughout my childhood, his evenings and weekends were spent ferrying me about, to football practice in the winter and cricket in the summer. Next year, he's stopping work for good, and I think he was looking forward to seeing me do those things with his grandchildren too. While my mum gave me a tearful bollocking after I called off the wedding, he's been mostly silent, which in some ways is much worse.

My mum's Sunday roast, with all the trimmings, is as delicious as always, and I'm gratified to observe Lucien eat a decent amount, although he politely declines her apple pie, a big error in my opinion. Conversation around the table never strays far from neutral topics, made easier when a cute toddler steals the limelight. She insists on climbing onto Lucien's lap, and he seems perfectly content to have her there, even if she does smear ice cream all over one of his YSL silk shirts. As my nosy sister quizzes him about work, he's charming company, deftly steering the conversation away from the personal, much to her suppressed irritation. I've brought colleagues home before—we're often at a loose end if one of our partners is also a shift worker, although they're usually blokes like me, clad in jeans and a rugby shirt—beer drinkers happy to argue about the recent purchases in the footie transfer window. If my sister is curious, she politely hides it.

After dinner, when we're all mucking in to clear up, my granny corners Lucien in the kitchen.

"I've got a present for you," she announces proudly, beaming up at him from behind her bottle-top glasses, her rheumy eyes magnified.

"Oh, yes?" smiles Lucien indulgently.

She ferrets around in the pocket of her housecoat. "Here it is. A handsome young man like you must have a pretty girl at home to give presents to."

Their exchange garners curious attention from both my parents. There's nothing overtly camp about Lucien's demeanour or mannerisms, particularly dressed as conservatively as he is. But there is something far too pretty about him which begs the question. Too graceful. My parents aren't especially homophobic, as far as I'm aware, and they've made Lucien feel very welcome, but it's just not what they would hope for their son. Hence the sudden interest in my granny's offering. Which saddens me as I'm all set to disappoint them massively. I'm still me, I want to shout. I'm still Jay, who loves his footie, who looks after his sisters, who has made them all proud. The disappointment won't happen today anyhow; I'm not ready.

Lucien holds out his hand for whatever trinket my grandmother thrusts into his open palm. Last time she gave me a gift it was a lint-covered Werther's Original, which looked as if it had spent three years lurking at the bottom of her handbag. Peering dubiously over his shoulder, I see a pair of pretty pink plastic hairclips, the sort of cheap tat my youngest sister used to spend her pocket money on in Superdrug. He studies them carefully, his lips pursed, clearly wondering how to respond. All eyes are on him; you could have heard a pin drop. Or a hair clip.

"So, Lucien," prods my mother as casually as she can manage. "Have you? You never said. Is there a girl waiting at home for you?"

Lucien glances at me for a moment and then at his audience. I've broken into a cold sweat; it suddenly feels like his answer is of utmost importance. I'm so not ready for the big coming out; I'm truly not. Not yet. Casting his gaze back down at the hairclips and then up again at my sweet, batty granny, he slowly smiles.

"I have actually. Thank you so much; they're very lovely. I think Louisa will be delighted with them, don't you, Jay?"

The tension in the room evaporates, and my mother reaches for her tea towel once more.

I risk a wink at him. "She certainly will, Luce. I think she'll look beautiful wearing them."

*

After lunch, we watch football on the telly with my dad, during which Lucien gamely pretends an interest in the fate of Wolverhampton Wanderers. My dad's already engaged him in an in-depth discussion about carpentry, and Lucien had obviously been paying attention when I fixed his panelling as he stood up well to the gentle scrutiny and covert assessment of his manliness. He even countered by asking if my dad had any recommendations for specialist sash window companies, which pleased me as there is an absolute gale blowing through our bedroom at Rossingley.

Our bedroom. Now I am truly getting ahead of myself. *My* bedroom is currently the eight-foot by four-foot box room in Ellie's and my little terrace, in which I can scarcely turn around without bumping into something. My feet hang off the end of the camp bed. The best night's sleep I've had in two months was at Lucien's, even with him clinging onto me all night like a barnacle and then chaining me at dawn to the bedpost. And his feet are bloody freezing.

At half time, my dad sends me on a pot of tea errand to the kitchen, which was most definitely prearranged as my mum and sister conveniently seem to be lying in wait for me.

"How's Ellie getting on, Jay?" asks my sister, giving me a shrewd look and not wasting any time.

"She's...she's okay," I reply, reaching into the fridge for the milk. "Well, as okay as can be expected. Failing her exams on top of everything else was less than ideal, obviously. She'd be much better if someone would put in an offer on the house so we could both move forwards a bit."

"Give her our love, won't you? I don't want her to think we've forgotten about her."

I hear a sniff and turn to see my mum has a tissue pressed to her nose. Christ, just what I need. My sister jerks her head, indicating to me to do something about it. With a sigh, I go over and pat her shoulder.

"Look, I've said I'm sorry, and I really, really am. But...but I just couldn't bloody go through with it, okay? I made a mess of things, and I'm sorry."

She brings her hand up and squeezes my fingers. "I know you are, love. But me and your dad, we're struggling to understand it, that's all."

Tears are rolling steadily down her cheeks, and my sister produces another tissue. "We're going out of our minds with worrying about you," she sobs.

God, I hate myself for upsetting my lovely mum so much. I'll carry the guilt for the rest of my days.

"You look so tired," she continues, shaking her head. "And Ellie's so lovely. You seemed so happy together. Is it something she did that you won't tell us?"

"God, no. Definitely not. Ellie's done nothing wrong."

I kneel on the floor, put both arms around her, and hug her familiar heaving body close. "Please don't worry about me, Mum," I beg, throwing my sister a pleading look. "I'm fine, honestly. I've just got a lot on. It will all blow over; we'll get the house sold, and I'll pay you back and..."

"It's not about the money, Jay," she sobs. "It's you. We can't understand you, that's all."

"I said I'm fine—please stop worrying. Let's talk about something else." I search around for a topic, anything at all. "Tell me how Aunty Lorna's getting on after her hip operation."

We take our leave when the football match ends, my mother insisting Lucien has his share of the apple pie in a Tupperware for later. Ten minutes down the road, I breathe a sigh of relief and look across at him to find he's sporting the two pink hairclips in his short blond fringe and attempting to keep a straight face. I snort with laughter.

"Do you think they fell for it, Louisa?" I laugh, trying to concentrate on the road and not on the ridiculous vision of loveliness next to me.

He shrugs. "Probably not. Pull over."

We're on a quiet stretch of road that I know well, and a little farther along, I pull into the carpark leading to Allen Downs, a patch of heathland popular with dogwalkers. At this time of evening with the light fading, the carpark is empty. I kill the engine.

"Why have we stopped?" I ask, unfastening my seatbelt.

"So I can do this," he answers and, leaning across, kisses me deeply. "I couldn't wait any longer."

Kissing across the front seats in a dark car is an underrated pleasure. We do it some more until, eventually, he pulls away.

"Listen, Jay. Let me tell you what I think, now that I've met them all." He rests his hand lightly in mine, twisting in his seat so he's facing me.

"First of all, you're lucky, you know? You've got a really nice family back there, who all care for you. They might not be the most expressive, but there was so much love across that dining table, and most of it was directed at you. You've made a decision they can't understand, mostly because you haven't told them your reasons, and they are obviously desperately worried about you. Perhaps that worry and frustration has been coming over as anger whereas, actually, everyone is feeling hurt and upset. They're not angry at all."

I sigh. He's right. Of course, he's right. I realised that when my mother collared me in the kitchen. "But how can

I tell them the truth? I'm dreading it as I'll upset them all over again. I can live with them being disappointed when they find out I'm gay—that's their problem not mine. And I'm not going to get all worked up if their attitude isn't perfectly PC—I'm too old to care about that, and they're too old to change. But I hate being a cause of all this worry when they have done so much for me. When I'm not calling off weddings, we're all very close, and I want to stay that way. Initiating a conversation about being gay will be awful beyond words."

Lucien frowns, a small vertical line appearing between his eyebrows. "And that's the only aspect of the whole situation that annoys me."

My confusion probably shows on my face as he carries on. "The only reason you should ever feel obliged to offer, to explain your actions, is that you realised Ellie wasn't right for you. That marrying her wouldn't have been fair on yourself or her. And you've done that already. Sure, it would have been a hell of a lot easier if you'd reached that conclusion slightly sooner, but at least you did it before you tied the knot and not after several years of married misery together."

He reaches up and tucks an errant clump of curly hair behind my ear. "I'm proud of you for having the balls to stand up and call the whole thing off when you did. Not everyone would have been brave enough to do that."

I still don't get it. "So why does that make you angry?"

"What makes me angry is that one day in the future, you think you will have to stroll into your parents' home, or your friends' houses, or the anaesthetic department, and announce that you are gay. And then suck up people's reaction to it. As if you almost have to declare and then apologise for being in a minority group. When your sister was seventeen, she didn't sit your parents down in the kitchen and declare that she was heterosexual, did she? She didn't come out to her friends one night and confess that she fancied men? Just as my brother, Oliver, didn't have to advertise to the world that he was straight. Frankly, whomever you choose to have sex with, whether male or female, is no one's business but yours."

I didn't peg Lucien as much of a defender of gay rights, and he probably isn't, but he's certainly passionate enough about this on my behalf. And it's kind of wonderful. "So what should I do then?"

He shrugs. "Nothing. You do nothing. You repeat the absolute truth—that marriage to Ellie wasn't right for you, you are deeply sorry you arrived at that conclusion so close to the wedding itself, and then you carry on. And sometime in the future, if you bring a boy home like you did today, and happen to hold his hand like a straight couple might do, or discuss your holiday plans together like a straight couple might do, then they can draw their own conclusions, can't they? But you don't need to explain yourself, or warn people—*Hey, guys, just a head's up. I'm gay, okay?*—because straight people don't, so neither should you. Being gay doesn't define you; it's just a part of you. And having said all that, you never know, they might surprise you with their response. As I said at the start, your family love you very much."

Resting my head back, I momentarily close my eyes. I'm so glad I took Lucien with me today. But I'm weary; the whole saga is dragging me down. I could sleep for a week. When I open them again, he's still looking at me intently, those pale-blue eyes imbued with warmth.

"The hair clips suit you, Louisa."

"They'd go better with one of my nighties, though, don't you agree? Perhaps the cream satin?"

I reach down to the button at the side of my seat, and it silently starts moving backwards. "Get your skinny arse over here; I need a cuddle."

Audi bucket seats are not designed to be shared by two tall blokes, especially when one of them is as beefy as me and the other has endlessly long legs. Somehow, I get him sandwiched in my lap sideways on, wedged between me and the steering wheel, those slender limbs stretched out on the passenger seat.

"Maybe the other way around would have been easier?" he questions as his head bumps against the interior roof. "Or, call me unadventurous, but waited until we got home?" Even with the seat fully reclined, his neck is at a less than ideal angle.

I shake my head. "I can't wait. I needed you on me now." A flush starts at my neck. His solid weight in my lap is soothing after my emotional afternoon.

"I like you above me and over me. Covering me." His hands start reaching under my shirt. "I thought...um...I thought that I'd be the one, you know, always on top or whatever. But actually, I want to be underneath you just as much." My face turns scarlet; I so wish I hadn't confessed that. I still haven't told him what I really want, but he's probably guessed by now. And anyway, I don't need any more words.

His soft mouth slants down onto mine, and closing my eyes, I let him kiss my worries away, ravaging my mouth until I've pretty much forgotten how to speak. My hand snakes automatically up his lean thigh until I encounter the warm heat of his shaft through the denim. I begin to undo his belt. Despite shagging his arse, being tied up by him and, sweet Jesus, being rimmed by him, I've yet to properly touch his cock.

"I feel about sixteen," he jokes, easing his arse up so I can loosen his chinos.

"I don't care," I growl. "I've been wanting to touch you all afternoon. It's been bloody murder."

"Yes, you were eyeing me rather hungrily over dinner, as though you couldn't choose between me or the huge slab of beef on your plate."

"Shit, do you think anyone noticed?"

"Who knows? But from what I've seen, the way they looked at us—your dad particularly—I think they can guess at the reason. And I think they'll be okay with it. Maybe not overnight but given time."

"I don't want to talk about my parents while I've got your knob in my hand."

I take the weight of it in my palm, a fine satiny layer of skin enveloping a steel kernel, before rubbing my thumb gently over the slit. Already wet with pre-come, I add to it by spitting into my palm. Slowly sliding my hand down the shaft elicits a sweet hitch in Lucien's breath. He's a mostly silent lover compared to me—he extracts all manner of embarrassing sounds out of me—so even this sharp intake of breath feels like a reward.

There's no room to do anything more than this in the car, but I don't mind because kissing fully clothed in the dark and giving him this simple hand job is strangely as intimate as anything we've done so far. He fucks into the channel of my fist as his soft lips find mine, and after he comes, spilling over my fingers with a breathy sigh, I bring my hand to my mouth and lick up every drop.

Chapter Thirteen

LUCIEN

Billy-Ray's funeral is a sad little affair, attended by a few staff from the ICU and a handful of relatives, none of whom ever bothered to visit him in hospital apart from his grandmother. Jay had insisted on coming with me and stands guard at my side throughout, giving me the strength to remain dry-eyed in front of curious work colleagues.

Any tears wouldn't have been wholly for Billy-Ray, although he was worthy of many, but the soulless crematorium brings back the horror of the consecutive funerals held at our little estate chapel—first my parents and then Oliver and Isobel. I endured those with only my cousin Freddie for comfort. The solid presence of Jay Sorrentino would have been most welcome.

Afterwards, I'm grateful to be sinking into the red leather seats of his car. Knowing without needing to be told, Jay's unfussy support shields me, from the quick press of my hand during the brief eulogy to the way he deftly steers us away at the end, after offering a few ineffectual words to Billy-Ray's shell-shocked grandmother.

I've hardly seen Jay since the trip to his parents, and I've craved him as sunflowers crave the sunlight. A hasty kiss in my office, an even hastier one against the back wall of lockers in the theatre changing rooms while two surgeons discussed a challenging abdominal operation barely three feet away from us, and a torturous department meeting with him sitting next to me along the row of seats, our knees touching and my cock throbbing.

He's been dreadfully busy, and I understand, I really do. They finally have a buyer for the house, and so the endless paperwork begins, as if the conveyancer is negotiating a deal for a shopping complex in Knightsbridge instead of a boxy two-up two-down just on the edge of Allenmouth town centre. Of course, in addition, we have those pesky things called jobs that take up an awful amount of time, and Ellie needs him, which I understand less well. But she's working for exams, trying to tease apart their shared lives, trying to find a flat of her own, and essentially, I'm at the end of a long line of commitments for him.

"Come to London with me," I urge as we drive away from the crematorium.

"What, now?"

"Yes, now. You're not rostered to be at work tomorrow, and I want to take you up the Shard. I should do it in Billy-Ray's memory."

"That sounds like a novel excuse."

He'd laughed when I'd told him about one of my final conversations with Billy-Ray. I'd been comforted to know that Jay was with him in his last few hours, even if I'd broken my promise to the poor boy.

Despite Jay's insane driving, I manage to nod off in the car. There's something indescribable about being with him that enables my whole body to relax, the nervous exhaustion I've stored up over the last eighteen months ebbing away from me. He must think I suffer from narcolepsy or something.

A phone call trumpeting through the Bluetooth speakers wakes me as we approach the M25, abruptly cutting off the background lull of sports commentary. A male voice I recognise but can't place launches into a tirade before Jay's scarcely said hello.

"Finally! You're like bloody Lord Lucan at the moment, Jay-Jay!"

Jay laughs easily. "Hi, Evan. How's it going?"

He mouths 'second-best man' at me, by way of explanation, and some chit-chat goes back and forth, essentially an exchange of derogatory comments aimed at each other. It's boy banter, something I'm able to recognise but in which I don't partake. I can put a face to the voice's owner now, one of the junior surgeons, a short, confident lad. Very keen and smart—one of the one's I find almost tolerable, in fact.

"So, Jay, fancy a pint later? Me and some of the rugby lads are going to the White Hart to watch the match."

"No, sorry, mate. I'm...er...not around."

"Where are you then? Ellie didn't think you were on nights?"

"No...um...I'm not. I'm driving up to London with a friend. I'll be back tomorrow."

There's a pause, an audible groan, and then some swearing.

"Oh for fuck's sake, Jay! You're with that posh twat again, aren't you? Jesus, what's got into you, man? He's so fucking weird."

Gosh, so this is a tad awkward. Jay glances across at me anxiously, and I blow him a kiss.

"Evan, I'm currently driving, and I've got you on speakerphone in the car. The posh twat is sitting here next to me."

"Hello, Evan," I say brightly. "How are you? I do believe we have an operating list together next week. Should be fun, don't you agree?"

It's rare to hear a surgeon apologise, let alone grovel, and it's a pleasing performance only marred at the end by Evan reminding Jay his presence is essential this coming weekend to celebrate his birthday. And he makes a point that Ellie will be there as well. Not for the first time, Jules's words echo in my head, and Jay's recent busyness with Ellie and the house and everything only serves to underline them.

We arrive at my family's pad in Mayfair, a vast Georgian residence that has been in my family since, well, Georgian times. It's undergone several modifications over the years, not least when my grandfather bought up the properties on either side. Jay becomes quieter and quieter as I direct him to the underground parking. I suppose this place is quite imposing, as is the estate, but sometimes I forget the effect it has on others as these properties are just parts of my life that have always been there. Ascending from the lift to the house, we are greeted by a pair of very pretty spangly silver Converse boots carelessly lying in the doorway, and a rather extraordinary green fishnet jacket thingy hanging up next to them. A pink feather boa is casually draped across the console table. They're difficult items to ignore, and they jar with the otherwise immaculate grand entrance.

"Bloody hell, I know you have an eclectic wardrobe, Lucien, but…"

I kick the shoes to one side and beckon Jay through into the hallway. "Oh, ignore those; they're probably Freddie's. He leaves his clothes everywhere. It's like a territorial marking."

Jay frowns at me. "Who the hell is Freddie?"

A teensy-weensy bit of possessiveness in that tone? Ooh, yes, how marvellous.

"Uncurl your fists, Jay darling. I've mentioned him to you before. He's my cousin and a very, very naughty boy. I let him stay here sometimes when he's hiding from everyone."

"Interesting footwear," he remarks, following me into the house. "Why is he hiding?"

"He's a model," I explain. "He's twenty-four, and he's usually trying to avoid either his father, his accountant, his dealer, the agency, or his exceedingly dull partner. Or sometimes all of them at the same time."

I turn and face him. "And I have an enormous soft spot for him. After the accident, he phoned me every single day for three months to check I was still breathing. And visited me whenever he could, despite his hectic schedule. Whereas I think most of my other relatives only saw pound signs and were hoping I'd fall into a spectacular depression and kill myself." I lean closer, my mouth to Jay's ear, and whisper, "Added to that, darling, Freddie's of the lavender persuasion. He's one of us."

Jay's lips quirk. "What, an anaesthetist?"

"Stop teasing and give me a kiss."

He does as requested, his arms circling my waist and pulling me close, his perfect soft lips warm against mine. When we're like this, I can almost believe he belongs solely to me. I snuggle closer, smelling him, burrowing into his neck, tasting him.

"Are you...are you...licking me, Luce?" he murmurs after a few moments, his hand roaming under my waistband and down to my arse.

"Possibly," I confess, my voice muffled against his skin.

"I hope I'm not going to wake up in the morning with a pink feather boa tied around my wrists."

I giggle and lick him again, my tongue tickling behind his ear. "Now, there's an idea."

He squeezes gently. "This Freddie of yours, does he look like you?"

"I'm an older, even prettier version. But, yes, he does. We are usually mistaken for brothers. You've probably seen his ads—he does the Jean Paul Gautier aftershave ones, some Ralph Lauren preppie stuff too."

Jay chuckles against me. "That figures." He surprises me by ghosting a finger over my cleft, and I wriggle with pleasure, pushing back for more. "Have we got time for me to fuck you nicely, Luce?"

In a sedate and leisurely fashion, I lead him by the hand to my room on the first floor, taking in a small tour of the priceless artwork on the walls, the ornate Louis XIV furniture in the salon, and the intricate plasterwork on the ceiling roses.

That's an enormous fib of course—we see neither to the left or the right as we canter up the stairs, pulling our clothes off as we go. Once in my room, he divests me of the remaining items, sweeps me up, and deposits me in the middle of the bed while kicking off his shoes and trousers before diving on top of me. My cock is as hard as a thousand-piece jigsaw, as Oliver used to say, and Jay's is, too, as he claims my mouth and our cocks tussle against each other. If we carry on like this, there won't be any fucking, just a soggy mess between us, and I come up for breath, panting a little.

"There's some stuff in the drawer," I say, indicating my bedside table.

"What, more Lurpak?" He laughs as he sits back on his heels and reaches for the drawer. "That's an unusual place to store the butter."

Then a split second later. "Whoa! What the fuck, Luce? I don't even know what half of this stuff is for! What the hell do you do with..." He's shaking his head as he rummages around. "No, don't tell me. I don't want to know."

"Oh, that little collection." I giggle as he comes back with my favourite vanilla-scented lube that I have specially imported from New York. I admire the Waitrose essentials range for many everyday household necessities, but lube isn't one of them. "It's all Freddie's."

He snaps open the lid and sniffs appreciatively. "You're such a fucking liar. Now, tell me what to do. I want to do it properly so that it's utterly perfect for you."

His matter-of-fact consideration blows me away. No one, and certainly not Jules, has ever wanted it to be all about me. I grab a pillow and shove it under my hips before bringing my knees up and widening my legs for him, all of me open and on display.

He moistens his lips with his tongue. "God, you're beautiful. So fucking beautiful."

Over the next hour or so, I begin to totally comprehend why Ellie isn't giving up on him without a fight. Because our sweet man really knows how to make love. I had my fair share of sexy times in my youth, which partly explains why young Freddie has me wrapped around his little finger. Everything Freddie's doing, I did myself—girls, boys, threesomes, kinky clubs. And I still managed to get up for work the next morning, which I frequently remind Freddie when he's whinging about having to spend a few days on a yacht shoot in Monaco after a heavy night out. But none of it, none of those casual, experienced partners, and definitely not Jules, come close to making me feel how Jay does. The house could be collapsing around us, and I'm not sure I'd notice.

He prepares me so carefully, so lovingly, he crooks his fingers so perfectly onto my prostate that I'm whimpering and begging by the time he lines up his cock. Entering me with one smooth slide, he whispers sweet nothings into my ear while he pauses, allowing me to get used to the feeling of fullness. I revel in the stretch and burn, wrapping my legs around him as it subsides, to be replaced by a glorious swell of pleasure. Not to beat about the pubic bush, but my Jay is rather well endowed. His cock is gorgeous, darker than mine with a thick violet vein pulsing along the underside. He's wider, too, and gosh, does he know how to angle it just so, so precisely. Drawing my legs up even higher so he's right at the hilt, his wiry pubes scratch deliciously against my balls. He slides one of his hands between our bodies, and with the tip of a wet finger, lightly touches where he's entered me.

"God, Luce. I love that you take me like this; I could come without moving, just watching you and kissing you."

I'm in agreement with him as he brackets my face with his arms and his lips find mine. Our hips begin moving regardless, in infinitesimal degrees, the scratch of his hairy belly an exquisite torture on my cock trapped between us. He's on his elbows but holding my hands in his by the side of my head, our fingers linked together tightly. I feel like I'm being fucked from the inside out, every push and retreat a silent *I love you*. When I come, it's with scarcely an increase in tempo, hands free, no wild rutting, no yelling climax, just a shuddering release followed swiftly by a hot liquid rush of heat inside me as Jay does the same.

"Sixteen generations of aristocratic cheek bones. Very nice. You remind me of that actor from *Twilight*."

We've cleaned up, kissed a hell of a lot more, and now we're stretched out in my bed, my head on that overgrown chest as usual, his thumb tracing a path across my cheek. I have to pretend I only vaguely know to what and whom he's referring. We haven't quite reached the stage in our relationship when I can admit that one of my guilty pleasures is masturbating to old Robert Pattinson interviews on YouTube with a dildo up my arse. I'm undeniably flattered, nonetheless.

"Which actor?" I answer coyly. "You mean...er, whatshisname, Robert...um...Richard... Patter... something?"

He shakes his head, the bugger. "Nah, not him. I mean the old guy who plays the girl's dad." He plants a kiss on the top of my head. "Of course I bloody mean him! The one who plays the main vampire, that my sisters used to love. Edward isn't it? Except that you are a lot blonder, skinnier, and have a few more wrinkles."

Charming. "I think the descriptor you are looking for, Jay, is slender, and unfortunately, us mere mortals do have that pesky problem of ageing to contend with."

"Are you going to tell me that I remind you of that stacked werewolf—Jacob?"

"No, certainly not!" *Because that boy can't hold a candle to you.* "Not after that dreadful comment about the wrinkles."

I love you has been on the tip of my tongue, ready to be blurted out since we arrived at the house. But, in the words of a well-known song, those three words are said too much and, in some circles, not enough.

When I was learning how to critique medical research papers, one professor advised me to always apply the 'so what' test. For example: smoking causes lung disease. So what? Well, if you stop smoking, you will have healthier lungs and live longer. Thus, it passes the 'so what' test. Another example: smokers are less likely to vomit after anaesthesia than non-smokers. So what? We're not going to encourage everyone to take up smoking prior to undergoing an operation. Thus, it fails the 'so what' test and, while undoubtedly an interesting fact, falls into the category of unhelpful research. Another example: I love you, Jay. So what? Declaring my love isn't going to make him love me back, although he'll feel obliged to come up with some sort of kindly response. So, for the moment, I keep my love to myself, curled up tightly next to my heart, and continue to lick his left nipple instead.

Chapter Fourteen

JAY

My night out with Evan and Ellie and the gang is a trial to be endured. I know Evan means well, and I appreciate the gesture. He's trying to bring me back into the fold, and a part of him is still hoping that if we carry on as normal, then everything will just slip back to how it was before.

I feel like I'm on a treadmill, with scarcely enough time to get off and take a piss, let alone time to breathe deeply and make sensible plans for my future. Evan's demands for his birthday celebration are the least of my worries, to be honest. Night shifts take their toll, and I've been doing shedloads of them recently as I'm paying people back for all the swaps I arranged for the wedding and the honeymoon. And Ellie doesn't make my night work easier. While she's not deliberately being noisy during the day, when I'm trying to catch a few hours' sleep, she's certainly not going out of her way to tiptoe around quietly in consideration of the bloke who's monumentally fucked up her life. As if I could sleep properly, anyway, on the camp bed in the spare room. I'm convinced it's a major contributor to my daily backache.

And yes, while on the subject of Ellie—another huge fucking row tonight. It had been bubbling under all week, as I missed the appointment with the conveyancing solicitor thanks to an overrunning emergency case in the operating theatre. I hadn't made the rescheduled appointment the next day, either, due to Billy-Ray's funeral, and then she'd demanded to know my whereabouts when I was in London. I'd been suitably vague, and she'd accused me of trying to deliberately sabotage the house-selling process.

Tears and undignified shouting followed, and that was just me. I'm so on the edge right now, I could fucking scream. To top it all, my sister phones just as I'm claiming five-minutes peace and heading for a quick shower. All I'm asking for is five fucking minutes standing under a hot jet of water and letting it spray over my aching back and pounding head, but I end up getting thirty seconds. As far as I can tell, the whole point of the conversation is to lecture me for the hundredth time how I've disappointed and upset my mum. No one apart from Lucien gives two fucks as to how I'm feeling right now.

I sink miserably into the back of the taxi, head still pounding and Ellie by my side, giving me the silent treatment. There is so much tension radiating from both of us that the taxi driver swiftly abandons his cheery chat and turns up the radio. From her tearstained face, she's clearly as miserable as I am. And it's all my fault, of course, as everyone is only too pleased to keep reminding me. Closing my eyes, I rest my head back and let my thoughts drift to Lucien, the only bright spot in my otherwise exhausting daily whirl. And I haven't even got time for him either. I wonder what he's doing right now, and I imagine him elegantly sprawled on that big squashy sofa in his cosy kitchen, sipping his beloved Campari while expertly completing the *Telegraph* crossword. I hope he's eaten properly. I'd give my right arm to be cuddled on that sofa with him, snuggling into his fluffy pink dressing gown, instead of in this cab with this lovely girl who hates me, and spending the next four hours with a group of people who think I'm a fucking idiot.

Our whirlwind midweek trip to London had been a far too brief happy hiatus. Lucien's London is very different to mine, very different to most people's, I imagine. His Mayfair home is extraordinarily grand. A housekeeper had stocked the fridge and prepared a light supper, and a concierge service had ensured we had the best window seats on the fifty-second floor of the Shard reserved for whenever we chose to arrive.

When this is all over, when Lucien has twigged that I'm a ten-a-penny ordinary bloke from Wolverhampton, living on my own in a grotty flat above a chip shop, I'll slot that night away in my memory as a perfect treasure, bringing it out only very rarely, examining it for flaws and forever finding it flawless. Because that night was when I realised, in amongst all the madness I've created, I'd fallen hopelessly, dangerously, gloriously in love with Dr Lucien Avery, the sixteenth Earl of Rossingley. He's spoiled me entirely for whichever man comes along after him. None will compare to his grace, his beauty, his wicked charm, his childlike delight in my oversized body, and his utter, utter sweetness.

There are certain districts in London where anything goes, and no one takes a second look. Not at two men, arm in arm, sauntering down a busy street, not even when one of the men is so head-turningly beautiful that my heart undergoes an alarming series of palpitations every time he leans up to kiss me.

He'd predictably pinched his cousin's ridiculous sparkly Converse and paired them with skinny white jeans and a fitted navy silk shirt, the pearls tucked safely inside. His eyes were made up with black kohl, and his fingernails matched. The overall effect was jaw-droppingly stunning; next to him I felt lumpy and provincial in my jeans and soft flannel checked shirt.

Banishing all thoughts of inferiority, I'd made up my mind to enjoy every second of it as we took our seats in the intimate booth. Lucien persuaded me to have an alarmingly purple-coloured whisky and blueberry-based cocktail, while he had a fancy margarita, the exclusive tequila apparently distilled from agaves that had been crushed between the thighs of fifty Mexican virgins or some such shit. Both of our glasses had way too many swizzle sticks and umbrellas; if my dad could have seen me, he'd have had a bloody fit. I'm not sure the gaudiness was quite Lucien's cup of tea either, but he reckoned Billy-Ray would have loved it, and we raised a bittersweet toast to him.

One cocktail had turned into three, and Lucien insisted I was the most handsome man in the room, even though my lips and tongue had turned purple and I looked as out of place as a pimp in a nunnery amongst all the glamorous fashionistas, Lucien being the most glamorous by far. Then back home, back to the mansion and the extraordinary wealth he wears so lightly. We stripped each other and dived into bed—black silk sheets no less, the kinky bugger. He did that simple thing I love, and of which I'll never tire, lying on top of me and kissing me to distraction, rubbing his cock against mine, smothering me in his scent and his long lean beauty. We could have lain on a bed of sacking for all I cared.

He's surprised me because, having had a hint of his kinkiness already and peeked at the surreal contents of his bedside drawer, he's prepared to carry on with the vanilla until I'm ready for more. And in my turn, I managed to surprise him because, in the early hours of next morning, I woke him with my lips around his cock, wearing nothing but a pink feather boa and a purplish smile.

Of all the fucking restaurants in all of Allenmouth Evan could have chosen to celebrate his birthday, he had to choose the Indian one I'd memorably visited with Lucien. The gang meet for drinks at the pub opposite, and I'm greeted reasonably cordially on the whole. A couple of the guys can't resist remarking that they are astonished I've turned up instead of pulling out at the last minute, but apart from that, the snarky comments are kept to a minimum. We'll see how everyone behaves a few pints down the line. I console myself with the knowledge that this is the last time I'll ever have to do this. Ellie can keep our mutual friends; it's the least I can do for her under the circumstances. I've just got to get through tonight.

There are ten of us altogether, made up of five conventional, heterosexual couples, and we enter the restaurant two at a time, like bloody Noah's ark. Ellie and I bring up the rear. A man on his way out patiently holds the door open for us, a takeaway carrier bag under his arm, and I unthinkingly steer Ellie through ahead of me, with one hand lightly at her back. We've reached an uneasy détente for the sake of Evan's birthday celebration, and she's actually smiling at something I say as we make our way in. Looking up to thank the door holder, I find my gaze locked onto a pair of beautiful pale-blue eyes that I know better than my own. My gorgeous, my fabulous, my very best man.

Visibly stunned, his own gaze flits between Ellie and me, a brief look of shock and pain crossing his refined features as he registers the apparent closeness between us, the final link in the caterpillar of happy coupledom blithely holding up his exit. Though as quickly as the look appears, it vanishes, and a blank mask descends. I'm not so cool.

"Shit… Hi, Lucien. Hi…" I tail off as he gives me a polite nod.

"Hello, Jay."

His tone is cool and crisp; he's summoned up the Dr Avery persona that strikes fear in our surgical and anaesthesia colleagues alike. Ellie is already through the door, and I grab his wrist as he leaves.

"Fuck, Luce. It's not what you think… Luce, wait."

I don't know what it is about exceedingly posh folk. Perhaps it's being raised by nannies and boarding schools. But fuck me, they're tough when they need to be, especially in public. The only sign that all is not well is the tightness of his grip on the plastic bag, his knuckles even whiter than normal. He looks at me as if we're barely acquaintances, let alone lovers, and pulls his wrist away angrily.

"Please don't do that," he bites out at me icily. "Go back to your friends and your girl; enjoy your evening and don't cause a scene."

How can he be so fucking calm? Realising I'm no longer at her heels, Ellie eyes us curiously from the doorway. Lucien looks over my shoulder and nods at her politely.

"Good evening." He smiles, and she gives him a faint smile in exchange. He returns his focus back to me.

"Enjoy your meal, and I'll no doubt see you in the department sometime next week," he says brightly for Ellie's benefit. With a final half wave, he turns and walks briskly away down the street. I watch him go, deliberating whether to follow.

"Come on, Jay. It's bloody freezing out here," she moans from the door, and I hesitate before reluctantly following her inside.

"Are you all right?" she asks as an afterthought, looking at me as if for the first time. "You look white as a sheet."

I mumble something about tiredness, scarcely able to speak as I trail after her. The single pint I had in the pub threatens to reappear; my heart pounds. I need to see him, I need to explain, he needs to know the truth.

"That was that weirdo Dr Avery, wasn't it?" says Rob, one of the surgical trainees, as we arrange ourselves around a big table.

"I didn't think vampires ate curry," remarks someone else to a chorus of laughter.

"Freak. He's fucking stalking you, Jay-Jay," laughs Evan, clapping me loudly on the back.

Whatever appetite I might have had has completely disappeared. I order at random and sit in a miserable silence as my friends raucously chatter around me. The food takes forever to arrive, and when it does, I pick at a poppadum, the texture turning to cardboard in my mouth, and I struggle to swallow it down. The broken pieces mock me on my plate. I can't make out any distinguishable country shapes, and there is no way I can contemplate eating a bloody curry.

Standing suddenly, clumsily pushing back my chair, all eyes turn to me as I throw down some money onto the table. "Sorry, Evan, I'm not feeling so good," I announce apologetically. "I think I'm going to have to head off early."

Everyone shows polite concern. Privately, they will no doubt put this down to more evidence of my recent bout of insanity, and I know I'll be the topic of conversation once I've gone. I don't give a shit. I'm out the door, flag down a cab, and head back home to pick up my own car.

*

Rossingley is swathed in darkness, the only sign of life a dim glow from the kitchen window. I knock loudly and push the door open before waiting for a reply. As if expecting me, Lucien sits at the kitchen table, primly dressed in his floor-length white cotton nightie, his pearls nestled against his chest. The curry is still in the bag, unopened next to him, and he glances up at me from the newspaper, raising his eyebrows.

"Don't you have a party to attend?"

"Don't you have a curry to eat?" I counter, nodding at the bag.

He turns a page, frowning slightly. "I rather lost my appetite."

"So did I."

I pull up a chair next to him, and we sit in silence for a few moments, his expression unreadable.

"Luce...I..."

"Please, don't speak. I have something I need to say to you first."

He carefully pushes the newspaper aside and contemplates me, his eyes roaming all over my face as if memorising me. He brings my fingers to his lips, holding my hand loosely in his cooler, slimmer one. With his other hand, he fingers his pearls. When he finally speaks, his clear voice is low and fluttery.

"I'm afraid I can't be your bit on the side."

Oh my God. I pull my hand away angrily. No, no, no, not now. Fuck, he can't do this to me, he fucking can't. "Is that how you perceive yourself?" I respond incredulously. "Because it's bloody ridiculous if you do." Almost shouting, I kick back my chair so I'm standing over him.

"No, but I need to be certain that isn't how you perceive me," he replies steadily.

He's too classy to come out and accuse me of cheating on him. Of stringing him along. He'll never scream and shout and demand to know what the hell I was doing on a couples night out with my ex-fiancée. I get that, but how the hell can the fucker sit there so calmly as he politely cleaves my world in two?

"Jesus, Luce, have you been paying any attention these last few months?" I rub my face in my hands and close my eyes. Dizziness washes through me, and I clutch tightly to the back of the chair to steady myself. *Please don't do this to me, please don't, I can't bear it. I'll beg if*

I have to, whatever it takes, just don't do this to me, not now.

He swivels round to regard me, then stands up, and gently taking my hand away from my face, holds it against his chest. "I need to be sure this isn't the moment for me to be saying goodbye," he says softly, and my heart silently crumbles.

Tears prick at my eyelids, all the tension, all the stresses, all the aggravation of the last few months threatening to flood out of me. I thought I'd reached rock bottom when I called off the wedding, but now I realise there are even further depths to plummet. Taking a couple of deep breaths in and out, scrunching my eyes up tight, I will myself not to fall apart. Is this it? Did I work up the courage to go to that shitty London club three bloody times to just jack it all in? To allow the most beautiful man in the world to turn his back on me? Did I call time on my straight life, alienating everyone who has ever mattered to me, to cave in without a fight? Am I really going to walk out of here and get back in that car and drive away from the one person who has kept me sane through all the madness?

Not fucking likely. Inhaling deeply, I straighten my shoulders and brush away my tears angrily, not giving them chance to fall.

"Saying goodbye? That's what you think, Lord fucking Rossingley."

Before he has a chance to fight it, my arms are around him, and he's crushed against me, my lips hot on his, my hands gripping him through the thin cotton of the nightdress. He's stiff in my embrace, but I carry on regardless because he's not fucking getting away from me.

Not ever. He likes all these muscles? Well, he's got them, and I'm putting them to good use pinning him down. I hope he took a big breath beforehand because I own this fucking kiss.

He may have grasped an inkling that I'll continue indefinitely if I have to because, finally, thank God, he's kissing me back. His lips open, his tongue finds mine, his body relaxes against me, his arms slide round my back. Now I have his undivided attention, I pull my mouth away, still holding him tightly.

"It's my turn to speak, Lucien," I say fiercely. "And you need to listen very carefully.

"You are not saying goodbye. You're not going anywhere, and I'll tell you why. Because I want it all. Everything. I want scary, pissy Dr Lucien Avery. I want the sweet, brave sixteenth Earl of Rossingley; I want the beautiful Lady Louisa. I want to paint your toenails luscious pink velvet for you. I want to paint your fingernails black for you. I want to paint the fucking walls of this stately home for you."

He giggles softly, a sound I'm planning on hearing every day for the rest of my life. "You make me sound like a DIY project, Jay."

I stop his words with another searing, brutal kiss. "Shut up and listen; I haven't finished. I want to do your fucking eyeliner for you. I want to dance in that enormous fucking ballroom with you. I want to watch red kites through those ancient binoculars with you. I want to visit my granny with you. And, Christ, I want you to wrap me up in your pearls and fuck me properly. I want to know how it feels to have you buried deep inside me."

"Is this while we're visiting Granny? Gosh, that will be quite the coming out, darling."

"No, you idiot. But I need you to know I want it all, Lucien Avery. All of it. All of you. Because...because sometimes I think I love you so much I'm going to fucking explode."

Silence, utter silence. He hasn't moved an inch. Only the sensation of his warm breath on the side of my neck, his nose brushing against...

"Lucien, are you...are you sniffing me?"

He wriggles in closer, almost climbing up my body. My dick automatically responds, swelling against him, but it's not about that, not now. This is so much more than lust and sex. Finally, he stirs, limpid blue eyes gazing up at me from under long blond lashes.

"Gosh. Can you say all those things again?" he whispers, then buries his blond head against my chest. I want to hear 'gosh' every day for the rest of my life too.

"What, all of it? I hadn't prepared it or written it down or anything, you know. I just vomited it all out."

"I'll settle for the last bit then, darling. That was quite special all on its own."

I push him away slightly so I can plant a soft kiss on his pale, smooth forehead. "I love you, Lucien. I love you more than I thought possible. You're not my bit on the side; you never have been. You're my front and centre. My heart."

*

Growing up, I was blessed with three older sisters, and I lived with Ellie for a couple of years, so I've endured plenty of romcoms in my time. I would even go so far as to say that the extensive oeuvre of Jennifer Aniston could be my specialist subject should I ever be crazy enough to want to appear on *Mastermind*. So I know, with the closing credits about to roll, it is the turn of the recipient of all those heartfelt declarations of love to return the favour. But then Lucien Avery has never starred in a romcom, and evidently not watched many either, because I get the distinct impression those three little words I'm desperate to hear are not forthcoming. Instead, he turns to the plastic bag on the kitchen table and holds it up to me.

"Do you want to share some of this? I'm guessing you skipped dinner."

Okay, whatever.

I'm disappointed, to put it mildly, but he knows how I feel about him at least, even if the feelings aren't mutual. I breathe deeply and frown. "Yeah, sure. But why aren't you having macaroni cheese?"

"Because a couple of months ago I met a handsome boy, and he gave me the courage to try some new things."

The sweet, hesitant smile of gratitude that accompanies this statement says more than 'I love you' ever could. I get out some plates and cutlery while he reheats the curry in the microwave. I make him a Campari and soda the way I've noticed he likes it, and get a glass of water for myself.

"There are a few beers in the fridge for you," he says shyly. "I wasn't sure which brand you liked best, so I bought a selection."

Beer and curry. Yep, I love you is so hackneyed; this man's declarations of love are pure poetry.

"The beer has a very long use-by date—I checked—so they'll keep if you don't get through them all tonight. Obviously, you won't because you're driving."

Had I misheard? Driving? After that little speech, I thought a bed and a shag for the night were pretty much guaranteed. "What the fuck, Luce?"

Smiling gently, he puts down his fork and lays a hand over mine as a stone lands heavily in the pit of my stomach, joining greasy, curdling lumps of chicken korma.

"Jay, listen to me, and see if you can do it without interrupting."

I immediately open my mouth to interrupt, and he stays me with a finger to my lips, shaking his head firmly. He indicates for me to push my chair back, then climbs onto my lap, slipping his arms around me.

"I've been thinking about what I'm going to say for a few days now; although, I confess, seeing you with Ellie threw me completely. Shhh!"

He pauses and plants a kiss on my forehead. "After we've finished dinner, you are going to go home. Next week, I'm rescinding my role as your educational supervisor and handing it over to a colleague because our relationship has rather stretched the boundaries of what's considered professional, to put it mildly. But as your current supervisor, until Monday at any rate, I'm instructing you to have at least eight weeks leave of absence from work."

"But..."

"No, shush, and listen to me. During that time, you are going to meet solicitors and accountants and do whatever else in the way of paperwork is required to sort out your house and finances. You are then going to help Ellie pack up and ensure she is settled into another place. She deserves every bit of help you can offer, and you are going to do everything in your power to remain friends because she is important to you.

"You are going to use the rest of the time to visit your parents, maybe take your dad to an Arsenal game and take your nieces and nephews out. Talk to your mother; I think she misses you. If you want to tell them that you're gay, then do so, but the choice is yours; it's no one's business but yours. Go and have a few beers with your second-best man and visit the gym or whatever it is you do to keep this delectable physique in such beautiful shape. I will be sending you some interesting medical articles to read, too, because I know you haven't had time to catch up on reading, and it's making you anxious."

I watch him in a daze as he takes a small sip of his drink and wipes the corner of his mouth delicately with an elegant fingertip. "And then, when your life is back on track and you have the space and the time, if you still want me, then I'll be here waiting for you. You are everything to me, by the way, just in case you didn't know already."

Tears trickle down my cheeks, and I hardly notice. It's that last sentence that did it, slipped in so casually in his whispery, fluttery voice that I might have missed it. *You are everything to me.*

There is nothing cold about Dr Lucien Avery, whatever people may think. He is the warmest, wisest, most generous man I know. And if giving me the chance to walk away from him when it's the last thing he wants isn't a true declaration of his love for me, then I don't know what is. His care and thoughtfulness are worth a thousand I love yous. Embarrassed, I brush the tears away, but he grabs my hand.

"It's okay to cry, Jay," he chides gently. "It's okay to be upset, especially in front of me. Gosh, you've seen me at my worst on several occasions. It's my turn to be strong for you."

"But I've never taken sick leave; what will people think?"

He waves my concerns away. "Who cares what anyone thinks? It's okay to admit that things are tough for you. Hey, you've called off a wedding, split up with your girl, started a new job, fucked a rather eccentric man, fallen out with family and friends, sold a house—there've been enough life events to keep you busy for ten years, for goodness sake!"

"Will you really wait for me, Luce?"

"I promise. If you still want me, I'll be here. However long it takes. No one else will drink your beer, and I've become rather accustomed to warm feet in bed."

Chapter Fifteen

LUCIEN

For the first forty-eight hours, I bang my head against a brick wall, figuratively and, on two occasions, literally, but my pale skin bruises far too easily and I decide to stop. I'm convinced I've made an error the size of the stately home in which I find myself roaming, alone instead of with Jay, pondering whether I should call him up again and announce I've changed my mind.

I'd been thinking of suggesting he take some leave from the hospital for a while. Being an expert myself in trying to present a normal façade at work while simultaneously attempting to deliver excellent patient care and juggling a few teeny, tiny issues in one's personal life, I couldn't bear watching someone I love—yes, love, adore, worship, idolise—go through similar unnecessary suffering. And while developing and honing an emotionless mask can be of benefit in many, many situations, I don't want Jay to ever acquire one. His openness and authenticity are some of the qualities in him I so admire. The broad hairy chest and never-ending supply of cosy hoodies are merely an added bonus.

It was seeing him outside the restaurant with Ellie that did it for me. My first thought was that he definitely has a thing for blonds. She could easily pass as my younger, less pretty sister with her long skinny legs and pale features. Meow! Undoubtedly, seeing them together like that was a shock, and so I behaved like an arse. But even as I walked away, I knew he'd follow later. Well, 90 per cent of me did anyway. I mostly believed every word he'd uttered had been the truth, but thanks to Jules and his sly insinuations, the other 10 per cent needed reassurance. Hearing the overpowered roar of that infernal car pull up on the courtyard within the hour only confirmed what I already trusted. That Jay is kind, thoughtful, and loyal, and he loves me more than he loves her. That's all that matters. Hearing him say the words with such passion, right here in my kitchen, was the stuff of the best Regency romance novels. But with added swear words...

So, Week One Without Jay passes fairly swiftly in a haze of swinging between congratulating myself for being a relationship genius and giving him space to pine over my absence, and the increasing certainty that I'm an utter twat for letting him go.

At the start of Week Two Without Jay, I begin to miss him, even though he was never completely mine to miss. Heavy limbed, my brain sludgy, I'm reacquainted with familiar symptoms of loss recognisable from the months after my family died. Symptoms that are precursors to a despairing, creeping grey fog continuing without end, like a dreary November. So I take a long overdue fortnight of annual leave from work, curl up in bed, and wait for the wretched fog to fully descend.

And I wait and I wait. By Week Three Without Jay, the fog still hasn't put in an appearance, so I get up, shower, pick out fresh clothes, force down some toast and, putting it bluntly, get on with my life. Because somewhere on the other side of town, perhaps having a pint in a pub with friends, or packing up removal boxes, or just lying in bed reading a book and having a well-deserved rest, is a man who loves me. And that love gives me the strength to endeavour to be my best self.

My best self is a surprise to Will, but he capitalises on my cautious good humour by asking me to consider a tour of all the estate properties. We have many small cottages and a few farms tied to the estate. Most are inhabited by estate workers and their families, or former estate workers, and a home for life at a reduced rent comes as part of the job package. My father and his father before him never served notice on tenants after retirement; they continue to live in the properties at peppercorn rates until they die or move away. I have no intention of changing this unwritten rule, and those who mock antiquated aristocratic patronage prefer not to notice the good, only dwelling on the bad. If a benevolent estate didn't exist, then quaint village properties like these would be snapped up by rich weekenders and city folk retiring to the country, pricing local rural families out of the market. But that's an argument for another day.

Anyway, there is a continual programme of maintenance (never buy a house with a thatched roof) required on these properties that has fallen behind since I took over the estate, a state of affairs that we need to redress. My father personally visited each tenant annually, and from now on, I will endeavour to do the same.

I'm nervous as I dress in my ancient Barbour and country cords, pearls safely hidden inside, and clamber into Will's old Land Rover to begin the social calls. My biggest fears are sympathy and kindness from people who have known my family since birth, people whose forebears worked at Rossingley before them. But as I sit in a succession of neat kitchens, drinking endless cups of tea and discussing chimney repairs, upgrades to central heating systems, and the like, the fear is gradually replaced by a sense of pride. Pride in my family for having generated such genuine respect over so many years and also in myself for not falling apart at the seams when I listen to all the bittersweet memories of my brother and father. When I finally arrive back home, emotionally drained and with an excruciatingly full bladder from being too polite to decline the hot beverages, the only thing missing is someone with whom to share my fascinating day.

Not every day is easy. Week Four Without Jay finds me finally generating the resolve to throw away the fags. The absence of nicotine makes me ratty and edgy. No change there then, and my colleagues in the operating theatre take the brunt of it. In particular, a cocky young surgeon named Evan feels the sharp edge of my tongue for keeping me waiting. Nothing personal. I experiment with vaping for seventy-two hours, but the sickly smell makes me nauseated, so I go cold turkey and continue to be a pain in the arse. I doubt anyone notices any difference.

Emily vaguely enquires as to Jay's whereabouts, and I'm suitably vague in reply. On several occasions Jules attempts to get in touch. I delete every text message and screen his phone calls. One of the techie theatre guys helpfully shows me how to send all his calls and messages automatically to a file labelled Old Junk.

Giving up my smoking habit and expanding my meal repertoire simultaneously is probably a step too far, but I resolve to give it a go anyway during Week Five Without Jay. And I fail spectacularly. After three consecutive nights of Waitrose salmon en croûte and broccoli, I'm jittery, anxious, and clutching my pearls like Miss Havisham moments before being engulfed in flames. The food control issues have been around since my time with Jules. I'm going to need the support of an understanding and patient boyfriend to wean me off my set menu of macaroni cheese. Some mountains are too hard to climb alone.

Overwhelmed by neuroses, failure, and rattling around on my own, I escape another bout of impending brain stodginess and fatigue by driving to London and allow myself to be subsumed into the world of my cousin Freddie, who's taken over the London house during a brief lull in modelling assignments. Twenty-four hours in the company of his youthful exuberance proves to be exactly what the doctor ordered. After hitting Harvey Nics as the doors open, we head for Versace, where he talks me into buying exquisitely delicate lace boxer shorts in every colour available, which I suspect Jay will adore ripping off. Back at the house, we proceed to get very drunk on stupidly expensive champagne before giving each other a makeover. In retrospect, as I gaze at the unrecognisable drag queen in the mirror, we should probably have done the make-up before the booze.

Week Six Without Jay starts with a firm knock at the kitchen door. A rather devilish young man introduces himself. Although I immediately dub him Heathcliff in my mind, he's actually named Reuben, and apparently, I employ him—he's one the estate maintenance guys. I hazily recall Will asking me to consider taking him on, despite his unusual background.

Rossingley has a long history of employing ex-prisoners, thanks to my grandfather's benevolence. This new chap, Reuben, learned his trade in prison, and although he has good references from his parole officer and the prison rehabilitation team, has struggled to find work. After establishing that his crimes hadn't involved stealing priceless valuables from country estates, I agreed to a trial.

It seems I have inadvertently developed a recruitment policy of which I wholeheartedly approve because in his worn black jeans, flowing white shirt, and dark waistcoat, young Reuben is stupidly handsome. And anyone who flouts conservative contemporary clothing conventions is fine by me, especially when it gives them the air of a rakish eighteenth-century troubadour. With his thick mass of spirally dark curls, held back in a loose bun, a few long tendrils escaping around his angular, clever face, his knowing green eyes slowly appraise me. I feel like Jesus lost for forty days in the Judean desert being tempted by the devil. And that's before he opens his mouth to speak, when that hot French accent hits me straight in the lower belly.

But it quickly becomes apparent that I prefer flattened Black Country vowels and a man for whom the pinnacle of sartorial elegance is jeans and a soft blue hoodie disguising a hairy chest, over lean, lithe gallic perfection. After showing Reuben to the rhododendron bushes that need cutting back, I leave him to get on with it. By Week Seven Without Jay, Reuben is popping in almost daily for a cup of Earl Grey, a slice of Battenberg, and my regular French lesson. He's adorably shy and scarcely has the nerve to look me full in the face, blushing prettily whenever he does. Most days, he precedes his visits with some manly gardening activity, and the herbaceous borders around the kitchen door begin to look rather spectacular. I decline his repeated offers to chop up the rest of wood because I'm still hoping to watch my boy Jay do that.

Week Eight Without Jay, and despite pretty distractions, my nerves put in a reappearance. What if he's met someone else? What if my Stallion has forgotten all about me? What if he's found that naïve cat-owning soccer fan he thought he'd meet? Over several Campari and sodas, I confess all to Heathcliff in halting, rusty French. He's probably now under the impression I'm in love with an Italian pony because vernacular terms really don't translate or rhyme well in French. Reuben is a patient if somewhat silent sounding board. When he agreed to the job, I'm sure he had no idea it would involve listening to the tipsy ramblings of a lovesick earl, but he doesn't seem to mind—those wide green eyes regard me kindly.

Week Nine Without Jay and his name reappears on the rota at work, although our paths don't cross as he's allocated a set of nightshifts immediately. I hover in my office early in the mornings with mixed feelings of excitement and apprehension, but he doesn't come calling. Unable to wear my pearls in a clinical environment, I start carrying them with me everywhere, turning them over in the pocket of my theatre pyjamas, running them through my fingers. I exist on a diet of apples and granola until Heathcliff notices my pallor and rapid weight loss during one of our French lessons and takes it upon himself to do something about it.

He orders me to eat something more substantial and rustles up a plate of scrambled eggs, warning me that he won't leave until my plate is clean. The scrambled eggs happen late on Sunday afternoon. My nerves are shot to pieces, and I'm slumped at the table in my comfiest white cotton nightie, grasping at my pearls. As a distraction, I'm doing my best to decline the future conditional of the reflexive verb *se défenestrer*, but gosh, it's hard to concentrate. If Jay doesn't put in an appearance soon, I'll be defenestrating myself. Heathcliff patiently watches me, those knowing green eyes full of concern. By now, he's fully up to speed with all of my foibles.

Our intensive lesson is interrupted by a loud thud, and on the first occasion, we mildly raise our eyebrows at each other, then continue with the lesson. Perhaps it was one of the stable doors banging, or one of the gardeners being particularly heavy-handed with a wheelbarrow. Another thud follows an instant later, louder, more of a *thwack* really, followed by a less heavy splintering sort of noise, and then a *thwack* again. We look at each other, Reuben frowning slightly. *Thwack*! It almost sounds as if...as if...as if someone has picked up the axe which happens to be lying on the bench by the backdoor and is...chopping firewood.

I'm peripherally aware of Reuben reaching for his coat and getting up out of his chair. A little dizzily, I stand, too, my heart threatening to leap out of my chest.

"Do you think that's him?" asks Reuben, smiling at me gently. "The guy you've been waiting for these past few weeks?"

"Yes," I reply, hardly daring to hope. "It is. But..."

"Breathe, *monsieur*, remember to breathe."

He'd prompted me just in time; the room had started spinning. I gulp in some air.

"The thing is, Reuben, I'm scared. I don't think I've been waiting for him for just these past few weeks. I think I've probably been waiting for him my whole life."

"Well, then you'd better go and see if he wants to come and join your life, don't you?"

"But what if this is just goodbye?" I wipe my wet palms down the cotton of my nightie before reaching for my pearls. "What if..." I say in a whisper, "What if he's only come here to ask me to return his hoodie? I don't think I'll be able to bear it, Reuben."

"From what you've told me about him, *monsieur*, he's no fool. And only a fool would walk away from you. Come on; I have a feeling that he's waiting for you too."

Chapter Sixteen

JAY

When I look up, he's leaning in a familiar pose against the door frame, one narrow hip cocked, his alabaster skin covered head-to-toe in white cotton, a hint of lace and pink satin at the notch of his sternum. After setting down the axe carefully, I straighten, and we regard each other for an instant. The voluminous nightie hides his body completely, but the skin stretched taut over his cheekbones hints at the weight loss since I last saw him; the purple smudges under his eyes show the strain. He seems younger and desperately fragile. He won't have eaten enough in my absence, he won't have slept enough, he'll probably have smoked too much. Can I handle this? Can I handle him and all the baggage that comes with this beautiful, lost man and his unconventional life? Do I really want to take this on?

Too right I fucking do.

There's a shadow behind him, and another figure appears, squeezing through the doorway past Lucien.

Red mist descends.

"Who the fuck are you?"

The figure has morphed into a bloke dressed up as if he's about to go on stage at the Globe theatre, and from his handsome features, he's leading man material. Ignoring my less than effusive greeting, he calmly holds out his hand.

"Hello, you must be the big horse I've heard so much about. I'm Reuben, and I'm just leaving." He turns to Lucien and gives his arm a brief squeeze. "I'll be here on Tuesday, okay?"

Lucien nods, never taking his eyes away from mine. As the guy retreats, he throws a quick comment in what I think is French over his shoulder, and for the first time, a small smile plays across Lucien's face.

"What did he say?"

"He says you've got a nice arse."

I sniff the air; there's an unmistakeable aroma.

"I can smell dope."

The corner of Lucien's mouth lifts again in amusement, pointy canines just visible. "I can't tell if that is a statement, a question, a hint, or disapproval."

That fluttery, fey voice; he could be reciting from the *Oxford Handbook of Anaesthesia*, and every syllable would still scream sex.

"All of the above, probably."

Lucien turns slightly, beckoning me to follow him into the kitchen. "Reuben works here on the estate. He's helping me to brush up on my French."

"And giving you weed."

"That's a reward for declining my verbs correctly."

We're in the familiar kitchen now. Nothing has changed, although I spot a replacement flowery pink butter dish near the fridge. A copy of the *Telegraph* lies on the long refectory table, open at the crossword page, next to a bowl of shiny green apples. My pale-blue hoodie is neatly folded on the arm of the sofa.

"Is that the only reward he's giving you?"

Lucien is backed up against the fridge, and I stand so close I can smell his fresh-air, countryside scent when I breathe in. He may need a good square meal, but close up, he's as stunning as ever. Those limpid blue eyes, with just a hint of eyeliner and framed in golden lashes, gaze up at me from his perfect pale face.

"Yes. On occasion, I've wondered if he'd like to give me more, but my heart's not in it."

"Where is your heart, Lucien?" I ask, and cage him against the fridge with my arms, leaning down into him so I can feel the puff of air against my lips as he speaks.

"Wherever you are, Dr Sorrentino."

*

Our first kiss is tentative, chaste, it's enough just to have him in my arms at last and crush him against my chest. "Fuck, I've missed you, Luce."

He giggles into my sweater. "I've missed that sweary mouth."

We kiss again, a little more firmly this time, his tongue mingling with mine. There's no rush, he's waited for me, thank God, and I have all the time in the world. My hands roam across his back, bunching up handfuls of fine cotton, loving the cool sweep of it across his smooth flesh. I reach lower, wanting to lose myself in the same smooth sweep across his delicious pert bum, wanting to drag a handful of cotton all the way up his long legs and rub it across his arse cheeks. With only this need in mind, I encounter what feels like the seam of boxer shorts underneath. Hmm, not what I was expecting at all.

Now, one of the divine pleasures of Lucien Avery dressed in a nightie or sheer negligee is the complete certainty that his entire block and tackle is swinging in the breeze underneath. When I fondle him, I have a perverse kick from the knowledge that the only thing separating us is a very fine layer of cotton, or silk, or satin. And trust me, it gets my dick hard like nothing else; I've had two months masturbating daily to exactly that thought.

"You've become a smidge prudish in my absence," I joke as he kisses me. I give the seam of his boxers a little twang against his skin. He hums his agreement and rubs his dick up against mine. Deciding there are far too many layers between us, I raise both sides of the cotton nightie and take it up and over his head.

"What the fuck!"

"Gosh, that sweary mouth again." He laughs, giving a delightful wiggle of his adorable tush.

I didn't even know stuff like this existed, let alone ever dreamed of having a gorgeous man modelling it for me. I can't lie; Lucien stark naked is good, really good, unquestionably good, but Lucien wearing nothing but the palest pink lace boxers, with a little black satin bow just where the tip of his hard cock is straining against the lace, comes a close second. Or maybe joint first place. A matching pale-pink feather dangles from his left nipple, and such a rapid surge of hot pleasure cascades down my dick that I fleetingly wonder if I've come in my pants. Sinking to my knees in awe, I run my hands down his sides until they rest at his hips before burying my face into the lace over his lower belly and his erect cock and just...breathe him in. Rubbing my cheek against him, I breathe and breathe and... breathe.

I feel like I've completed a steeplechase, not the one the horses do, but the one that those insanely skinny, fit athletes run at the Olympics; the one where they race round and round a track for bloody ever, and just as they find a rhythm, they have to negotiate a hurdle or a water jump without falling or skidding or succumbing to injury, every obstacle seemingly designed to prevent them from safely reaching the finish line. And as I kneel on the cold stone floor of Lucien's kitchen, at his feet with my arms around his waist, filling my lungs with his musky warm scent, his long fingers softly carding through my mop of hair, I know I've surmounted every barrier thrown in my path and finally reached the end.

I have no idea how long I remain that way. Too long, evidently.

"Is this some sort of tantric blow job technique you've been honing while you've been away, Jay?"

Never let it be said that Dr Lucien Avery is subtle. As he pushes against me, I respond by licking the length of his cock through the lace, coming off at the tip where already I can taste his salty wetness through the delicate holes in his underwear. No doubt I'm developing a wet patch of my own, and I adjust myself through my jeans before giving another firm lick.

"As much as I adore these, they're coming off."

I'm much better at blow jobs since my first foray in Spangles. And I have the added advantage of a pat of Lurpak butter nearby. Seconds later, like a pro, I'm sucking on his knob while simultaneously reaching for the butter and palming my own dick. I hear the first heavenly 'gosh' as one buttery finger breaches his arse and then another as I twist it and rub against his prostate.

"Jay, Jay, I'm going to...Jay..."

I bring my mouth off him with a wet pop and, regaining my feet, walk him backwards to the sofa, shrugging out of my clothes and toeing off my trainers. "Not until you have me buried inside you, Luce."

With a groan of pleasure, I sink down on top of him as he spreads wide, welcoming me in. I had imagined our union, after such a length of time apart, would be loving, spiritual, and sensual, but fuck, I've missed having my dick in his arse as much as desert plants miss rain. The feeling is mutual; within seconds, we're rutting like sex-starved cavemen—I'm definitely sounding like one, even if Lucien is keeping his powder dry. He's limber, and with his legs over my shoulders, I tunnel so deeply that I come with a shriek, and he's right there with me, accompanied by a mountain of whispery gosh's. I could drown in his gosh's.

*

"I was incredibly brave in your absence," Lucien declares a while later. We're in the four-poster, limbs wrapped around each other, those ice-block feet tucked into the crook of my knees. I'm naked, but I've insisted he put on another pair of those ridiculous lacy things, and he's humouring me. Honestly, once you get to know him, Dr

Avery is a complete softie. Dr Avery-the-softie is currently licking my collarbone like a cat, although I'm trying to ignore it because it's ticklish.

"I know you were," I say, "because I tracked down Will and phoned him every few days for an update. There was no way on earth I could have walked away and not known what was going on with you for two months. I'd have been worried sick. So Will agreed he'd have one of his guys visiting the house regularly for me. Of course, I didn't realise what a gorgeous stud he'd lined up for the job, otherwise I'd have been back like a shot."

"I even managed to stop smoking,"

"Good. Maybe your sperm count will recover sufficiently for you to have all those albino babies that you want. I'm happy to start trying for one now, if you like." I give him a quick squeeze, and he snuggles down.

"Did you miss the reproduction lectures at med school, Jay, darling? That's not how it works."

"We're going to keep trying anyway. And we need to get some more meat on these bones. That's my main priority."

Will had warned me he didn't think Lucien was eating much or sleeping well, but it was still a shock when I saw him the first time. Yet, mentally he's strong, stronger than I've ever seen him. He's full of ideas for the estate, and I happily let him rabbit on. Now that I'm back and filling the fridge, the food thing should be a piece of cake, so to speak. And on the few nights we've previously spent together, as long as he does his octopus thing and sprawls all over me, he seems to sleep like the dead. Fortunately, I'm rather fond of octopuses.

"Are you here to stay, darling?" His tone is deliberately light, but I sense an undercurrent of anxiety.

"If I told you a suitcase and three boxes full of my crap are piled up in the car, would that be the correct response?" I ask, and feel him grinning against my skin. "Homeless and penniless. I'm quite the catch, Lord Rossingley."

*

He wakes me with a kiss at dawn. I'm lying flat on my belly and my first instinct is to check that I'm not tied to something. It's like living with Cato, Inspector Clouseau's manservant—I never have a bloody clue what to expect next. Lucien's delicate fingers trace a line down my spine, and I shiver as he follows them with his tongue. Closing my eyes again, I stretch and relax into the sensation of his hands massaging my muscles and his tongue trailing in their wake. Now this is the sort of wake-up call I could become very used to, and I rub my hardening dick contentedly against the under sheet.

A pleasant waft of vanilla invades my nostrils at the same instant a warm, lubed fingertip invades my arse. Lucien drapes himself over the top of me, leaving his finger just inside. A slight change of position and he adds another, stretching me slightly wider. With an involuntary gasp, I arch my hips back and into him, a silent request for him to give me more.

"Was that a 'yes please', darling?" he murmurs into my hair, crooking his fingers just enough to make me groan and push back even further. I'm inelegantly humping the sheet.

"Here, have this." He shoves a pillow under me, and I continue my pleasurable humping, my hips lifted higher while he finger fucks my arse. I'm so over my initial embarrassment when he first did this; now I can't get enough. He adds more lube, all the while kissing and nibbling at my neck, his own hard dick grinding against my hip, wet against my skin. He hasn't explicitly said what's coming next, but he doesn't need to. I've wanted this for a while, and I'm more than ready. I make to turn over, but he stops me.

"It will be easier this way for your first time, trust me Jay. Spread your legs a little wider."

I tense as the fingers disappear, and he manoeuvres so that his dick lines up against me. As he blankets me with his body, hot, whispery kisses land on my skin. So when he breaches, I cry out as if I've been unexpectedly slapped. It really fucking hurts. He shushes me, and more hot wet kisses land on my shoulders as he drives slowly in, each inch in its turn an agonising stretch and fullness I can't put into words and am not sure I totally welcome. But it's bearable because it's Lucien, and he's telling me how much he loves me as he inches in further. And when, finally, he's all the way to the hilt and his balls are squidged up against me, he stills, waiting for me to accommodate the sensation of someone trying to stuff a proverbial camel through the eye of a needle. I use the pause to remind myself that millions of blokes do this all the time and love it—Lucien loves it, and he's taken it a hell of a lot rougher than this. So instead of screaming at him to 'take that goddamn thing out of me', I count to twenty in my head and wait for the sting and burn to pass because Lucien promises me that it will.

When Lucien starts moving, slowly and carefully at first, and I gingerly push back, then, it's not too bad. Maybe a generous four out of ten. Even my flaccid dick perks up against the stupidly luxurious goose down pillow, and I think to myself that, okay, perhaps maybe not every day, but if it makes Lucien happy and he really, really wants to, then...

"Oh my God, oh my God... Fuck, Lucien that's good...don't stop, never stop, please, Luce, Luce, Luce..."

Lucien's breath is like fire burning into my ear, his sweat-slicked body up against mine, his hands grip my hips, his heavy balls slap hard against my arse.

"That's right, Jay, come up onto your knees. Just like that, yes, oh...oh Jay, you're so beautiful, oh gosh...oh gosh..."

He bangs so hard against that sweet spot I swear my teeth rattle. I'm being fucked to smithereens from the inside out by the fabulous, breathtaking, unique sixteenth Earl of bloody Rossingley. Again and again, he hits the bullseye so precisely, until the urgent, primeval sound of his balls slapping and his heavy panting are completely drowned out by my shrieks and groans of utter, utter ecstasy. I'm seeing stars, moons, satellites, whole fucking universes, all the time thinking why the fuck did I wait so long? My orgasm roars through me, cannoning all the way from the tips of my toes to the roots of every single hair on my head, and I hose out onto the million-thread Egyptian cotton and goose down underneath. I'm not just boneless, but bloodless, cell-less, atomless, most definitely brainless, and ready to sell my soul to him.

"Gosh, I'm not sure I'll be resting my head on that pillow anytime soon," says a bemused fluttery, whispery voice from somewhere nearby. I'm lying on my back, although I don't remember turning over.

"Fuck the pillow, Luce," I respond sleepily, reaching out for him.

"I rather think you just did," he replies mildly, and I'm octopused once more.

"Tell me it's not a school day," I groan as he nestles closer, sniffing me somewhere around the back of my ear.

"It is a school day. And you have an operating list with Dr Avery, starting in one hour and...ooh...fifty-three minutes."

"Is Dr Avery in a good mood today?"

Inhaling deeply, Dr Avery, Lady Louisa, and the sixteenth earl lifts his head and grins at me, showing every single one of those pointy small teeth. I'd walk to the ends of the earth for that heart-stopping smile.

"Rest assured, Dr Sorrentino. Dr Avery is in a most excellent mood."

Epilogue

JAY

6 months later

The annual Anaesthetic Department summer party is usually a sleepy affair. An old gag, my dad would heartily approve. Everyone was flabbergasted when Lucien agreed to host it—most of all me because although I'd made the suggestion, I hadn't considered for a minute that he'd actually say yes. But the Dr Lucien Avery now graciously attending to his starstruck guests is a far cry from the haunted, lonely man I met almost a year ago.

It's not been all plain sailing—breaking the macaroni cheese diet is proving harder than I imagined, and of course, his grief is never far away. Family birthdays and anniversaries come and go. Oliver's birthday was particularly tough, but we got through it with a lot of tears, tantrums, and Campari. And love, lashings and lashings of love.

A life of coupledom clearly agrees with him, and we've settled into a quiet routine. In between shifts at the hospital, Lucien manages the estate, and I cook dinners and complete manly chores. While I'm occupied with those, I swear he invents novel ways to wake me up in the mornings. All I can say is I wish I'd never brought that bloody pink feather boa back from the place in Mayfair.

Our colleagues and their families mill around on the lawns in front of the house, and an exclusive outside catering company serves a broad selection of drinks and buffet-style foodstuffs. So it's probably a little grander than the usual department get-together, where everyone volunteers to bring a dish and the result is a surfeit of soggy salads and cheap Prosecco.

Most people are somewhat surprised to see me greeting guests alongside the host—well, a lot surprised actually. I've kept a low profile both socially and at work since my time off, mostly because we've scarcely left the bedroom. Naturally, there have been a couple of rumours, and Evan has pinned me down once or twice. Lucien picking me up from his wedding reception was a particular point of gossip, but as he regularly reminds me, what goes on behind locked doors is no one's business but their own. An Englishman's home is his castle and all that, in our case quite literally.

This afternoon, I take a perverse pleasure in the moment Dr Leitner remarks that it is very good of the sixteenth earl to loan Lucien the use of the main house and grounds for the party, and would he be putting in an appearance? Smothering my laughter, I gravely point him in Lucien's direction and then watch with fascination as his complexion becomes redder and shinier. He then dogs Lucien for the rest of afternoon, attempting to ingratiate himself, and generous soul that Lucien is, he refrains from pushing him into the lake.

Finding an empty bench under a shady cherry tree, I sit on my own for a while, gazing across the estate. But mostly gazing at my future husband, although I've yet to officially propose. He's doing well for a guy who, a year ago, wouldn't let anyone through the front door. He's dressed in what I call one of his 'I'm a mature, conservative gay' outfits, which is a toned-down version of his New Romantic gear crossed with his work clothes, although there's no mistaking the outline of the nipple adornments underneath his snug shirt, and the string of pearls is boldly displayed on the outside. Today, his eyes are beautifully ringed in kohl, smoky and seductive, his lips a pale-pink gloss, both of which will no doubt set Annabel and Emily chattering for weeks. He's the best-looking woman here by a country mile.

I actually half expected Lady Louisa to put in a full appearance as she gives him courage when he needs it the most. That would have been okay, too, I guess, although this outfit is probably a little easier for most of them to swallow. To be fair, he can wear what the hell he likes because he's the Mad Earl and master of all he surveys. Anyhow, I've got plans for Lady Louisa later when everyone has gone, involving a new grey silk negligee and very little else.

When I said I'd been lying low, it's true, apart from a couple of trips to visit my parents. Lucien has accompanied me on both occasions. There has been no big coming-out moment, nor will there ever be, but even a blind man couldn't miss how in love we are. And yeah, so maybe I did plant a titchy kiss on his cheek on the driveway while my mum was still probably waving goodbye at the kitchen window, but he looked so adorable clutching his Tupperware of bread-and-butter pudding and my dad's offering of the latest Jack Reacher novel that I couldn't resist. He's invited my relatives to stay next weekend—sisters, nephews, nieces, granny, everyone. I think he's cautiously excited about becoming part of such a large, rambunctious family. Reuben has been instructed to build a treehouse especially for it, just to keep the kids entertained.

Talking of families, Lucien's going to start looking at surrogacy next year, and I'm cool with that too; he's already made preliminary contact with an agency in Sweden. I'd like one or two of my own kids at some point, although we're going to have a couple of little alabaster rug rats first—an heir and a spare—before the curly Latinos are allowed to feature. I'm imagining them toddling across the lawn, just as a pair of slender pale arms encircle me from behind. I lean back into him as he buries his nose in my hair.

"Gosh, you were miles away, darling. What were you thinking?"

"Oh, nothing much."

"Go on, tell me."

How much I love you? How I don't think I could have survived another day on this earth without you? How we will watch our grandchildren playing on the lawn from this same spot one day?

"I was thinking that the guttering on the north wall of the orangery is looking like it needs a bit of attention. It's probably just blocked with leaves. I might get the ladders out later, when everyone has gone, and have a quick look."

"I had some slightly less worthy activities planned for later, darling, although equally strenuous."

I bring his hand up to my lips. "The guttering will have to wait for another day, then. Heaven forbid I keep the sixteenth earl waiting."

He sits next to me, and soon his head finds my lap, as it commonly does, his long legs stretched out along the bench, my fingers curling in his fine blond hair. We watch quietly as a pair of red kites swirl and swoop high above the grounds, one vigorously chasing the other, a seemingly haphazard game of tag played out against the blue skies, oblivious to the chatter and laughter from the lawns.

Soon, we will have to return to the house and our guests. But for now, this moment of peace under an old cherry tree, with my one true love, is nothing short of perfect.

Acknowledgements

Looking after extremely sick patients is a privilege. While this isn't strictly speaking a medical romance, Lucien and Jay are both front-line doctors, and I have drawn on my own experiences as a hospital doctor in creating aspects of their story. I wrote this book during the Covid pandemic, a period of history that has been an extraordinary challenge for all hospital staff. Thus, I'd like to take this opportunity to thank my medical colleagues for all their hard work and support during this difficult time.

In addition, I'd like to thank my publisher, NineStar Press, and above all, my editor, Elizabetta, for her endless patience and encouragement.

About Fearne Hill

Fearne Hill lives deep in the southern British countryside, a stone's throw away from the private country estate providing her inspiration for Rossingley. She looks after varying numbers of hens, a few tortoises, and a beautiful cocker spaniel.

When she is not overseeing her small menagerie, she enjoys writing contemporary romantic fiction. And when she is not doing either of those things, she works as an anaesthesiologist.

Email
fearne.hill@fearnehill.com

Facebook
www.facebook.com/fearne.hill.50

Twitter
@FearneHill

Website
www.fearnehill.com

Instagram
www.instagram.com/fearnehill_author

Pinterest
www.pinterest.co.uk/fearnehill

Other NineStar books by this author

The Last of the Moussakas

Coming Soon from Fearne Hill

To Catch a Fallen Leaf

Rossingley, Book Two

Rossingley is gloomy as hell in the misty dawn light, the neoclassical, whiteish-grey façade of the main house hinting at all kinds of ghoulies and ghosties and things that go bump in the night. The taxi driver clearly thinks so, he's twice offered to drop me off halfway up the drive so I can enjoy the walk. Unfortunately for him, I'm not so easily spooked, having grown up on a country estate myself—a tad smaller than this one, admittedly. Even though the achingly familiar looming cattle and whispering trees don't give me the willies, it doesn't automatically follow that I like them—goodness, no, not at all. Give me the swinging, bustling streets of London or New York any day. I can't fathom how Lucien stands it living here, week in, week out. No shops, no gossip, definitely no hot men to ogle; he's wasting his best years, in my opinion.

I'm hoping he's still an early riser because I didn't phone ahead to warn him I was coming to stay, and it's bloody freezing out here. I only made up my mind a few hours ago, and no one appreciates an unexpected night-time call, especially Lucien. His life was comprehensively shattered by the mother of all out-of-hours phone calls a couple of years ago, so if he saw my number appear on his screen at three in the morning, he'd immediately assume the worst.

I'm not exactly dressed for the inclement January weather, having expected to be spending the night at my father's London home. I'd flounced out of Vincent's place after our miserable row wearing only the tightest pair of chocolate-coloured skinny jeans, which are threatening to guillotine my balls, and a rather divine, yellow silk Paul Smith shirt. I was not anticipating having to shout at the housekeeper through a Belgravia letterbox before eventually being told by her beefy husband to "bugger off," and then flag down a taxi.

Three hours later, and I'm rather regretting hotfooting it out of Vincent's without at least putting on a coat first. I'm not sure I even packed one in my small suitcase. Thank heavens Lucien's clothes will fit me because if I have to wear these trousers for a single hour longer, I'll be auditioning for the soprano section of the Rossingley church choir. And if I do find myself twiddling my thumbs in the godforsaken countryside for a few days, he's going to have to ferret out a whole new wardrobe for me because my London togs will be extremely ill-suited to the terrain.

After paying off the taxi driver, I make my way around to the back of Rossingley house, the gorgeous, flimsy shirt soaked within seconds. As I alighted from the cab, I stepped straight into a puddle, so water is seeping through my Gucci loafers. I squelch noisily as I peer into the house. A dim glow emanates from the kitchen window, and through the material of the blinds, I make out a tall, slim figure pottering about. Thank God. I send a short text, and five seconds later, the figure is stationary for a moment before moving towards me in a more purposeful fashion. Several bolts are unfastened, and the heavy back door opens.

"Gosh, Freddie darling! Oh my goodness, how marvellous to see you! I was only saying yesterday how I hadn't heard from you and was missing you dreadfully! Oh, darling, you look to be freezing, and so wet, like a drowned rat! Come in, come in; stand by the warm Aga, and let me give you a hug!"

And that is the point at which I burst out crying because my wonderful cousin Lucien, who never tells me I'm a disappointment, who never claims I bring shame on the family name, who never judges my lifestyle, and who makes me feel as if I'm one of the most important people orbiting his universe, strips me of my wet clothes, wraps my shivery body in his fluffy pink dressing gown, manoeuvres me so my bottom is warming against the Aga, and allows me to bury my face into his neck. All the fear, all the shame, all the uncertainty, all the jetlag, and all the exhausting bravado of the last forty-eight hours comes pouring out in the form of hot, salty tears.

"Darling, darling Freddie, tell me what's wrong? Why didn't you call me? Look at you! Oh, don't cry darling; please don't cry. Let me make you a cup of Earl Grey, and you can tell me what's happened, so I can make it right for you."

Cue more tears and more cuddles. Eventually, he calms me down sufficiently so that, between ugly sobs, I give him the bones of it. It's not a particularly edifying tale. I finish by showing him my father's caustic email.

"Gosh, delete that rubbish at once, and don't think about it again! I shall be having some strong words when

I call him later. How dare he use your mother's name against you like that? Especially when he didn't care much for what she thought when she was alive."

I have no idea what I've ever done to deserve Lucien's unconditional love and support, but if there was ever a time I needed it, it's now. He's a wonderful person to have on your side, and I don't envy my father being the recipient of that particular dressing-down.

I'd thought a lot about my father's email and treatment of me as the taxi drove through the night down the M4 towards Rossingley. Granted, he has a right to be angry. I've fucked up. He's been waiting for an excuse to tear me apart, and I've gone and thrown one in his lap. I'm an eternal disappointment to him. After Eton and Cambridge, my father entered politics at an extremely young age and rose to his current elevated seat swiftly. I was expected, nay, groomed to follow. And what did I do? Eton, Cambridge, and a swerve into modelling. And partying. Not to mention other men—that's a whole box of disappointment right there on its own. A degree from Cambridge and a lucrative career isn't enough to satisfy him; I should be heterosexual (oops), clean living (oops again), and mostly invisible.

Several times over the last few years, I've contemplated severing all ties with him. Thanks to my own income and my mother's legacy, I have financial independence, but apart from Lucien, he's all the family I have. We've never been close—his new trophy wife and all those years spent at boarding school saw to that, but I haven't ever given up hope that one day we could maybe have something between us. Because for some stupid fucking reason I can't bloody fathom, I really care what he thinks. I crave his approval, which in a grown man is frankly pathetic.

"I don't know what to do or where to go, Lucien," I get out between fresh outbreaks of hideous crying. "I think my father is about to disown me, which the bitch wife is, as we speak, no doubt strongly encouraging. Malcolm, my agent, says I have to dry out or get out, and Vincent... Well, I've called time on Vincent. I've asked him to box up my stuff and send it here—I couldn't think of any other address to give him. I don't think he will, though. He'll make me go back and get it myself, knowing him."

"Good riddance, too, Freddie, darling. Vincent, I mean, not your stuff. Leave the sorting out of that to me; we'll have it sent down within the week. That man had his heart in the right place, but gosh, he was so controlling. And in cahoots with your father. I hated seeing how he treated you."

"No more Excalibur, though," I giggle through my tears.

Lucien laughs with delight. "No, no more Excalibur, thank goodness. Last time you invited me for dinner, I could scarcely keep a straight face when he showed me his first edition of *The Sword in the Stone*. All I could think about was him attempting to get his floppy sword in your arse after I left!"

He hugs me close. For the first time this week, the tension in my shoulders drops and my heart rate steadies. Lucien senses it.

"My home is always your home, Freddie darling, you know that. And the New York thingy will blow over. We'll decide what to do about your father when you're rested and more settled. Now, dry your eyes, and don't you worry about another thing."

Cue another flood of tears.

My agent, Malcolm, had scouted me at a private party at Annabel's nightclub while in my final term at Cambridge, and instead of going on to complete my planned doctorate, I began modelling. It's mostly fun; I'm good at it, and I love, love, love dressing up. Which, according to my father, makes me a super-shallow underachiever.

I have a desirable, unusual look: pale, aristocratic, slender, and slightly androgynous. I also have two small symmetrical moles situated exactly 4.5 cm on either side of my upper lip, which the agency bookers go wild for. That naughty sailor straddling a giant Jean Paul Gautier aftershave bottle in this month's *Tatler*? That's me. The troubled young man on the inside cover of *Vogue*, moodily staring into the sunset, swathed in Ralph Lauren cashmere? Me too. Prada sunglasses in the broadsheet Sunday supplements? Check. The Oscar-winning performance, five days ago, of an incontinent, dying junkie slumped outside Macy's on West 34th Street? That was me too. A fondness for cocaine and too many lunchtime Negroni's had me waking up in a hospital bed, handcuffed to one of New York's finest. And not handcuffed in a kinky, fun way. Arrested for possession of an illegal substance and public vagrancy, I was released on bail and hotfooted it into the nearest first-class flight cabin back to Blighty. Those free Prada shades came in very handy.

I'm not the first model or minor member of the aristocracy to excessively embrace the sex, drugs, and rock-and-roll lifestyle, and I won't be the last. But when your father is the current Home Secretary, tipped to be a future prime minister, and renowned for his traditional conservative stance of being tough on crime and drugs, then my behaviour is no longer viewed as merely decadent and brattish, but cannon fodder for a ravenous British tabloid press. They haven't got hold of the story yet, thank God, but it's only a matter of time before it breaks.

My father and Lucien's father were brothers, and while this is undoubtedly a genetically accurate description, the filial similarity ends there. Lucien's father was one of the nicest men you could ever hope to meet, whereas mine is a complete dickhead. And while I didn't spend my school holidays confined to a broom cupboard under the stairs, sometimes it would have been preferable to constantly failing to live up to my father's expectations. Yes, so I've been an utter tit on this occasion, but I have to do something to get his attention once in a while. Sometimes, he makes it quite clear his life would be so much simpler if I didn't exist.

At this point, it would be easy to conclude I'm a fairly spoilt, unpleasant, shallow, and superficial young man, and I deserve everything coming to me. And that would be absolutely right. But Lucien doesn't think so. He looks at me the way I always imagined a kindly older brother might if I'd had one, or perhaps how my mother had before she became too ill. As if he's spotted a grain of goodness inside me, even if no one else can see it. As if I'm a really important piece of his world jigsaw, and he doesn't want to lose me. And for that alone, I utterly adore him. At the moment, he feels like the only person in the world who cares.

Also from NineStar Press

First Impressions by C. Koehler

When Henry Hughes and Cameron Jameson meet for the first time at a Coming Out Day party, it's anything but love at first sight. In fact, it's an unmitigated disaster, despite a scorching physical attraction.

Henry, whose social anxiety gets the better of him, humiliates Cameron, and when Cameron finds out about Henry's past in adult films, he assumes he dodged a disease-covered bullet. Yet as Henry runs into Cameron again and again, he realizes he might have misjudged the younger man. He also realizes that Cameron won't let go of his own initial view and thinks Henry is an unmitigated ass. First impressions are lasting impressions, and Cameron seems to misinterpret all of Henry's words and deeds.

It's not until Henry confronts Cameron that Cameron realizes just how wrong he's been, but he thinks he's lost his chance. Yet when disaster strikes Cameron and his friends, Henry rides to the rescue. Will Cameron be able to put aside his pride and shame to accept Henry's help and his heart?

Give Way by Valentine Wheeler

Kevin McNamara's life after retirement is...fine. He has friends, a few consulting gigs, and an ex-wife he's finally on good terms with. But when he meets an intriguing stranger—a rarity in close-knit Swanley, Massachusetts—in his apartment lobby, he can't stop thinking about him or about the unexpected attraction that knocked him flat.

Awais Siddiqui never thought he'd want to come back to his childhood hometown, but when his grandmother falls ill, he's the only one who can move back to help. Awais figures he'll be back in a big city soon enough—but then a silver fox on his route catches his eye.

It's never too late to accept a second chance at love.

Something Borrowed by Yolande Kleinn

When public defender Trevor Ortega finds himself dateless for his ex's wedding, faking a relationship seems like the perfect solution. Less perfect is his thoughtless impulse to invite Sebastian Greer—friend, federal judge, and former boss—as his plus one. It would be a solid plan if not for one problem: Trevor's been in love with Sebastian for years, and each fraudulent touch will remind him of everything he can't have.

Trevor doesn't know why Sebastian agreed to his scheme, but there's no backing out now. It's only one night after all, and what's a little heartbreak between friends?

Connect with NineStar Press

www.ninestarpress.com

www.facebook.com/ninestarpress

www.facebook.com/groups/NineStarNiche

www.twitter.com/ninestarpress

www.instagram.com/ninestarpress

9 781648 902963